"Connie, to me you are still a
little girl in braids—and
you always will be."

Her cheeks flamed with inner heat. The only sound was
the warbling of a meadowlark. Constance found her
fingers curling around the carving secreted deep within
her pocket. The unfamiliar knot began to grow in her
abdomen again.

"Well, I am not a little girl any longer, Temple," she said
softly.

Temple chuckled and looked away. He took a bite of
cornbread and chewed in silence, but Constance could
see he was well pleased with himself.

The knot in her middle twisted and churned. She
reached up and pulled the netting down over her face,
grateful for the opportunity to avoid being seen, and
made herself a promise.

Before this expedition came to an end, she was going to
make Temple Parish acknowledge the fact that she was
not a child…!

Dear Reader,

Linda's Castle's new book, *Temple's Prize*, features a hotshot young paleontologist who discovers that his challenge to his former professor and current rival will be taken up by his daughter instead. A battle of hearts and wills ensues as the two fight their mutual attraction and struggle to keep their eyes on the prize rather than each other. Don't miss this wonderful tale.

His Secret Duchess is a heart-wrenching new Regency tale from Gayle Wilson about a nobleman presumed dead who returns home after seven years of war to discover his "secret wife" on trial for murder, and a son whom he must rescue from a vengeful merchant. And popular author Suzanne Barclay returns to her bestselling series, THE SOMMERVILLE BROTHERS, with her newest medieval novel, *Knight's Rebellion*, the stirring tale of the leader of a band of outlaws who finds himself unable to resist the mysterious woman whom he has rescued.

And when a homeless schoolteacher is taken in by the wealthy uncle of one of her students, falling in love is the last thing on their minds, in Pat Tracy's new Western, *Cade's Justice*, the first book in her terrific series set in Denver, Colorado, called THE GUARDSMEN. Another great read from an author who always delivers a fast-paced and sexy story.

Whatever your tastes in reading, we hope you enjoy all four books this month.

Sincerely,

Tracy Farrell
Senior Editor

Please address questions and book requests to:
Harlequin Reader Service
U.S.: 3010 Walden Ave., P.O. Box 1325, Buffalo, NY 14269
Canadian: P.O. Box 609, Fort Erie, Ont. L2A 5X3

LINDA CASTLE

TEMPLE'S
Prize

Harlequin Books

TORONTO • NEW YORK • LONDON
AMSTERDAM • PARIS • SYDNEY • HAMBURG
STOCKHOLM • ATHENS • TOKYO • MILAN
MADRID • WARSAW • BUDAPEST • AUCKLAND

ISBN 0-373-28994-4

TEMPLE'S PRIZE

Copyright © 1997 by Linda L. Crockett

Books by Linda Castle

LINDA CASTLE

is the pseudonym of Linda L. Crockett, a third-generation native New Mexican. Linda started writing in March of 1992, and *Temple's Prize* is her fourth book from Harlequin Historicals.

When not penning novels, Linda divides her time between being a wife, mother and grandmother. She loves speaking to aspiring writers and teaching them what she has learned. Her best advice—write from the heart.

Linda believes one of the greatest benefits she has received from writing historical novels is the mail from the readers. She encourages and welcomes comments to be sent to: Linda Castle, #18, Road 5795, Farmington, NM 87401. Please include a SASE for a reply/bookmark.

Dedication:

I thank God for the miracle of each day and the love of my family. Especially Bill, for all the times you have cheerfully taken us out to dinner because I forgot to cook. For all the mornings you let me sleep in while you go to the salt mines. For all the hours you act like you are truly interested in hearing about people who live only in my mind and on the printed page, you still have my heart. Your tender love and care are the essence and soul of my writing. I am proud to be your wife.

And Brandon, for all the times you have sat in my office, patiently waiting for me to write one more line—one more paragraph—for forgiving me when my eyes glaze over and I start plotting in the middle of a conversation, thank you. Each day you gracefully step closer to manhood. If you continue as you have begun, you will make a real hero.

To Logan, for all the times you have come to give me a hug and a kiss when I was mentally lost in some other time and place. You instinctively provide what I need, you forgive me when I have been too busy to go to the park or to the movies, and I am so very grateful. You are a unique treasure, my darling. It is a privilege to live with you and watch you grow.

I am thankful I am Mom to you both. What would life be like if I had boring, uninteresting children who never gave me plotlines or graying hair?

Without you three I could not do this—and I doubt I would even want to. I adore you all more than words can say.

A special nod to Pattie Steele-Perkins. I hope you know what a large contribution you make to this whole crazy process. Thanks.

Chapter One

"Confound it, Constance Honoria, I will *not* allow that scoundrel to steal Montague's endowment from this university!"

"Now, Papa." Constance tried to placate her agitated father. "Remember what your doctor said."

"Confound him, too. I refuse to stay home while that bounder goes in search of the prize. I have survived jungle rains, snakebite and insect infestation." He flung the newspaper he had been brandishing like a weapon across the crowded office. It narrowly missed several native clay pots Constance had been meticulously illustrating while she cataloged them into the university archives.

Professor Charles Herbert Cadwallender rose unsteadily to his feet. Even with the aid of his cane, it was obvious the heavy plaster cast on his leg was cumbersome to manage. When he glanced away Constance picked up the newspaper and looked at the photograph on the front page. She could see why her father was in such a state. The caption below Temple Parish's handsome visage declared him on the way to becoming the most noted scientist and explorer of 1889. That alone would be enough to send her father into an apoplectic fit—without mention of Filbert Montague's rich endowment.

"Papa, I'm sure Temple will earn—"

"Earn? Earn? Temple Parish has never earned anything in his life!" The aging professor leaned heavily on his cane beside a table strewn with odd rocks and bits of broken bones. His spare weather-hardened body vibrated with indignant fury. "Temple has charmed or cajoled or committed outright thievery to worm his way into the scientific community ever since I hired him as my assistant."

Constance pushed the wire-rimmed spectacles up on the bridge of her nose, and as she did the past came into sharp focus. She remembered the day her father and Temple had parted company as if it were only yesterday. That was the day Temple Parish had pulled on her braids, winked at her, kissed her forehead and walked out of her life.

"Something must be done! Dandridge University is going to lose out on a one-hundred-thousand-dollar endowment unless I can find a way to go on that dig."

"Papa, would it help if I went to see Temple—if I talked to him? Maybe we could reach some sort of understanding."

"Constance Honoria Cadwallender, haven't you been listening? I am talking about Temple Parish—the blackest-hearted pirate to walk God's earth since Captain Kidd!"

Constance tilted her head and frowned at the idea. She had, thought of Temple in many different ways over the past ten years, but as hard as she tried to conjure up the image, she simply could not consider

Temple something as outmoded as an ancient, unscrupulous pirate.

It was just silly. And even though people whispered his name in the hallways of the university, and just because her father refused to discuss him at all, there was really no cause to think that he would be unreasonable about this little problem.

Constance pushed up her glasses. There had to be a civilized and sensible way around this dilemma and she intended to find it.

"Mr. Parish?" The fledgling reporter was clearly in awe.

"Please, Thaddeus, call me Temple." Temple smiled, hoping to set the eager young man at ease. Noise surrounded them as the elegant dining room started to fill with refined, well-dressed women and their evening escorts. Temple glanced down at his dusty clothes and worn high-topped boots and realized he was sorely out of place in New York's finer dining establishments. The clothing he wore would have been out of place no matter the time of day. He unconsciously rubbed his finger across the raised scar on his cheekbone.

"Mr. Parish—Temple, I mean?"

"What? Oh, I'm sorry, Thaddeus, go ahead with your interview." Temple leaned back in the comfortably padded dining chair.

"Do you have any comment on the criticism that Professor Cadwallender has been giving you in the *Sentinel?* Would you like to rebut his recent comments?"

Temple's scalp prickled but he kept a broad smile pasted on his face and forced himself to remain calm.

"I respect C.H. very much. I have nothing but respect and admiration for him. I only hope his advancing years do not prevent him from accepting this challenge. It would be a great boon to Dandridge University if he could at least make a good showing—for the sake of his reputation."

While Thaddeus Ball scribbled in a small dog-eared pad, Temple allowed his gaze to skim over the women seated around him. Feminine whispers accompanied flushed cheeks. Several smiled and let their eyes linger a moment longer than polite society dictated was proper. He smiled back, even though none of them caught his interest. The *Sentinel* had been running a series of articles about him and had managed to paint him to be a combination of Louis Lartet, the discoverer of Cro-Magnon man, and Casanova, the world's greatest lover. In truth Temple was no more than a weary wanderer in desperate need of a bath, a bed and a woman who could understand multisyllable words—not necessarily in that order, of course. As he glanced around the room he realized he would be lucky to find even one of those three in his present environment.

"Well, Mr. Parish—I mean, Temple, is there anything else you would like to tell our readers?"

"Yes—tell them that C. H. Cadwallender was the best teacher a man could have, but I fully intend to be the first explorer to find and catalog a new species of extinct reptile and name it for Filbert Montague. I am confident my quest will be a short one. You can tell Mr. Montague to get that one-hundred-thousand dollars dusted off, because it will be going to Ashmont University, the institution of my choice, very soon."

Constance read the newspaper article again. She found it hard to believe that Temple Parish could be bristling with so much confidence, but there it was in black and white. He had issued a blatant challenge to her father, and the prize at stake was the endowment promised by Mr. Montague. She sighed and set the paper aside.

"Papa will be beside himself," she told the mynah bird eyeing her from its black iron perch.

"Awrk," the bird said. "Beside, beside, beside."

"Be quiet, Livingstone. This is serious. I have to find some way of helping Papa and the university." Any chance of trying to reason with Temple was out of the question now. Even if he were inclined to make some private and amicable arrangement with her, the newspapers would hear of it and everyone involved would risk being discredited by Dandridge University and her father's stuffy, narrow-minded colleagues.

She pushed her spectacles up on her nose and tried to think. Sunlight was streaking through the beveled glass transom in the hallway. The parquet wood floor was striped in shadow and light. Livingstone hopped down from his perch to the round oak table and started shuffling through the day's mail. He picked up several envelopes and then dropped them to the floor. Then he found a letter more to his liking. While Constance was preoccupied he began to pierce the paper with his sharp pumpkin-colored beak.

"Give me that—you nuisance." Constance jerked the envelope from Livingstone's bill. "You pesky little thief."

She held up the perforated letter and looked at the damage with a critical eye. "Now look what you have done."

Luckily it was addressed to her, C. H. Cadwallender. Papa was beginning to grow impatient with her pet. He was far too talkative and his habit of ruining anything he got his beak into had begun to wear on her father's nerves.

She ripped open the tattered envelope, tossed it into a wicker wastebasket and began to read the letter. A frown creased her brow. Constance retrieved the discarded envelope and read the address again.

"C. H. Cadwallender," she mused. She refolded the letter and replaced it in the envelope. A smile curved her lips. It was a natural mistake, since she and her father had identical initials.

"Perhaps Papa can go on that dig after all." She urged Livingstone to step onto her hand and returned him to his cage before he destroyed anything else. While she picked up the scattered mail from the hall floor a plan had begun to form in her mind. By the time the uneven tap and click of her father's cane announced his arrival home, Constance was ready.

She opened the door and greeted her father with a kiss to the cheek. "Good afternoon, Papa."

C.H. hung his hat on the tall oak hall tree. "Honoria. You seem in particularly ebullient spirits—what has made you so buoyant?"

Constance straightened her collar, nudged her spectacles up on her nose and looked her father straight in the eye. The time had come to tell him her plan. "Come sit down, Papa, I have something to discuss with you."

C.H. hobbled to his chair and flopped down awkwardly. Whenever Honoria got that glint in her eye he knew he was in for stormy weather. Constance placed the ottoman in front of him and gently put his foot in the middle with a pillow beneath it. When he was as comfortable as she could possibly make him, she drew in a deep breath and told him of her plan.

Professor Cadwallender stared at his daughter in disbelief. She had come up with some bizarre schemes in her life, but this one was the most far-fetched yet.

"I can do it, Papa. I am a better digger than many men and I know how to map and grid by using the system you taught me. I can do it—I am sure I can be successful." Constance heard a challenge ringing in her own voice.

"It's ridiculous. It's no place for a female on her own. To even consider it is preposterous."

Constance felt her own pride surging forward. She wanted this chance to prove herself. "I have gone on many digs with you in the past."

"That was entirely different, Honoria. Those were *my* digs. If you went to Montana you would be completely on your own."

"Would you rather see Temple Parish win by default?"

She knew her words had hit their intended mark when her father's lined face turned three shades of crimson.

"That bounder!" Professor Cadwallender struck his cane against the fat pillow elevating his cast. A spiral of dust wafted into the still air of the overcrowded study

"I am capable of succeeding, Papa. And I would be able to make detailed sketches for Dandridge's archives." Constance reassured her father again.

He looked up at her and tilted his head much as Livingstone did when studying a new toy. "Are you sure, Honoria?"

"You can depend on me, Papa—I promise you won't be disappointed. You have my solemn oath, I will not allow Temple Parish to win."

C.H. sighed in resignation. "All right, Honoria—go. Go and show that ungrateful Temple Parish what we Cadwallenders are made of."

Temple propped up his feet and stared out the window of the train car as mile after dusty mile of terrain rattled by the window. The fine film of grit that coated the glass added a soft sepia tone to his view of the world.

Other than an occasional antelope springing away with a flash of its white rump, and the sporadic long-eared jackrabbit bounding alongside the tracks, Temple seemed to be the only person in the train car who was not napping. Not a sound came from the other passengers. It was the kind of quiet that grated on Temple's nerves—the kind of quiet before a god-awful thunder-boomer raced across open country, or some terrible disaster swept into his life—or he was cursed to have a month's worth of nightmares about his mother's death. He rubbed the scar on his cheek and directed his thoughts to his recent departure, forcing the old pain below the surface of his consciousness.

He would reach the tiny town of Morgan Forks tomorrow morning. There, he was to meet with the local man Filbert Montague had hired to guide him to the ravine where a cache of bones was rumored to be. From that point on it would be a soft job.

All he had to do was dig out some unknown critter—and most everything being found was unknown—ship it back to New York and watch Filbert

Montague hand over the money to Ashmont University.

"After reasonable expenses," Temple muttered to himself. The cash he had managed to save from his last dig was rapidly dwindling. He had hoped Ashmont would be grateful enough to offer to finance a new expedition, but they had not. Luckily Filbert Montague's inflated ego and fat bank account had solved his problem. "For the moment," Temple muttered aloud.

The job would be easy and quick, hardly so much as a challenge. He knew he should be happy about that, but he was still sorely disappointed that C. H. Cadwallender had been unable to make the trip. It had been a ten-year-old thorn in Temple's side that old C.H. never gave him his due, just as he had never given him the benefit of the doubt.

Temple was good at what he did—perhaps he was even the best—and he was itching to prove it to C.H. and the rest of those stodgy old fools at Dandridge who had been so quick to pass judgment on him ten years ago.

He wondered why it should mean so much to him, after all these years and all these miles, but deep down inside he knew. All he had wanted since C.H. found him living in the streets and started teaching him the science of the past was to measure up in the old man's eyes. He longed to show C.H. and his fellow academics that book learning was not the *only* way. And he needed to hear them admit that he was just as honorable, just as fair, as somebody who had not grown up in the gutters of New York. Temple had been forced to learn his methods through backbreaking work, but they would not acknowledge his skill or forget the rumored scandal that still clung to his name like dust to his boots.

Temple leaned back in the seat and pulled his shapeless felt hat down over his eyes. It was a constant source of irritation to him that he could not simply let the past go. To the professors at Dandridge he was the street rat, a guttersnipe, and that was that. Temple knew he might as well take a nap and forget his ten-year-old frustration. Besides, when he returned to New York and accepted Filbert Montague's endowment, those same snobby professors would finally be forced to admit he had done what one of their faculty had not been able to.

That would have to be enough, because that was likely all he could ever expect from C.H. and his kind, he told himself as he shifted in the seat and tried to find a comfortable spot.

Constance lifted the veil on her traveling ensemble and allowed herself a better look at Temple. She had chosen a seat at the back of the train car, and in truth, she doubted he even knew she was there.

His battered knee-high boots were carelessly resting on the back of the seat in front of him. Dull brown pants were stuffed tightly into the high tops. Other than that, all she could see was the crown of his worn hat. His tawny hair, which he always wore a little longer than was considered fashionable, was concealed along with the dark brown eyes she remembered so well.

She smiled in anticipation of his reaction. It had been ten years and she had grown up. Even Temple Parish would have to see how much of a lady she had become since he left her father's house. Constance had planned their meeting and the shared expedition down to the last detail, including taking the liberty of contacting the man Mr. Montague had hired to be the guide for C. H. Cadwallender and Temple Parish.

Constance felt a small shiver go through her body.

She had always dreamed of working side by side with Temple, as his equal. She couldn't wait to sit down and have a serious discussion with him about the hominid bones found in China, or the theories about what had actually happened to all the amazing creatures that were being unearthed.

Yes, Constance mused, it was her girlhood fantasy come true. Working with Temple Parish in the middle of Montana. And perhaps she would finally learn what had caused the terrible estrangement between Temple and her father and why the other professors at Dandridge said his name with contempt and then only in whispers when they thought she could not hear.

After she returned to New York with the specimens and received the praise due her, perhaps her father would stop treating her like a child. And maybe, just maybe, she could bring about a reconciliation of the two men she cared for.

Chapter Two

Temple stepped off the train and looked around. Morgan Forks wasn't much of a town—in fact it wasn't a town at all. It was a sorry collection of run-down stores and a couple of saloons. There wasn't even a proper hotel on the dusty street.

"Oh well, I've worked in worse locations." He winked at the small, gap-toothed boy who had suddenly materialized to carry his cases from the depot. "Point me in the direction of Peter Hughes," he told the lad.

The child took off straight as an arrow in the direction of the closest beer hall. With a town so small, it followed that the center of activity would revolve around the watering hole.

Once inside, Temple threaded his way through a maze of empty tables. The wooden floor was coated with a thin film of dust where his boots left faint prints with each step. It did not escape his notice that his prints were the only recent ones. A bartender swiped at dull glasses behind a long plank while a whipcord-lean man was resting his boot on a spittoon.

At the very back of the room Temple spied one

occupied table. A grizzled old man with a two-weeks' growth of beard was focused on a glass of amber liquid. His dusty clothes and overall appearance put Temple in mind of a prospector, the likely choice for a guide into the Montana badlands. The boy led him to the table without hesitation.

"Are you Peter Hughes?" Temple asked.

The old man looked up and acknowledged his presence with a small lift of his hoary brows. "Yep."

"I'm Temple Parish." Temple extended his hand.

Peter's brows rose higher as he stared at Temple's callused palm but he made no move to grasp it. He returned his attention to the glass and took another sip of his drink.

Temple let his hand fall to his side. "Are you the man hired by Filbert Montague?" He heard the impatience in his voice. It had been a long trip by train and he was anxious to find the bones and return to New York.

"Yep," Peter grated out.

Temple frowned. It was obvious Peter Hughes was a cantankerous old galoot who liked to have every syllable yanked out of him by the roots. Under different circumstances Temple might have enjoyed the struggle, but right now he simply wished to be taken to the canyon he had heard about.

"Are you ready to guide me to the canyon?" Temple was becoming irritated.

"Nope."

The succinct reply took Temple aback. "Well, when *will* you be ready?"

"Don't know." Peter Hughes finished the amber liquid in his glass and looked up at Temple suggestively. He placed the empty glass on the scarred table-top with precise and exaggerated movements.

Temple sighed. "Barkeep, another drink for—my friend."

"Thanks," Peter said with a toothy grin.

"Don't mention it. Now can you tell me when you'll be ready to take me to the canyon?"

"In 'bout five minutes, I'd guess."

"Five minutes, huh? What is going to happen in five minutes that requires us to wait?"

"That's when the other fella I'm taking is supposed to show up."

Temple felt the hair on his nape prickle. C. H. Cadwallender was in New York, with a broken leg. Temple had the sensation of being manipulated and he didn't like it.

"What fella?"

"Mr. C. H. Cadwallender, I believe the telegram said."

"Cadwallender?" Temple couldn't believe it. Had C.H. found a way to make it? Could he have persuaded the doctor to cut the cast off early? Happy anticipation surged through Temple. He pulled out a chair and sat down at the table, suddenly willing to sacrifice a few minutes. The boy who had carried his bags was still standing patiently beside him watching the exchange from beneath sun-tipped lashes.

"Here, son, for your trouble." Temple flipped him a shiny silver dollar. It was a silly and damned extravagant thing to do, but the boy reminded Temple of his own youth, when a tip from a gentleman meant the difference between eating or going to bed hungry. The child caught the coin in one hand and scurried away grinning.

Temple and Peter Hughes sat in stiff silence while the minutes ticked by. A sort of drowsy lethargy crept over the dusty barroom. It didn't take long for Temple to grow restless. He glanced at his pocket watch in annoyance.

The more he thought about it, the more absurd the notion. C.H. was not here. This was obviously somebody's idea of a joke—a bad one—and Temple wasn't known for his sense of humor. "I thought you said C. H. Cadwallender was supposed to be here." He glared at Peter and returned the timepiece to his trouser pocket.

"I am here, Temple," a cultured feminine voice said from behind his back. "I'm ready to go now."

Temple stood up so quickly he knocked the chair over in his haste. He turned to find himself staring at a voluminous canvas coat and large-brimmed hat covered by a veil of netting designed to keep insects out. He blinked in confusion at the apparition.

"What? Who the hell are you?" he asked the overdressed female.

Constance peeled up the netting and pushed her spectacles up on her nose. She peered at Temple, who didn't seem to have the slightest notion who she was. "I am Constance Honoria Cadwallender—C.H.," she said with a pleased grin. "I am going to be accompanying you to the canyon. I am ready now, if Mr. Hughes is quite prepared to leave." She glanced at him and saw him gulp down a mouthful of his drink. His eyes seemed to bulge and she realized that Mr. Hughes was not quite ready—as a matter of fact, Mr. Peter Hughes had fallen off his chair because he was laughing so hard at the look on Temple Parish's face.

Constance looked at Temple for reassurance, suddenly unsure of herself, but instead of comfort in his eyes, she found him glowering at her as if she were somehow the cause of Mr. Hughes's odd attack of mirth. It was perplexing, but men, with the exception of her father, had always perplexed her.

Mr. Hughes fell silent for a moment and she thought it was a good sign, but then he glanced at Constance and the skin around his eyes wrinkled ominously. His eyes watered.

"Oh, for pity's sake! Don't start that again," Temple blustered. The man behind the bar was chuckling and Constance wondered if she had interrupted some joke.

She started to ask Mr. Hughes, but he staggered up from his chair. He rushed to the doors and stepped through them before a loud guffaw erupted from him. He more or less tumbled into the street. A little puff of dust wafted through the doors screeching back and forth on rusty hinges.

"Astonishing!" Constance shook her head.

Temple turned and took a step toward her. When he stopped, he was close enough for her to see him clearly—even if she hadn't been wearing her spectacles.

"Temple—I am pleased to have the opportunity to work with you." Eager enthusiasm rang in every word. "I've dreamed—" Constance saw him flinch and she tried to harness her excitement. "That is, since I was a child I have been looking forward to working with you."

One thick brow twitched above his hard unyielding brown eyes.

Constance swallowed down her elation. She had expected Temple to treat her with the same friendly irreverence they enjoyed as children. Now she realized, with a certain uncomfortable jolt, they were no longer children and his expression was decidedly less than friendly. She pushed her spectacles up on her nose and tried to deal with her disappointment while she waited for some civil response, but Temple continued to glare at her in disapproving silence. She felt more awkward and painfully aware of each passing minute. Then he cleared his throat.

"Madam, I don't know what your scheme is, but I am sure I have never met you before. I undoubtedly would have remembered the incident." His eyes disdainfully swept her from the top of her hat to the toes of her shoes.

Constance stiffened at the undisguised condescension in his voice, but then she told herself she was being silly. Perhaps he didn't realize who she was. Then a happy thought popped into her head. While Temple had been busy making a name for himself all over the globe, she had had the benefit of seeing his face in the New York newspapers at fairly regular intervals over the past ten years. He, on the other hand, had not seen her since he left her father's brownstone, when she was an awkward girl in braids.

"Of course, how silly of me. I just now realized, you don't recognize me."

"That, madam, as they say, is a rather large understatement," he said stiffly.

She shook her head as if to physically throw off his words while she continued to explain. "It has been years. Papa sent me—to dig with you," Abruptly she stopped and corrected herself. "Well not exactly to dig *with* you. What I mean to say is that Papa sent me to dig *for* Dandridge University."

Temple inhaled sharply and then he leaned an inch closer and peered into her face. He tilted his head to the side and squinted as if he were seeking a new perspective. While he studied her his breath fogged her spectacles.

"But surely it can't be." He sounded doubtful. "Connie?"

"Yes! Yes, I'm Connie." She repeated the name that only he called her. Now things would progress more smoothly.

"Little Connie?" He swept his eyes from the large hat on her head, down the heavy protective coat, and stopped at her sensibly booted feet. "The same little Connie who used to follow me around? Who always had her nose in a book—and an answer for any question?"

Constance found it oddly annoying that Temple was compelled to remind her of childish habits. After all, she was now no more a child than he was. She had not seen fit to remind him of the capricious escapades of his youth. "I only wanted to help," she muttered softly.

"C.H. sent *you*?" he repeated.

Perhaps if she explained the entire situation to Temple, he would understand. "Papa had a little accident, you see, his foot..."

"He sent you to challenge *me*—for the endowment?" Temple cut her off as if he had not heard her.

Constance pushed the spectacles back up on her nose and stared up his lean weathered face. "Well— I was hoping that we could compromise—work together for the good of the scientific community. The endowment is large enough for both—"

"C.H. sent his—daughter? Little Connie?" Temple

kept cutting off her sentences, as if he were completely unaware of her attempts to explain.

Constance blinked and glanced around. The bartender immediately looked away and started rubbing a cloth over the top of the plank counter. She felt awkward, and this was not going at all as she had imagined—not at all.

"C.H. must have grown dotty," Temple said harshly.

"Why would you say such a thing, Temple?" She took a step backward so she could see him without straining her neck to look up.

"Connie, *little* Connie, you must see how laughable the whole idea is." He wiped at his eyes and grinned sympathetically at her. He pushed his hat back on his head and a strand of sun-kissed hair poked out at an odd angle.

"I don't find it laughable at all, Temple." How ironic that she had traveled so far from New York only to find herself on such familiar ground. This was territory she trod frequently, each time she offered an opinion or suggestion to one of her father's colleagues. "You may not be aware that I am a qualified anatomist. I am more than competent enough to handle this kind of exploratory expedition."

"Competent? Exploratory expedition?" Temple swept the soft-brimmed hat off his head and slapped it against his knee. The smile on his face grew wider. "Connie—" deep throaty chuckles interrupted his sentence "—you...have the most delightful sense of humor. I never realized it when you were a little girl. I remembered you as being rather serious, but you do have a devilish funny side."

Constance opened her mouth again but her words

were frozen in her throat by Temple's laughter. It started low in his belly, as only true amusement can. Then it came rushing forward, rolling like thunder as it gathered strength and rumbled out of him.

Temple grabbed hold of his ribs and chuckled with amusement. Constance realized, with a surge of uncharacteristic anger, he was laughing *at* her. Only her upbringing made it possible for her to stand there, stiff as a poker and watch, and while she did, any inclination to compromise and work *with* Temple Parish withered away. In fact, while Constance twined her gloved hands together in disappointment she found her thoughts racing ahead. And while more and more heat rose in her cheeks, her mind was focused on only one thing.

She was determined to silence Temple Parish's arrogant laughter, and the best way she could think of to do so was to claim Filbert Montague's prize.

The setting sun cast a reddish glow to the floor of the small room Mr. Hughes had procured for Constance above the saloon. She paced across the vermilion radiance while he apologized for his earlier behavior. He managed to do so without ever once breaking into guffaws, though once or twice she saw the skin around his eyes crinkle.

"I wish to start for the canyon immediately. Mr. Hughes."

"I'm sorry, miss," he said sheepishly. "But I—uh, I have wasted the better part of the afternoon. The trip is a long one and best started at sunrise."

"I see," Constance said. It was a reasonable enough request to wait until tomorrow morning to begin the journey but she was feeling neither calm nor reasonable.

"I'll come and get you loaded up at sunrise, miss."

"Thank you, Mr. Hughes. That will be fine." Constance opened the door and let him out into the narrow empty hallway. The sound of Temple's voice down below in the bar made the hair on the nape of her neck prickle. She so seldom lost her temper, it was not an experience she was accustomed to.

Constance shut the door behind Mr. Hughes, but even with the door closed, she could still hear the baritone rumble of several men in conversation. A sharp bark of amusement shattered the silence of her room, and heat rose in her face.

As the sun dropped from sight and darkness claimed her room a new sound was added. Plinking piano music vibrated through the floor against the soles of her shoes.

A sudden explosion of laughter echoed up the stairs. A hot tide of indignation climbed into her cheeks again.

"He is still laughing at me." She walked to the small neatly made bed and sat down. Constance tried to ignore the hilarity but the sound continued to hammer at the closed door. Temple's reaction to her suggestion really was the most baffling and insulting thing she had ever experienced.

"Most confounding." And infuriating, she finally admitted to herself. For the first time in her memory, Constance was seething with anger.

Another barrage of baritone chuckles wafted up the stairs. Constance found the image of her father's elderly colleagues swimming in her mind.

They frequently looked at her with bemused expressions—or patted her hand and offered her some patronizing explanation about *why* she couldn't participate in their scholarly activities. In fact she almost expected it from them. But to have Temple Parish, of all people on earth, sitting downstairs, in a barroom in Montana, laughing at her.

It was simply unthinkable.

"And humiliating." Constance rose from the edge of the bed. Her long skirt rustled while she walked to the small door. She opened it a crack and heard a renewed torrent of mirth blend with the slightly off-key piano music.

"That is quite enough from you, Mr. Temple Parish." Her ears burned with heat each time his deep, well-modulated voice caught her attention. She pushed her spectacles up on her nose and opened the door a few inches wider. "Quite enough, indeed. I believe it is time we came to an understanding, Mr. Parish." She took a deep breath and squared her shoulders before she started down the hallway.

Temple had the glass halfway to his lips when he glanced up and saw her on the staircase. She was swathed in black bombazine from her jawline to the toes of her very sensible and unattractive shoes. The creamy oval of her face was almost lost beneath the coil of heavy chestnut hair. Her eyes were hidden behind the thick rectangles of glass perched on the bridge of her nose. Her shoulders and neck were rigid and set with unyielding indignation.

She was furious, and it showed in every stiff step she took down the steep poorly lit stairs.

Temple watched her progress and realized with some amusement that he had become quite adept at putting women into a high state of emotion——whether he intended to or not.

"Mr. Parish, I would have a word with you." Constance felt the silence rush through the room like a blast of cold northern wind. The men who had been having a jolly time at her expense ducked their heads and turned away from her in embarrassment.

The music ceased with one last awkward sour note that rang through the silent room like a death knell. Temple glanced at the piano player in unmasked annoyance, but the man only shrugged and slid off the stool. He slunk to the bar, turned his back and ordered himself a drink. It tickled Constance to see all the men casting furtive glances at her in the dusty streaked mirror behind the bar.

Temple turned to face her, the only man in the room who could, it would seem. The look in his eyes was frosty and she heard her father's words echoing in the back of her mind: *the blackest-hearted pirate to walk God's earth since Captain Kidd.*

She tilted her head and studied his face. After a moment's thought Constance decided it was just possible that description was too kind. In fact, she thought with a large portion of silent sarcasm, it was more likely a terrible slight against poor Captain Kidd than it ever was to Temple Parish.

Temple cleared his throat and drew her attention. "Please, by all means, Miss Cadwallender, won't you join me?" Temple swept his hand toward an empty table. He smiled, but his eyes did not warm. He was playing the gallant for the benefit of his audience, who were watching every move reflected in the mirror from beneath their lowered hat brims.

Well, let him posture and preen for this rowdy

group, she mused silently. She intended to add to their entertainment in ways Temple had never even imagined. With a rustle of stiff fabric and petticoats, she nodded stiffly and seated herself in a straight-backed chair.

"May I offer you some refreshment?" Temple raised his own glass while he leaned back. He flopped his arm over the back of the chair and settled himself comfortably. The look on his lean weathered face left no doubt that he considered himself master of this— or any—domain.

"No. Thank you." Constance replied in curt clipped tones.

He looked at her with only mild interest, his dark brown eyes sweeping over her face carelessly as if he had seen all he needed or wanted to see at their first meeting. He tipped the glass to his lips and drained it.

Constance studied him closely. If she squinted her eyes, and used her imagination, she could almost see him with a gold earring in one lobe, a wicked dagger between his clenched teeth.

Yes. He was a pirate, a philistine, an ingrate and every other terrible thing her father had called him over the past ten years. She had not possessed the intelligence to recognize it as a child, but she saw him clearly now. He was a handsome brute, without scruples or conscience. It was going to be a pleasure to see that self-assured grin disappear from his lips.

Constance met the arrogant gaze of Temple Parish and felt a warm flush in her cheeks. At that same moment ten years of childish dreams crumbled into dust at her feet. She raised her chin and forced herself to smile as if her heart were not beating too rapidly in her bosom. He needed to be taught a lesson in manners and in the abilities of a modern thinking woman.

"Mr. Parish, I have given our predicament some thought."

"Have you?" He flashed her a wider, but no less false, smile. His straight white teeth contrasted starkly against the tanned flesh of his angular face. She noticed the raised white scar on his cheek.

"Yes, I have," Constance replied evenly.

"Well, I'm happy to hear it. It was a long way for you to have traveled in vain, but then again the trip wasn't a total loss for you. I mean, after all, we have had a pleasant reunion—haven't we?"

She shoved her spectacles up on her nose. "Is that what we've been doing, Mr. Parish? Having a reunion?"

His smile slipped and for a moment was replaced by a frown but within seconds the dazzling smile was back in place. "Of course, Connie, it has been nice to see you after all these years. I had hoped it would be C.H. who came but... Tell me, what have you been doing to keep busy?"

"Oh, this and that." Constance smiled stiffly.

"Really? Do you still accompany C.H. on expeditions?"

Constance heard the brittle tone of Temple's voice and realized he was more than just a little interested in what her father had been doing. Once again the old rumors about Temple raced through her mind.

"Papa has been lecturing rather steadily for the past few years."

"Is that so?" he asked with mild interest.

"Yes, but he did unearth some wonderful things in

South America a few years ago. I have been cataloging and illustrating them for Dandridge University.''

Temple stiffened perceptibly at the mention of Dandridge. "I'm sure you do fine work, Connie. Dandridge is no doubt lucky to have you.'' There was a note of sarcasm in his compliment.

"How nice of you to say so. And I have managed to acquire one or two other skills since we last met.'' Constance continued to study his face from behind the protective barrier of her spectacles.

"Really? You must tell me, what else do you do?'' Temple's words were dripping with open condescension.

"As a matter of fact, Mr. Parish, I am a digger,'' she said flatly.

His brows shot up, but other than that he managed to suppress any further reaction. "You don't say, Connie—a digger? A female digger? I have never heard of such a thing.''

He nodded to the bartender and held his empty glass aloft.

Constance glanced at the man who grabbed a tall bottle in his hand, then she turned back to Temple. "I am quite competent, as I told you. So competent, in fact, that I intend to complete the expedition my father sent me on, Mr. Parish.''

His smile slipped at the same moment the bartender appeared at Temple's elbow and began pouring liquid into his glass.

"You what?'' he asked loudly. His question echoed through the silent barroom. Several men leaning on their elbows actually turned around and gaped at him.

Constance nodded and continued. "You heard me correctly, Mr. Parish. I intend to leave Morgan Forks tomorrow morning at sunrise, but before I go, I wanted to issue you a new challenge to go along with the one we have both accepted from Mr. Montague.''

"Challenge? Me?" Temple brought his arm down from the back of the chair. He no longer appeared to be uninterested in what she had to say—in fact he was perched on the edge of his chair, leaning across the table toward her as if he were on tenterhooks, waiting for her to speak. His dark eyes were trained on her face with single-minded intent. His long fingers were splayed out on the scarred tabletop. "You are challenging me?"

"Yes, that is if you are up to the task," Connie replied smoothly. It was difficult to continue staring at Temple now that he was mere inches from her, but she did so without blinking until he at last glanced away.

"What task did you have in mind, Miss Cadwallender?" His voice was brittle with suspicion and his pet name for her had conspicuously vanished.

"The challenge I am issuing you is this, Mr. Parish. In addition to the endowment Mr. Montague is offering, I am proffering you a personal challenge as well. There will be no money involved, so you may not be interested…"

One brow shot upward when her intentional barb hit its mark. "What kind of a challenge, Miss Cadwallender?"

She leaned forward. Constance had never been very good at public speaking, but she cleared her voice and took a deep breath. She wanted to make very sure that every man who was lined up at the bar heard her clearly. "This challenge would affect only your pride—your ego, Mr. Parish."

"Speak your mind, Miss Cadwallender." His brown eyes narrowed down to predatory slits and there was open hostility in his voice.

"I not only intend to find a previously unknown species of dinosaur for Mr. Montague, I intend to do it on my own and long before you can even locate one." She spoke loudly.

The impact of her words settled on the interested occupants of the room and drew a deep murmur from the men who were bent in speculative conversation.

"You're mad," Temple said in a whisper only she was meant to hear.

"Perhaps, but the challenge stands. Are you declining—admitting you are not up to the task?"

"What?" Temple snorted.

"Are you admitting I am the better digger?"

Temple stood up so quickly the chair legs screeched on the floor. He glared down at her. "You're female."

"How very astute of you to notice, Mr. Parish." Constance forced herself to remain sitting and watch Temple even though it made her neck cramp to do so. A collection of emotions raced across his face and through his eyes while they held each other's gaze.

"It would be ridiculous for me to compete with a—a—woman. I would be a laughingstock."

"I fail to see why, but if you would rather admit that I—a Cadwallender and a female—am more competent and capable..." She shrugged then placed her palm on the table as if she were rising from her chair.

A wide rough hand closed over her own and stilled her movement. Constance tilted her head and looked up.

Temple sucked in a breath that seemed to be too much air for one man to hold in his lungs, then suddenly it left him in a great angry rush. "I will never admit to that!" he bellowed.

"Then I assume you are accepting my challenge?" Constance glanced at the mirror, but now every man was turned, watching. She experienced a measure of satisfaction when she saw every pair of expectant eyes was trained on Temple's face.

"*Miss* Cadwallender!" Temple nearly vibrated with indignation. "I would much prefer you exercised some sense, remembered where you belong and returned home."

"I am not leaving until I find those bones," she said calmly.

His face turned three shades of red. "Then it appears I have no choice but to accept your challenge. I would be most happy to prove who is the better—digger." His voice was a tightly controlled rumble.

"Good." Constance nodded stiffly at him. Then she scooted her chair backward. It took some effort for her to pull her hand from beneath his, but finally she was able to stand up. "Now if you will excuse me, I shall see you tomorrow morning at sunrise."

When she turned on her heel she heard a soft hiss as Temple drew another furious breath between his tightly clamped teeth. All the way to the staircase she was smiling.

She was going to enjoy this—very, very much.

Chapter Three

"So, you see, Mr. Hughes, I want to make sure that my messages are sent back to my father on a regular basis." Constance stopped pacing.

"Yes, Miss." Peter stifled a grin. He was seeing more excitement than he'd had since he fled New York City with Tweed's stolen money and the Tammany thugs on his heels. Miss Cadwallender had a conniving streak beneath all those proper manners. He couldn't help but like her. He had been mighty surprised when the bartender had sent a message for him to come back to the saloon—that Miss Cadwallender had to speak to him. For a bit he had half expected her to tell him she was packing up and heading back to New York, but she set him straight about that notion quicker than he could skin a cat.

"Mr. Parish has been known to be—well—unorthodox," She twisted her fingers together and tried to explain why she was making these preparations. After she had goaded Temple into accepting the challenge, it had occurred to her that she needed a tiny edge—just in case.

"Yes, miss, I can see he might have that inclination," Peter agreed solemnly.

"Not that I'm asking you to do anything unethical—I would never ask you to do that, Mr. Hughes."

"No, miss."

"I just want to make very sure that I don't fail my father or Dandridge University,"

"Yes, miss, I understand. I can see a lady like yourself would never suggest anything that wasn't on the level."

"I'm so glad you understand, Mr. Hughes."

"Yes, miss, I do—I do understand." Mr. Hughes nodded his head rhythmically while he spoke.

"In the past there have been rumors that Temple, I mean Mr. Parish, has been known to employ methods that were considered—uh—corrupt." Constance wrung her hands and paced up and down the bare floor of the room. The solitary kerosene lamp managed to illuminate the small room quite well. Her pulse was still beating unevenly and she admitted to herself that she had never before been quite so excited. All her preparations and precautions were necessary and completely legitimate since she was dealing with Temple Parish. Any sensible individual could see he was a man without principles. She really had no choice, Constance told herself.

"Securing this endowment is very important to my father's reputation and it is vital to the university. It is extremely consequential to me as well," she admitted while she stared at the moon hanging in the Montana sky.

"Yes, miss, I see that you are real serious." Peter kept his eyes on her while she paced up and down. The heavy black material rustled with each tense step.

"I am so pleased that we have come to this understanding, Mr. Hughes. It does take a burden from my shoulders. When we leave tomorrow I shall rest easy in my mind now." She walked to her carpetbag and dug down deep inside it. "And I insist that you take something extra, for your trouble."

"Miss, that really isn't necessary," Peter began.

"No—I insist. This is not part of the original agreement you made with Mr. Montague and his agents. I wouldn't feel right about you doing these things for me, unless you allow me to compensate you for your inconvenience."

Peter stared at Miss Cadwallender. Behind the thick spectacles she had soft brown eyes fringed with thick curved lashes. They reminded him of a fawn's eyes, innocent and trusting. A light dusting of freckles was sprinkled across the bridge of her nose. He felt a strange and unexpected protectiveness toward her, as if she were a favorite niece.

"Please, Mr. Hughes." Constance extended the handful of money. "Please take it, I would feel much better if you did."

"If you insist, Miss Cadwallender, but I'd do it for nothing—for you." Peter felt heat in his cheeks when the words tumbled out, but it was true. He liked this young woman. And, he realized, he was going to have a jolly good time watching her turn Temple Parish's arrogant hide inside out. He shoved the bills deep into his pocket while a grin crept across his lips.

She blinked behind the thick eyeglasses. "You are so kind, Mr. Hughes. I cannot tell you how your assistance will speed my work. Thank you once again."

"Is there anything else, Miss Cadwallender?" Peter

stood. It was getting late and he needed to get some sleep.

"No—nothing I can think of, Mr. Hughes. You have been most tolerant of my situation."

"Don't mention it, miss." Peter stepped out onto the landing before the chuckle bubbled from his throat. Young Miss Cadwallender was crafty. She had the kind of mind old boss Tweed would have admired. Peter took two steps toward the narrow stairs before he heard a strange hissing noise. He stopped and tilted his head to listen. The noise was a little like the sound a bobcat makes. Peter squinted his eyes and peered down the narrow hall.

"Psst." The sound came again.

Peter whirled around and found Temple Parish hiding behind a half-open door at the opposite end of the narrow hallway.

"Psst." Temple Parish waved his hand at Peter. "Come here."

Peter raised his bushy eyebrows and pointed at his own chest in doubt.

"Yes—you. Come here," Temple whispered harshly while he gestured with his hand once again.

Peter walked down the hallway toward the partially open door, puzzled by Parish's strange behavior. When he reached the door, Temple opened it wide enough to grab Peter's shirt with one hand. He jerked him inside the room and shut the door behind him.

"What the devil is this all about, Parish?" Peter jerked his shirt from Temple's fingers. No wonder Miss Cadwallender was nervous; having to deal with this hothead would make a body plumb jittery. "What's the matter with you?" Peter demanded.

"I need to talk to you." Temple Parish snapped.

"Couldn't it wait until tomorrow morning when we leave?" Peter straightened his shirt and glared at Temple.

"No. I wanted to discuss our arrangement—before you guide us to the site tomorrow morning."

"Oh." Peter nodded knowingly. "Are you backing out—admitting the lady is a better—uh—digger?"

"Not on your life." Temple stood with his boots spaced wide apart. He crossed his arms at his chest and gave Peter a scathing glare. "The very notion is ridiculous."

Peter shrugged. "I was just asking." He glanced at the narrow bed, smooth and untouched, and the single wooden chair in the room. "Can I sit?"

Temple blinked rapidly, as if he had only just become aware of the furniture in the tidy little room. Peter had a notion Temple had been wasting as much shoe leather pacing up and down the floor as Miss Cadwallender had been doing a bit ago.

"Sure—sit. Would you like a drink? I have a bottle in my valise."

If Parish was starting out with the pretext of a drink, Peter assumed the subject was going to be a ticklish one.

"I could drink—" Peter grinned and eased himself into the chair "—as long as you are buying."

Temple tossed a battered leather valise onto the bed. He unfastened the buckles on the worn straps and pulled the ancient satchel open. He dug into the contents like an angry badger through loamy turf. Finally he brought out a bottle of whiskey. Peter had not seen that particular brand since he left New York.

"Sorry, I don't have any glasses," Temple apologized.

"Don't need any." Peter took the bottle by the neck, uncorked it, wiped off the lip and took a long swallow. The full-bodied liquid burned pleasantly down his gullet. It left a wave of memories from the old days in its wake. Peter pushed the dim recollections aside and focused on Temple's face. "What did you want to talk about?"

"About tomorrow." Temple clasped his hands behind his back and started to pace the room. His expression was darker than a rain cloud. Peter took another pull on the bottle and waited.

"When I find what I'm after, the bones, and I leave—" Temple stared at Peter with his brows pinched together "—I—know little Connie, I mean Miss Cadwallender, will be very disappointed. I just want to make sure you will stay with her, see that she gets back on the train safely, after I am gone. Will you do that?"

Peter grinned in amazement. He had expected quite a different request from Temple. The way Parish was talking now, if Peter didn't know better, he would have sworn that Miss Cadwallender was a child, instead of the calculating and very capable lady she appeared to be. But Peter decided to go along with Parish's scheme, at least as long as he was serving aged whiskey.

"Sure, I'd be happy to keep an eye on the little lady. Course, you know this is an extra service. This is above what I had agreed to do for Mr. Montague. I would have to have—compensation." Miss Cadwallender's term rolled cleanly off his tongue.

"Of course, I wouldn't expect to have it any other way," Temple said dryly. He strode to the bed and dug deeper into the valise. He pulled out a soft leather pouch. He brought out five silver dollars and put them in Peter's waiting hand. "There is one other thing, Hughes."

Somehow Peter had known there would be. "And what is that, Parish?"

"I want to be sure that my messages reach the telegraph office here in Morgan Forks without interruption. I need to be sure Mr. Montague is informed of my progress daily and he is notified the very moment I find his dinosaur for him."

"Can't do that." Peter shook his head.

Temple glared at him with his sun-lightened eyebrows pinched together. "What do you mean, you can't do that? Can't—or won't?"

Peter grinned and took another drink of the smooth whiskey. "I can't send telegrams to New York daily, 'cause the trip to the canyon takes a full day and a half in good weather."

Some of the tension left Temple's shoulders. "Oh—I see. Well, then I would like you to get word of my progress to Mr. Montague as quickly, and as regularly, as possible."

"Are you asking me to bring your messages into town for you?" Peter was having a good time. Temple Parish was as prickly as a porcupine when it came to this competition with Miss Cadwallender.

"Yes. I won't be leaving camp, or stopping until I find what I'm after. Just see my telegraphs are sent to Mr. Montague's agent." Temple lifted one brow. "I don't think Miss Cadwallender needs to know anything about our arrangements."

"You're right about that. It will be our secret," Peter promised solemnly while he gave Temple an exaggerated wink.

Temple frowned at him. "It's nice to know I can—uh—depend on you, Hughes. Little Connie—that is, Miss Cadwallender should be no trouble to you at all."

"I'm sure you're right about that, too, Parish," Peter agreed while he fought to keep a straight face. "I don't think she'll be one whit of trouble to me, but you might ought to worry 'bout yourself."

The sun was poking holes in the dusky eastern sky when Temple climbed aboard the wagon and settled himself between two large wooden crates. He hitched up his boot and rested it on a mound of canvas-covered supplies.

"What is all this?" he demanded.

"My supplies," Constance answered from behind the netting extended over the big-brimmed hat. She stood beside the wagon staring up at Temple. His eyes narrowed as they slid over her traveling costume. Then his expression altered until it was identical to the one he wore yesterday when she reintroduced herself.

Constance stiffened beneath his arrogant gaze. She was still bristling with anger over Temple's attitude toward her. She had come to expect this kind of patronizing folderol from her father's colleagues, but never from Temple Parish. She had already checked her list of supplies and tools before Mr. Hughes loaded them in the back of the wagon. Now she paused and looked at her trunk, where Temple's boot heel was propped. He was squeezed between her crates like a sardine in a tin. He fidgeted and wedged his broad shoulders between two boxes. Constance found herself smiling behind her insect netting. Seeing how her crates and trunks bothered Temple, she was almost sorry she hadn't brought more.

"All set, Miss Cadwallender?" Peter Hughes lifted her up.

"Yes, thank you, Mr. Hughes." Constance settled herself on the hard wagon seat and forced herself to ignore Temple's scowl.

Temple moved but his hip connected with the sharp edge of a crate. He could not believe that anybody could need so many supplies. He turned his head, thinking to tell Connie as much, but all he could see was a swath of insect netting and sand-colored canvas. She was camouflaged from head to foot and perched stiffly on the high wooden wagon seat behind him. It was unnerving.

"If you need anything, miss, you just say so." Peter's voice dripped with a sincerity that set Temple's teeth on edge.

Temple frowned and mugged a face at Peter's words. How could she possibly need anything? Hell, she must have half of the state of New York packed into all the damned boxes, trunks and crates that surrounded him.

Peter climbed up beside Connie and picked up the reins. Temple pulled his hat low on his forehead, determined to ignore her on the trip to the canyon, but no matter how he turned his body to find a comfortable position in the wagon bed, his gaze kept returning to the huge hat and insect barrier that obscured her face.

He tried to turn and raked his shoulder on a metal latch. A hot tide of anger coursed through him. He was angry with little Connie. That surprised him. Not that she hadn't done plenty to make him angry years ago before he left C.H.'s house, but he had always spoiled and indulged her. Now it was different—he was different. Silly little Connie had gone too far by challenging him. He wished she would go home—wished she had not used his ego as a weapon to goad him into this ridiculous competition. She could not win. There was nothing ahead for her but humiliation and defeat.

Acknowledging that made him angry as well. Being orphaned on the streets of New York had given Temple a thick hide, but C.H. and his doe-eyed daughter had gotten under his skin way back then. Evidently they were still able to make him itch—after all these years.

Temple pushed his hat back on his forehead and shoved the old memories to the back of his mind. He took out his knife and cut a thick slice of wood, about the size of his index finger, from the closest pine crate. While Peter and Connie chatted, and the wagon rocked back and forth he whittled. The repetitive task allowed his mind to wander aimlessly.

Connie laughed at some comment Hughes made. Her girlish giggle reminded Temple of the old days. Even though it was stupid, he found himself straining to hear what was being said. The sun rose higher in the sky while Temple's shoulder knocked against the crates. He tried to adjust to the lumbering sway of the wagon while he diligently whittled.

The spring sunshine of Montana felt good. This country and setting were so different from the cold spring day when C.H. had found him alone and bloody in the park.

He snapped his head up, shocked at his mind's persistence in dredging up old memories. It had been eighteen years since he had been taken in by C. H.

Cadwallender. Too damned long ago to matter. Temple had put a million miles and a hundred countries between him and Dandridge University since that day, and yet here he was on a wagon with C.H.'s only child. And as much as Temple hated to admit it, it did matter. Winning the prize and showing C.H. that he was more than a street rat mattered very much.

"When I find those damned bones for Montague, C.H. will no longer have to be ashamed of taking me in," Temple muttered under his breath, and the sound of his own voice startled him.

He glanced up to see if Connie or Hughes had heard him, but neither one of them had changed positions or lessened their steady conversation. He went back to his whittling while thoughts of Montague's endowment flooded his mind.

He was not going to allow little Connie to stand in his way. With a rich endowment for Ashmont he might finally have a measure of respectability, and that was worth any price—any price at all.

Chapter Four

Temple watched the herd of antelope bound by. Hughes grumbled about the animals taking so long to cross, slowing the wagon's progress toward their destination, but Connie was standing up in the wagon watching. At least Temple thought she was. The thick folds of her dress made it difficult to tell much of anything about the position or shape of her body.

The huge herd gamboled across the wagon trail to disappear over a gently sloping rise into a hollow. When the last white rump vanished from sight, Connie clapped her hands together in childish glee.

"Oh, Mr. Hughes, they are extraordinary," she declared as she settled herself amid the mound of sand-colored cloth. "I really must do some sketches of the local wildlife. It would be lovely to have a set framed for Papa's office."

The mention of that dusty room made Temple's jaw muscles tighten. His insatiable curiosity forced him to sit up. "Is he still in the science wing of the Palmer Building?" He continued to whittle, never looking away from the hunk of pine even though he was paying close attention to Connie and her answer.

A rustle of stiff fabric telegraphed Connie's intent to swivel around on the hard wagon seat. It took a few minutes for her to manage to move all the material surrounding her body.

"Yes—he is," she said.

He could not see her face behind the netting, but her voice held a tone of undisguised amazement.

"It was so long ago when you left, I am surprised that you would remember such an insignificant thing as the exact location of his office."

He shouldn't remember. But every small incident and minute detail was as clear as if it had been yesterday instead of ten years ago when he lived with C.H. and Connie.

"I have a good memory." Temple bent his head lower to concentrate on the hunk of wood, wishing he had kept his mouth shut. His brows pinched together in annoyance and he promised himself that he would not allow his curiosity to get the better of him again.

"Yes, you certainly do." Constance turned back to face the front of the wagon. The team was trudging slowly and Peter slapped the reins against the rumps of the horses as if he were anxious to reach the canyon. The wagon lurched forward and Temple neatly sliced the tip of his thumb with the razor-sharp blade.

"Damnation, Hughes. You've made me nick myself." Temple stuck his thumb against his tongue to stanch the flow of blood. The faint taste of iron filled his mouth as blood oozed from the stinging gash. The wagon jerked again as it came to a halt.

"What is it?" Constance demanded. She had somehow managed to climb over the iron railing at the back of the seat—quite a feat considering the amount of cloth that surrounded her. She was kneeling, or he believed she was kneeling, beside him. One thing he was sure was that her huge skirt was ballooned near his thigh and she was pressing him tighter against one trunk. Her fingertips grazed over the flesh on his exposed forearm. "What has happened? Let me see."

As if she could see anything through the netting, he thought sourly. He took his thumb from his mouth in order to speak. "It's nothing."

She grabbed his hand with both of her smaller ones. "You have cut yourself." A thick glob of blood welled from the wound. The cut was not deep enough to be serious but wide enough to bleed freely.

"It's nothing to worry over," he grumbled. She ignored him and turned his hand this way and that, examining his thumb while he dodged the brim of her outrageous hat.

"I'm not going to bleed to death, Connie, now let me go." Temple felt awkward, sprawled on his back among the canvas with Connie hovering over him like some sort of apparition from a child's dream.

"It could become septic, Temple. Allow me to tend it now." Authority rang in her voice and it only served to make Temple more annoyed.

"While you see to Mr. Parish, I am going to take a little walk." Peter climbed down from the wagon seat and ambled off toward a scanty grove of squat pine trees, leaving Temple to fend for himself.

"It is a tiny scratch." He managed to wrench his hand from Connie's determined grasp. The fact that she was now calling him Temple and not Mr. Parish did not escape his notice during their tug-of-war.

"I don't want to win Montague's endowment because you were too injured to give it your best," her smooth voice pronounced from behind the barrier of her netting.

Renewed fury sluiced over Temple. He wanted to deliver a suitable retort, but her thorny declaration had left him momentarily speechless. A hot tide crept up his face to his hairline.

"Very well, Miss Cadwallender, do your worst," Temple grated out. He shoved his hand toward her, offering the injured thumb for her to inspect.

"I am pleased to see you are at last being sensible," she muttered while she searched through a small carpetbag. He had the uncomfortable suspicion she was smiling behind the barrier of cloth. In fact, he could practically hear laughter in her voice. When she had found what she was looking for, the massive hat once again turned in his direction. "Now kindly hold still so I can put some antiseptic on this cut."

A gust of icy wind blew over them and he actually heard a muffled giggle. But surely it was a trick of the wind; little Connie would not laugh at an injured man.

Would she?

Temple used his free hand to close his knife and slip it inside his trousers. Constance put something related to liquid fire on his thumb.

"Holy blue blazes, Connie!" The stinging liquid made his eyes water. He glanced around for the piece of wood he had been carving when she had descended upon him, but between her ministrations and the antiseptic he had no luck in finding it.

"There now—that should keep your thumb clean and dry." Constance gathered her skirts and stood up. Temple was stunned to see his hand swathed in white gauze. His thumb was bound to three times its normal size. Now he looked almost as ridiculous in his bandage as Constance looked in her hat.

"If this bandage is meant to stanch moisture you must be expecting a flood." Temple climbed to his feet and leaped from the back of the wagon before she had a chance to object and bind him further.

Constance couldn't imagine why Temple was so annoyed. After all, she had done him a good turn by cleaning the cut. She watched him enter the copse of low shrubs near the pine trees. The sun was high overhead and she was a little warm in her traveling ensemble.

Her eyes swept over the countryside while she gathered the gauze and mechanically popped the cork back in the bottle of antiseptic. Short mossy-green tufts of grass sprouted here and there, but in the deepest ravines and beneath the squat pines, there were actually small patches of snow on the ground. Constance replaced the items in the small box and returned it to her carpetbag. She had climbed halfway over the wagon seat when something caught her eye.

It was a piece of pale pine wood wedged in a flap of canvas on one of her crates. She picked it up and turned it around in her fingers while she looked at it. A most peculiar tightness manifested itself in her middle while she studied the tiny figure in her hand.

It was a young girl with thick plaits trailing down her back. She was dressed in full skirts and a pinafore.

"It's me," Constance whispered to herself. It was the very image of the way she had looked when Temple stomped out of her father's house ten years ago.

The sound of masculine voices drew her head up. Temple and Mr. Hughes appeared at the edge of the bushes. Impulsively, and not really sure why, she thrust the little carving into her pocket and scrambled back over the seat before they reached the wagon. She was grateful she was wearing her insect bonnet, because she was quite certain that a most unbecoming flush had stained her cheeks.

When the sun had climbed to the center of the sky, and Constance's stomach had growled noisily several times, Mr. Hughes stopped the wagon in the middle of a small meadow. A sprinkling of hardy wildflowers were blooming near the tough sprigs of grass.

For a moment Constance was struck by a sharp pang of homesickness. She excused herself and went off for a few moments of privacy. She stuck her hand inside her pocket and felt the carving again. She had never taken another person's belongings before and she wasn't sure why she had done so now, but when she wrapped her fingers around the small object she felt less homesick.

After relieving herself, Constance made her way toward the wagon. Temple was unloading the large wicker basket Mr. Hughes had brought along. Sunshine caught the pale strands of Temple's hair and turned it to liquid silver. A hard knot formed in Constance's stomach while she watched him. The pale collarless shirt strained across the width of his neck and the shoulder seams stretched with each movement.

"Miss Cadwallender, you best come have some of this fried chicken," Mr. Hughes called out to her.

"Yes, thank you, I will," Constance replied, trying to swallow her embarrassment, wondering if Mr. Hughes had seen her staring at Temple. She quickened her pace toward the wagon but when she reached it, she hesitated. For some reason, the idea of sitting down on the bleached fallen tree trunk beside Temple filled her with an odd sort of dread. She saw him glance up at her from under thick lashes while she lingered, unsure and hesitant.

"Miss Cadwallender—" there was a mocking edge to Temple's voice "—I would not want to win this challenge because you were too weak from hunger to put up a proper effort." One sun-gilded brow rose above taunting brown eyes while a corner of his mouth curled upward. "Or perhaps you have come to your senses and have decided to concede that I am the better digger. If you leave today, you could be back in New York by week's end."

Constance's anger bloomed anew. Whatever had been wrong with her a moment before, whatever silly notion had caused her to hesitate had faded when Temple's dare left his mouth.

She stepped over the end of the log that Mr. Hughes was sitting on and plopped down beside him, peeling up the netting to expose her face. She accepted the piece of chicken Mr. Hughes offered and tore off a huge bite with her front teeth while she glared defiantly at Temple. Each time he told her to leave, the more determined she was to stay. She chewed with enthusiasm but the truth was, she couldn't even taste the food.

"Hungry?" Temple asked with an arrogant tilt of his head. Sunlight made the scar on his cheek gleam stark white against his lean, tanned flesh.

"Starving, Mr. Parish—absolutely starving," Constance answered around a mouthful of fried chicken.

"Good. To be a proper digger, a man—oh, excuse me—a person must eat well and keep up their strength." He grinned and tossed a chicken bone out into the grassy meadow.

"Be assured, Mr. Parish, I am more than up to the task." Constance swallowed the last bite then tossed her chicken bone alongside the one Temple had thrown.

He chuckled and reached for a chunk of corn bread. "Maybe, but I think you won't stay. Without C.H. around, I think you will find this task daunting. I expect you will be returning with Mr. Hughes when he brings the first load of supplies."

She stared at him with narrowed eyes while she pushed her spectacles up on her nose. He was so sure of himself—so arrogant. A thousand tart replies ran through her head but none seemed harsh enough.

"Mr. Parish, I wish you would refrain from calling me that childish pet name," she heard herself snap.

He stopped nibbling the corn bread and stared at her for a full minute. Then one side of his mouth tilted upward in a boyish expression of repentance. "Childish? You think my name for you is childish? Connie girl, to me you are still a little girl in braids—and you always will be."

Her cheeks flamed with inner heat. Silence hung between them. The only sound was the warbling of a meadowlark off in the distance. Constance found her fingers curling around the carving secreted deep within her pocket. The unfamiliar knot began to grow in her abdomen again.

"Well, I am not a little girl any longer, Temple," she said softly.

Temple chuckled and looked away. He took a bite of the corn bread and chewed in silence but Constance could see he was well pleased with himself.

The knot in her middle twisted and churned. She reached up and pulled the netting down over her face, grateful for the opportunity to avoid being seen, and made herself a promise.

Before this expedition came to an end she was going to make Temple Parish acknowledge the fact that she was not a child. And she was going to claim Montague's prize.

She stood and marched toward the wagon. "Can we be on our way, Mr. Hughes? I am most anxious to reach the site so I can begin digging."

Her words brought Temple lurching to his feet. He cast one quelling gaze in her direction. Constance stood by the wagon, with her elbows akimbo, watching him toss jars and crocks into the basket.

The look on Temple's face and the stiff set of Miss Cadwallender's shoulders brought a low rumble of laughter welling up inside Peter. He glanced back and forth between them and tried to gulp down his humor. They would both skin him alive if he started to laugh right now, he was sure of it.

He shook his head and muttered to himself. "It is going to be a long afternoon, and an interesting one, if I have my guess."

After hours of riding in the wagon in tense silence, Peter glanced at the western sky. The sun was hanging low and yet Miss Cadwallender had not asked to stop. He had noticed that each bump and sway of the wagon brought a tiny gasp of discomfort from her, but the young miss was determined and strong willed.

After the words she and Parish had exchanged at lunch, he knew she would not ask to halt—no matter what. She would try her best to hide her weariness and continue for as long as the men wished to travel, just to prove herself to Temple Parish. And then tomorrow she would be all done in and the bounder would have an unfair advantage. The idea didn't set well with Peter. He pulled up on the long leather reins.

"This looks like a real good place to make camp for the night." Peter shoved the foot brake in place and swiveled in his seat, ready for Parish's complaint.

"We're stopping already?" Temple levered himself up and lifted the brim of his hat. He glanced at the surrounding countryside from his snug trough between the crates and trunks. "Isn't it a little early? We have at least one more hour of good light."

Peter stared at Temple and tried to keep a straight face. It wasn't easy, especially since the big man was wedged between two crates, with his back against one and his boots propped up against another. He was practically bent double.

"The horses need rest. So do I," Peter lied. "We're setting up camp here." He jumped down from the wagon and moved toward the head of the team.

Temple shrugged and scooted the hat up to its proper position. "Suit yourself, Hughes." He dislodged his body from the crevice and stood up. "I could use a little stretch myself."

Constance tried not to notice when Temple jumped down from the back of the wagon. He extended one leg like a cat who had been curled up too long. She remained in the wagon and watched him from beneath the shelter of her netting while he raised his arms and bent his body into a backward arc. Mesmerized by the glint of the crimson sun on the hard planes of his form, the vision of the boy she remembered merged with the reality of the man he was today.

There was a width to his shoulders and sinewy muscle in his upper thighs that had been only a promise of things to come when he left her father's brownstone in New York. Now, as the rays of waning sunlight illuminated his chiseled face in a bronze glow, a painful catch manifested itself in her throat.

How could Temple Parish be so heartbreakingly handsome and so absolutely infuriating at the same time?

"Miss Cadwallender?" Peter Hughes's voice jolted her; she blinked in confusion. She found him staring up at her with his hand extended, waiting patiently to help her from the wagon. Embarrassment sluiced through her.

"Oh, I'm sorry." Once again the insect netting on her hat kept her unbecoming blush from being seen.

"Nothing to apologize for, miss. Give me your hand and I'll help you down. You might want to take a look around while I set up camp. Just be sure to watch for snakes and bears."

"You know, Hughes, if you keep coddling Miss Cadwallender, she will be at a loss when you leave us alone out here." Temple sauntered over and leaned against the side of the wagon. "She will scarcely be able to manage without you."

Constance tilted her head to look at him, expecting to see his customary scornful smile but instead his brows were furrowed together as if he might actually be worried about her. The very notion nearly made her laugh aloud. It was absurd to even consider that Temple might have a single minute of concern on her behalf.

"I assure you, Mr. Parish, I am quite capable of fending for myself now and I will be able to do so when Mr. Hughes has returned to Morgan Forks.'' Constance swiped some of the trail dust from her coat while she spoke. ''While traveling with Papa, I set up camp on more than one occasion.'' She expected him to stomp away in a fit of temper, but he continued to lounge against the side of the wagon while he toyed with the large gauze bandage on his thumb.

He was no more than a yard from Constance and a capricious breeze brought a whiff of his distinctive odor to her nostrils. Without conscious thought she tried to analyze—to catalog—the scent. It was part wood and dust mingled with crisp Montana air. It was a man's smell, different from the way any man at the university ever smelled. It was impossible to name in one word except to say it was all Temple's scent, a bit wild, a bit reckless and wholly stimulating.

''So, old C.H. drug you to hell and back after I left,'' he mumbled under his breath. Constance watched him continue to stare at the earth in front of his boots. She realized it was not a question that he asked of her, but she heard the question hidden in Temple's soft words.

''After you left, Papa found himself in need of a new assistant. I was the only logical choice.''

Temple's head snapped up. He speared Constance with the flinty look in his eyes. ''Why were you the logical choice?''

Constance started at the sharpness of his question. ''I received the same education Papa had given to you. It was natural that I should begin to accompany him when he went looking for scientific relics. After all, there wasn't anybody else he had been training. He had invested a lot of time in you....'' Her words trailed off.

Temple's brows shot up. "Is that your way of telling me that I took too much of C.H.'s attention? How you must've rejoiced when I left."

The memory of lying in her bed while silent tears streamed down her face came rushing back. Temple's departure had ripped her tender fourteen-year-old heart in two, but she refused to let him know that she cared so much—then. "I meant it was perfectly natural for Papa to begin taking me with him on all his scientific expeditions, Temple, nothing more."

"Connie—you may have been given a gentleman's education by C.H. and all of his colleagues, but taking you to primitive locations around the world was hardly natural. The field is certainly no place for a growing girl—and it is no place for you to be now." He stared at her with eyes full of ice and contempt. "Go home, Connie. Save us all a lot of trouble and just...go... home."

If her netting had not been in place Temple would have seen her own brows rising in astonishment at his measured words. "I will not go home. So you may as well quit asking—or rather ordering me to do so."

He kicked a loose stone with the toe of his boot. It was difficult to put what he was feeling into words. Images of Connie as a child assaulted him each time he looked away from the veiled and swathed form of the determined person before him. "C.H. should've taken better care of you—he should have made sure you had an opportunity to be a..." His sentence trailed off.

Constance felt the heat climbing into her face. "A lady? Is that the word you are searching for?" She placed her hands on her hips and waited for his answer. He finally glanced up at her and she saw a new expression in his face. Eyes that were normally hard and cynical as agate now held something more elusive than the fragrance that wafted around him.

"No, Connie." He stared straight at her netting and for a moment she wondered if he could see her face. "I was going to say that you should have spent your youth at home. C.H. never should have dragged you across the world looking for bits of bone and broken rocks. It wasn't right. And it wasn't right for him to send you to do his battles now."

He gave her one last look, then he turned and walked away. She watched him and wondered why she felt the ridiculous urge to call him back.

Mr. Hughes had ingeniously used the wagon and three pieces of canvas to erect Constance a shelter for the night. He stood back while she examined it.

"Thank you, Mr. Hughes, it is wonderful, but I really could have managed with a bedroll. I have slept in the open many times."

"It was nothing, miss. I want you to be comfortable." He continued to test the strength of the canvas while he talked. Constance saw him smile each time she gave her approval to some small detail.

"The wind comes up of an evening, miss, and it turns cold, even this time of year. I wouldn't want you to take a chill."

"You are very considerate." She smiled and pushed her spectacles up with one finger.

Peter found himself staring at Miss Cadwallender in amazement. She had removed her netting and the full-length duster that she had worn over her traveling dress. The glow of the campfire cast a rosy blush across her smooth cheeks and the thick lustrous hair piled carelessly on top of her head. The small rectangular spectacles reflected crimson flames each time she moved her head to look at the simple lean-to.

"I have had to erect all manner of contrivances for shelter while traveling with my father, but this is really most remarkable."

Constance smiled and touched the canvas in an appreciative manner and he felt a burst of pride. At that moment Temple walked around the canvas lean-to.

"Top-notch, Hughes. I couldn't have done better myself. It reminds me of the camp I set up last year in the mountains of South America."

Miss Cadwallender stiffened and Peter saw the expression in her eyes change. He moved back into the shadows and busied himself while the two glared at each other.

Constance felt her good mood evaporate while she glared at Temple. The South American trip he mentioned had been only last summer and she had read more about it than she ever would have wished while the newspapers followed his progress. "Would that have been the camp where the American heiress tried to snare you in her butterfly net?" She knew her voice was a touch too sweet and a bit too sharp to be sincere—and she saw by the way Temple's brow shot up that he knew it also.

A wicked grin began to spread across his face and she regretted mentioning it.

"Constance Honoria, I do believe you have been reading *on dits* in the New York society columns. What would your father say about your choice of reading material?" Temple wrapped his long fingers around the suspenders hooked to the buttons on the waistband of his trousers. His cocky grin grew wider while he watched her. She wished she could simply disappear, but Temple's gaze held her as firmly as any leprechaun in a child's fable.

Temple couldn't help but grin at Connie. While he watched, her eyes widened behind her glasses, but suddenly she inhaled deeply and pulled herself up straighter than an aspen's trunk.

"Well, Mr. Parish—" her voice was composed even if her hands were trembling "—I imagine he would say it was the one place neither of us ever expected to find your name printed."

The smile faded from Temple's face and his mouth became a thin line. His craggy jaw hardened while a knot formed in her belly.

"Touché." Temple inclined his head and released his grip on his suspenders. "That barb certainly found its mark."

Too late Constance realized time had not dulled the raw pain he felt about his background. She regretted her comment almost as much as her reference to his South American trip, but she could not apologize.

He took a step toward her. She forced herself to meet his gaze without backing up so much as an inch, but in order to do that she had to bend her head back in a most uncomfortable position.

"You should become some deserving professor's wife. Then only one man would have to suffer the rough side of your tongue."

She stared unblinking into his flinty eyes. She pushed her spectacles up on the bridge of her nose and tried to tell herself that he could not be that tall and intimidating.

"Actually, Mr. Parish, only one man *is* suffering the rough side of my tongue, as you put it." Constance narrowed her gaze and watched him clamp his lips into a hard taut line.

Peter stood at the corner of the shelter and watched the couple staring at each other like a pair of bighorn rams during the rut. Neither one was willing to give an inch. But while they glared at each other, Peter sensed a power between them. The air felt charged, as if a great booming storm were about to come sweeping down from Canada.

Then he knew.

Temple Parish and Constance Cadwallender cared for each other. But if either one of them knew it, or admitted it to themselves, they were not about to admit it to the other. Peter caught himself smiling while he shook his head in amazement.

It was going to be a long and interesting summer in Montana's badlands. And whether they knew it or not, the young competitors had a lot more at stake than a bunch of bones.

Chapter Five

An unfamiliar sound brought Constance awake with a start. She saw nothing but darkness inside the lean-to. She turned her head and discovered that the flap to her enclosure was open a few inches on one side. Through the small slit she caught a glimpse of the camp. The campfire that had been a golden blaze when she dozed off was now nothing more than a circle of red embers. A crescent spring moon bathed everything in a dusky lavender wash and provided just enough light for her to make out nearby shapes.

She sat up and drew her knees up to her chin, while she pulled down her thin cotton gown tight around her ankles. The sounds of nocturnal creatures kept the night from being completely silent.

In New York, she frequently crept downstairs and into the secluded garden behind the brownstone just to stare at the night sky. But this Montana night was different. It was silent and compelling and seductive. Constance loved the silence, and living in the city she rarely enjoyed it. Only on expeditions to faraway and primitive places did she ever truly find the kind of peace she craved.

She crawled to the front of her tent, wanting to stare at the night, wishing to allow the almost silent night to seep into her soul.

As she emerged from the tent she saw two motionless forms positioned on either side of the smoldering fire. The steady rattle of Mr. Hughes's snores brought a smile to her lips. For this brief span of time she could enjoy a moment of solitude, a short respite from the tug-of-war that was going on between her and Temple.

Constance reached for her day coat but hesitated just short of touching it. She had grown tired of the bulky garments and insect netting that covered her face. She relished the freedom of movement she experienced while not wearing her boned corset under her sturdy dress. A capricious breeze fluttered over her cheeks and she realized how much she missed the feel of the sun and wind on her face. She drew in a breath and tasted the wilderness on her tongue.

Temple Parish might not believe it of her, but Constance loved this wild outdoor life as much as any man ever could. When she was in the field, in North America or some foreign exotic country, her senses sprang to life. She found herself rising before dawn from sheer excitement, and the possibility of discovery made it difficult for her to sleep at night. Right now she was eager for the dawn—anxious for the dig—and more than ready to show Temple Parish she was no longer the little girl he captured in his wooden carving.

Constance heard peeps, croaks and other feral sounds she preferred not to identify as she crept from her shelter. She was sensible enough not to stray too far from camp, but she did walk to the back side of the lean-to and look out across the unbroken expanse of black velvet prairie.

She raised her chin toward the heavens. Her unbound hair tickled the lower part of her spine through the thin fabric of her gown. The ebony sky invited her to reach toward it, and she found herself doing that, as if she could actually touch the soft texture and allow a handful of stars to trickle through her fingers like droplets of water.

Constance squinted her eyes and for a moment she thought she could pick out the constellation of Orion. Without her spectacles she could not be sure, but she preferred to believe it all the same.

The sound of wood scraping against wood brought her spinning around in surprise. She drew in a breath and held herself rigid while her eyes swept the crimson and ebony embers that marked camp. Now only one dark shape remained near the dying bed of coals.

Creeping forward, Constance searched for the source of the sound. She squinted her eyes and made out a looming shape in the half-light. When she heard a whispered string of descriptive expletives, she knew it was Temple fumbling around in the back of the wagon.

The sound of another crate being shoved across the wooden bottom of the wagon grated through the night and temporarily silenced some of the creatures around her but Mr. Hughes continued snoring.

"What is he up to?" she whispered to herself.

Constance hid beside her tent and watched while the dusky gray outline of Temple's body shifted and moved against the night. He stood up straight and she saw him drag his hand through his hair in obvious frustration. The sound of his deep-voiced cursing wafted to her from among the mounds of canvas and crates. Then his tall form bent over and she heard the sound of him rummaging through folds of canvas.

"He is looking for the carving." While Constance watched him searching through the back of the wagon, a smile tugged at the corners of her mouth. It gave her a silly surge of satisfaction to know Temple was looking for the very thing she had already found. After his surly attitude and continued disdain for her skills, she was happy to have a moment of pleasure—no matter how small or trivial.

Perhaps it was an omen, she thought. She had found the carving that he was searching for in vain. She was positive she would find the bones Mr. Montague was interested in.

Temple stood up once again and she fancied that he looked in her direction. She held her breath almost feeling the heat of his eyes upon her. But after a minute of peering into the darkness, he went back to his search and she released a tense breath. She crept around her lean-to and tiptoed back inside with a smile curving her lips.

A mournful howl silenced all the other night sounds for a moment and in that short measure of time, Constance heard the sound of flesh meeting wood. And then she heard Temple mutter a string of salty oaths.

She was chuckling softly to herself when she turned over and snuggled down inside her blankets.

The first thing Temple did when he woke was check his bruised shin. He had stumbled against one of Connie's damned trunks while he was looking for that silly carving last night. It annoyed him that he couldn't find it—it annoyed him that he had made it in the first place. He squatted by the morning campfire and pulled down his pant leg, but the ridiculous mound of gauze caught on his bootlaces. He lifted his hand, stringing shredded gauze like a spider's web.

"Damn foolish thing." He ripped the remaining bandage from his thumb. "I swear," he muttered under his breath, "I am going to ignore Miss Constance Honoria Cadwallender. If she has no more sense than to stay, then so be it. Filbert Montague's dinosaur bones are the only thing I'm interested in." Temple wadded the bandage up and tossed it into the fire.

It had occurred to Temple during his sleepless night, that C.H. had sent Connie in his stead because Temple had always looked out for her. The old fox knew Temple was the better digger—everybody knew Temple was the best digger. But C.H. was shrewd and ruthless. Perhaps he was counting on Temple having a soft place in his heart for little Connie. And perhaps C.H. and Dandridge had hoped that he would allow sentimentality to get in the way and enable them to claim the prize.

"Well, it isn't going to work, C.H." He swore.

Did his old mentor really believe that his brotherly feelings for Connie would prevent him from claiming Montague's endowment? If so, then he was in for a big surprise. Temple could ignore little Connie Cadwallender. He was going to find the bones and get away from Connie and the Montana territory just as quickly as the train could take him back to New York. And when he accepted the endowment for Ashmont, then every professor at Dandridge University would finally have to admit Temple Parish had made it to the top on his skills—and not in the way they claimed.

It was midday when Peter pointed to the great gouge in the earth.

"This is the starting point of the Devil's Spur." He inclined his head toward the cleft in the earth. Temple levered himself up from his spot between the trunks so he could get a good look.

The earth was treeless and barren here, the weathered soil a dusty gray. Erosion and wind had cut fantastic hollows and gullies in the ground, and there to his right lay a fissure. Temple allowed his gaze to wander up the cut. As far as he could see, there was a great laceration that grew progressively wider and deeper.

"Is this where the bones were found?" Temple asked.

"At the far end," Peter said without turning around or allowing the team to slow. "The Morgans have a mine near here. One of their hands had been doing some blasting nearby and found a big chunk of earth with little fish bones and such in it."

"I am so glad they contacted the university," Connie said from behind her netting.

Until that moment, Temple had almost forgotten she was there. Now his anger and frustration washed over him again. He slid back into the small space between the trunks and crates. He didn't want to talk to her—didn't want to think about her. It made him itchy and mad all at the same time—and all he cared about was getting Montague's prize.

Temple pulled his hat low over his forehead and stared out the back of the wagon. The day wore on while he watched the Devil's Spur grow in size. By afternoon the sides of the canyon were at least thirty feet deep and the middle of the cut was flat and wide enough to set up camp in.

The slice in the earth must have been caused by

some cataclysmic event aeons past. In the long deep trough grew bitterroot, and small shrubs. On either side of the flat expanse in the middle, the earth rose in great striated walls. The afternoon shadows made the impressive rent look somewhat ominous.

Constance was excited and eager to begin digging. The ribbons of color reminded her of a child's lollipop. She rose from the wagon seat and allowed her eyes to sweep over the primal landscape.

She had discarded the netting earlier since there were few biting insects. The cold spring breeze fluttered over her bare cheeks while her mind raced ahead, plotting the most logical location of bones.

"It is truly remarkable, Mr. Hughes," she said.

"Yep." Peter stared at the deep gash. "This is on the Flying B Ranch but you are a long way from the house. Lake Nowhere is just over that rise."

"Lake Nowhere?" Constance frowned. "What a strange name."

Peter shrugged. "You are in the middle of nowhere, miss. Like I said, the owner of the Flying B has some mines near here and they do fish in the lake from time to time, but other than a few cowboys checking for strays or taking supplies to the mine, people tend to shy away from this section of the badlands."

"What do they mine?" Constance was truly interested in this otherworldly landscape.

"Manganese—lead. There used to be some gold but I think the veins have played out."

"This is a wonderful opportunity to document and catalog the area." Constance sat down. "I will be spending the first few weeks I am here sketching the terrain."

"Sketching?" Temple sat bolt upright so fast he

raked his ribs on a trunk latch. It smarted almost as much as his pride. He had sworn he would not be drawn into a conversation with Connie, but her ridiculous words could not go by unquestioned. "You are planning to sketch?" The question tumbled out of his mouth while he managed to stand up.

"Yes. I have been responsible for the sketches of all Papa's expeditions. I see no reason why I should not treat this dig like all the others." She frowned up at Temple. "Is there some reason why you find it so unusual?" She felt herself growing more defensive as he stared at her with wide eyes.

He shook his head and laughed. "Connie, you sketch as much as you want. I am grabbing a shovel and finding those bones as soon as camp is set up. While I'm headed back to New York you can do all the pretty watercolors you like." He vaulted over the side of the wagon and walked away chuckling. "I'll think of you when I accept Mr. Montague's check."

"You are very sure of yourself, Temple." Constance stood up and hitched up her skirt so she could step onto the big wheel of the wagon. She perched there for a moment while she watched the man who continued to patronize and belittle her at every turn.

"I have good reason to be sure of myself." He paused long enough to spear her with a glance. "I have worked hard—and enjoyed some degree of success over the past ten years. This dig is no different. I intend to get the bones and be out of here before you are even settled in." He turned his back on her and started to walk away.

She hopped down to the ground with a swish of the heavy material. "Then by all means don't let me detain you." She shouted at his wide back. "Which side of the gorge do you wish to set your camp on?"

Temple lurched to a stop. He turned to Constance with a blank expression on his face. His hat was shoved back on his head, tawny hair jutting from under the brim. He squinted his dark brown eyes against the bright sunlight.

"What do you mean, 'which side'?" He crossed his arms at his chest. Sinewy bands of muscle bunched beneath the rolled-up sleeves of his pale shirt.

He looked strong, virile and too handsome. It just wasn't fair that he could be so good-looking and yet be so maddening. Constance shook her head to banish the image of him as man. She had to focus on him as ruthless competitor.

"Under the circumstances we cannot pitch our tents cheek-to-jowl. We need space between us." She swept her hand forward to indicate the wide rift of earth. "We have to be organized in such a way that there can be no question, no dispute, over which of us is the clear winner of Mr. Montague's endowment." She shoved her spectacles up on the bridge of her nose. "Surely you agree."

After a moment of contemplative silence, he cleared his throat and one brow lifted. He dragged the hat off his head and raked his hand through thick hair that glistened in the sunlight.

"All right, I see your point. How do you propose we split up the supplies Mr. Montague sent?"

She was not having much success ignoring the way the afternoon rays made his eyes gleam like polished agates.

"In half would be the most logical method," she managed to say.

Temple swallowed hard. He tried to banish the image of danger that Connie might encounter if she were alone. "Where do you intend to camp?" he asked, while he cursed himself for breaking his vow to stop feeling responsible.

"You pick which side of the gorge you prefer, then I will be free to choose what is left." Constance offered reasonably.

Anger flashed through Temple. He had the overpowering urge to shake some sense into her silly little head. She had no idea how rough this dig could become. This was the West, not some well-clipped and tended park. How could C.H. let his only child put herself in this kind of danger? The more he thought about it, the more anger and frustration boiled up inside him.

"Fine—I'll take this side. This side looks just dandy. Is that all right with you?" Temple slapped his hat against his thigh. Dust rose from his pants in a little puff. Then he muttered a curse and stalked away.

"There is no need to become peevish, Temple. The opposite side will do fine." Constance turned to see Mr. Hughes watching her. He was wearing a tight-lipped expression, so unlike his usual habit of being on the verge of laughter. Men were so difficult to understand.

"Mr. Hughes, if you would be so kind as to deliver the remainder of the supplies and my three trunks to the other side of the canyon after Mr. Parish has removed his half."

"Yes, miss, I would be happy to do that, miss." Peter hopped into the wagon seat and picked up the reins. Temple was already hefting crates and boxes from the back of the wagon. Each time he dropped one onto the earth, he muttered a different expletive. He paused once to glare at Constance. For a moment she thought he was going to say something to her, but he shook his head and went back to unloading the wagon.

"Mr. Hughes, I need to stretch my legs after that long ride." Constance allowed her eyes to scan the ravine once again. "I will take my sketching box, for I might see something of interest along the way. I will meet you on the other side—and erect my own tent later." The last few words were more for Temple's benefit than for Mr. Hughes's. She expected to hear a disparaging remark from her rival but he kept his lips clamped tight and ignored her.

Peter grinned and nodded his graying head. "Yes, miss, that sounds like a fine idea. I will have to take the team back the way we came and come around the end of the canyon. The sides slope down kind of gentle here, so just watch your step. It shouldn't take me more than a couple of hours to reach the other side. Will you be needing anything else to take with you?"

Temple snapped his head up and stared at Peter. His scowl was darker than a thunderhead. "Of course she doesn't *need anything*, Hughes. Haven't you been listening? She is more than competent. She is a bloody wonder," Temple snapped. "If she meets up with a grizzly she can explain to him that she is a most accomplished anatomist, or she can sketch him." He put his arms akimbo while he spoke. "I am sure the bear will be most impressed by Miss Cadwallender's long list of accomplishments." Temple clasped his wide hands at his waist. "He will be so awed that he will forget all about wanting to *eat her*." He was practically bellowing by the time he spit out the last two words.

"Really, Temple, you are astonishing." Constance had no idea what Temple was going on about, or why Mr. Hughes had doubled over in the seat with laughter at this latest outburst. She didn't understand what possessed either one of them, but she had grown tired of trying to figure them out. She tucked her sketching box beneath her arm and starting walking.

Temple hammered his tent stake deep into the earth with the mallet. He stood up and surveyed his work with a critical eye. The canvas was taut, the lines pegged securely into the Montana dirt. He had placed the opening to the east so the morning sun would warm and wake him, or so he told himself.

When he looked up from the mouth of his tent it was Connie's camp that greeted his eyes on the other side of the gorge. And just as he expected, Peter Hughes was busy erecting Connie's tent while she was meandering through the bottom of the canyon.

A wave of some emotion swept through Temple, but he couldn't quite define it. It might have been irritation that the old goat went out of his way to pamper Connie, but it just as easily might have been something else.

"I am not jealous," Temple muttered aloud while he hit the last stake with the mallet. "The idea is preposterous."

But he glanced back at the neat camp growing on the other side of the hollow and found unexpected emotions flooding through him.

"I couldn't care any less. She is on her own." He

kicked a tent stake with the toe of his boot. The rope twanged in response.

After he came to live with C.H., Temple had always been the one who fixed things or solved problems that were beyond Connie's ability. He had been her hero.

Now he stared at the tent poles and struggled to deny he was disappointed that he was not the one she would come to when she needed help here in Montana.

The sound of paper fluttering in the canyon drew Temple's attention. He walked to the edge of the cut and looked down. There, about thirty feet below him was Connie. She was sitting on the dirt with her sketching pad in her lap. Her dark chestnut hair had tumbled free along her back and the sunlight skipped over her delicate cheek and deposited tiny diamonds on her smooth skin. The scene could have been from a watercolor study, such a bucolic picture she made.

Temple shook his head and steeled himself against the wayward thoughts and feelings.

She was his enemy—his competitor. Temple Parish had survived the past ten years by never forgetting the most important thing in his life was winning.

He never gave an edge to those who were against him and Constance Honoria was very much against him as long as she was aligned with C.H. and Dandridge University. He had never forgotten what happened ten years ago. With the exception of the death of his mother on that freezing January night, his departure from C.H.'s house had been the most traumatic and painful event in his life. He couldn't allow himself to hurt like that again, he thought as he took a step closer to the edge.

Constance was concentrating on an interesting stony outcrop when a scatter of gravel rained down on her hat. She shielded her eyes against the sun with the side of her hand and scanned the ridge above her.

Much to her surprise, Temple was standing on the edge, about three stories above her. She pushed her spectacles up on her nose and met his unmoving gaze. A strange thing happened to her insides while they stared silently at each other. She couldn't identify the odd emotion that gripped her. It was very curious that looking at him could cause physical reactions—but it did nonetheless.

Her breath caught in her throat and her mouth dried out. It was most extraordinary. Constance swallowed hard and managed a thin smile but Temple did not return it. In fact, she could have sworn his dour expression darkened before he spun on his heel and disappeared from her view beyond the rim of the canyon.

"Remarkable," she muttered. She did not remember Temple having such a sulky and prickly personality. Her ten-year-old memories of him all involved playful teasing and capricious pranks. It saddened her to think the years had hardened the laughing boy he had once been into the scowling man who now challenged her.

Constance looked up at the opposite side of the gorge and saw the top of a tent come into view. "Oh dear, this will not do." She stood and gathered her sketching supplies and tucked the box under her arm. By the time she had managed to climb the natural stairs of the rock path to her side of the canyon she was winded and covered with dust. "Mr. Hughes, you must not do this. Temple will never take me seriously as a competitor if you continue to treat me like a helpless child."

Mr. Hughes looked at her with his brows arched high. And then, true to form, he burst out laughing.

By nightfall Constance was settled at her new camp. She dipped the last bite from one of the tins Mr. Montague had sent. Her dinner had been passable, the smoky attar of the open fire soothing. She sighed and allowed her eyes to linger on the lavender-dusted terrain. With Mr. Hughes gone and Temple across the gorge, she had complete solitude. It was wonderful. Constance closed her eyes and pretended that she was the only human at the gorge.

Temple stared at the amber glow of Connie's campfire across the canyon and grew more restless with each passing minute. He wrapped his fingers tighter around the hot cup of coffee.

It was quiet—the kind of quiet that rattled his nerves and leached away his patience. He hated the silence. When calm descended upon him he was no longer able to push aside his painful memories. Silence was what came with a killing New York blizzard—quiet brought death to poverty-weakened women like his dear mother.

He swallowed hard and forced himself to sip the hot brew. Control was a thing Temple cherished and worked hard to maintain, but as he sat in the unforgiving hush of the Montana night he could not help but wish he had hired a small crew. Then at least he would have had someone to talk to during the hard hours between dusk and bedtime.

"But Connie probably wouldn't like that—she'd say it was unfair, not ethical." He shook his head and realized he was talking to himself. "I better find those bones in a hurry or I'll be a babbling fool."

Temple stood up and tossed the contents of the cup

into the dying fire. It sputtered for a moment, then a dying hiss accompanied the last stubborn flame as it flickered out. He went into his tent and yanked off his boots. He was not really tired, but he could not bear to sit in the dark and watch Connie's campfire. At least sleep would block out his memories and if he rose early he would get a jump on Connie. The sooner he found those damned bones, the sooner he could get out of this forlorn place. It never ceased to amaze him that he had fallen in love with a profession that ensured he would spend time alone.

The morning air was crisp and slightly damp when Constance stretched herself awake. She opened one eye and saw that full dawn was still a half hour away.

She took off her thin cotton gown while chills danced up her thighs and arms. Shivering against the cold, she slipped into her chemise and sturdy mustard-colored dress. She thrust her stocking-covered feet into her boots and laced them tight around her ankles. Then she quickly piled her hair on top of her head and stuck a few pins in to hold it.

She got her fire started rapidly, but when she started making coffee she discovered all the water barrels had accidentally been unloaded on Temple's side of the gorge. If she had done any real cooking last evening, instead of eating from tins, she would have noticed it then and could have trudged over for a canteen full, but she had been so enamored of the stark lonely prairie that she had not even noticed.

Now she stared at Temple's camp across the wide chasm that separated one side of the canyon from the other. There was a natural gentle staircase of boulders on each side, and the distance between them was no more than half a mile. It was an easy walk but she saw nothing to indicate he was awake yet.

Pink ribbons were beginning to unfurl in the eastern sky behind her as she stood there, with the empty coffeepot in her hand. She wondered if she should hike to his camp and wake him. Or should she wait until she saw him moving about? His disposition had been volatile; the thought of rousing him early did not inspire much enthusiasm in her.

Constance glanced around. She found herself wondering how far the lake Mr. Hughes had spoken of was from her camp.

"Surely not too far, or else he would not have mentioned it," she muttered.

Constance sighed and shoved her spectacles up on her nose. Temple had been testy enough lately. She didn't want to set him off on the first morning of the dig.

"No, not on our first morning." With one final glance at Temple's silent camp, she set off in the general direction Mr. Hughes had indicated.

The morning sun arced over the horizon before Constance had even lost sight of her tent. The terrain was a bit rocky but walking was not difficult. She was amazed at the diverse fauna that grew in the somewhat harsh landscape. Sagebrush, greasewood and alderwood were scattered on the craggy hills and in the deepest ravines or shaded areas, small patches of snow remained as if to remind her that nature maintained a tight grip on this austere land.

By the time she found the lake, a long shimmering finger of water between two craggy knolls, the sun had burned off the morning dew and taken most of the chill from the thin air. The day promised to be clear, perfect for her to sketch the strata of the canyon walls for Dandridge's archives.

Constance hiked up her skirt and squatted beside the pebble-strewed shore. She dipped the edge of the coffeepot in the gently lapping water and watched the water flow into the speckled blue gray cavern. When she looked up, a fish silently jumped out in the middle of the placid lake. Sunlight turned the trout's slippery scales to an iridescent rainbow. A smiled tugged at her mouth. She would much prefer a fresh fish dinner to eating from the tins. Surely she could sketch for a few hours and then return to the lake for an afternoon of angling.

Papa had drilled her since childhood about being prepared for anything, so as usual she had packed her fishing gear and a few other items she would probably never use. It would be nice, this time, to put some of that cumbersome gear to use.

She was lost in her own world, standing on the shore, watching the watery silver ribbons, when strong fingers bit into her shoulders. She was roughly spun around and found herself staring into a furious face.

"Where in God's name have you been?" Temple leaned close enough to fog her glasses with his angry breath. She was taken aback by the hard polished gleam in his agate eyes.

"I came to the lake for water. Temple, you are hurting me." Constance glanced at his white-knuckled hands biting into her upper arms.

Temple blinked and removed his hands. "Sorry." He managed to stop glowering at her but his body remained rigid and his eyes blazed. "What do you think you are doing—going off—so early?"

"Was there something you needed?" Constance

pushed her spectacles up and peered at Temple. His hair was disheveled, and his shirttail flapped loose beneath his suspenders as if he had jerked his clothes on hurriedly. "Did you come looking for me?"

He glanced at Constance and the gleam in his eye intensified. "No. Yes. I mean to say that is… " His mouth compressed into a tight uncompromising line before he turned and stalked away, leaving her standing by the lake.

"Temple? Is there anything wrong?" Constance called out but he didn't stop.

"No, Connie, everything is just fine—just fine." He shook his head in disgust. What in blue blazes was the matter with him? He had gotten up early and gone to Connie's camp on the pretext of offering her assistance with her cooking fires, but when he found her gone…something inside of him had just snapped.

He slowed his furious pace and dragged his fingers through his hair. Connie had told him that she had traveled all over the world with C.H., not to mention the fact that ten years had passed since he had needed to watch out for her. So why had his gut twisted with fear when he had found her gone?

"Old habits die hard," he grumbled bitterly.

He hated to admit it, but he knew exactly what was the matter with him.

He still felt responsible for Connie. When C.H. had found him beaten and hungry in Central Park and brought him home, little Connie had accepted him without question. To show his appreciation, he had appointed himself her guardian. And no matter how furious he was at her now, nothing she ever did could wipe away the feeling of gratitude he had felt in her simple acceptance.

Eighteen years had gone by since he first laid eyes on her as a little girl, but when he really forced himself to admit the truth, he realized little had changed. Temple felt obligated to keep Connie safe, and that made him angry with himself—because she was his rival. He couldn't allow himself to go soft where she was concerned, not with Montague's endowment and a chance to humble C.H. hanging in the balance. And yet, when it came to Connie, he knew he could never be completely ruthless.

It was going to be difficult, but he was going to have to make sure Connie did not claim more of him than she already had.

Chapter Six

Temple tossed another shovelful of earth into the growing pile. He rammed the nose of the shovel into the damp earth and hopped into the sizable hole he had created within the half-mile-wide gully between his and Connie's campsites.

"What have we here?" Temple knelt in the depression and knocked away some loose earth with his hand. He leaned closer and blew away some more dirt. A sly smile plucked at the corners of his mouth. The vague outline, something only a professional would recognize, was a giant vertebra encased within the sandy soil.

"Miss Cadwallender, you should hurry with your sketching because I am already on the trail of the prize." Temple rubbed appreciative fingers around the rough edges of the ancient bone. He glanced up over his shoulder at the spot where Connie had been sitting all morning.

She was gone.

He stood up and scanned the horizon with concern gripping him. A flutter of yellow fabric brought relief flooding through him. She was climbing the natural stair to her own camp. A ragged sigh escaped him. It was only natural that he keep a close watch on his competitor, to know if she found any sign of bones. After all, he couldn't let her accidentally discover something without his knowing about it. That was the only reason he was so anxious to know where she was. There was *no* other reason, he told himself.

Temple climbed from the hole, satisfied that she was out of harm's way for at least a while. She was probably going to go rest in her tent. She was probably exhausted from the rigors of their primitive camp. It was ridiculous to think he had any interest whatsoever in her beyond the fact that she was his rival. In his eyes she would forever be a child and C.H.'s little girl—two facts that assured his total disinterest.

Constance drank the last of her tepid coffee, tossed out the dregs and opened one trunk. She bent nearly double to dig all the way to the bottom. The tiny carving Temple had made caught her eye when she was burrowing into mounds of cloth and supplies. She touched it lightly with her fingertips and admired the simple details. The braids, the pinafore, a perfect little girl's mode of dress.

"A very little girl," she muttered. She pushed aside the statue and pulled out a sturdy if somewhat ancient cane pole. A dour Scot named Hamish had taught her to fish with the prized cane. As she picked it up she realized a considerable length of time had elapsed since she had used the pole. She wondered if her old mentor would be disappointed in her skills—if they had grown rusty from disuse.

She flicked her wrist, going through the motions of casting before she ever left her tent. Not satisfied with the feel of her single imaginary attempt, she threaded the line, put a hook on it and tried again. This time she flicked her hand, feeling long unused muscles stretch and bend as she sent the hook and line floating backward over her head.

"What the—watch out—!" The alarm in Temple's voice brought her wheeling around, wide-eyed. He was standing at the entrance of her tent with her fishing hook firmly embedded in the crown of his hat. Several coils of line had somehow looped across his face, over the bridge of his nose and dangled down his cheek in a mass of knots.

Constance frowned at him. "Temple, you have snarled my line." She had been patient with him, but this was really too much. She could not believe his clumsiness. He had continued to belittle her skills and yet he was so awkward that he kept getting into difficulty. First he sliced upon his finger and now this. And, she thought sourly, he had an annoying habit of showing up uninvited. She could almost believe it was intentional—done to annoy her.

She walked nearer to him, balancing her pole in one hand while she surveyed the damage he had done to her hook. With an impatient shake of her head, she placed her pole on the floor of the tent and reached up to start the laborious task of removing the snarled line from his hat.

He flinched as if reluctant to have her touch him.

"Do be still, Temple, you will ruin my hook if you don't stop fidgeting."

Temple's eyes widened and his mouth gaped open in a manner that reminded her of a large-mouth bass.

"Ruin your hook? Ruin your *hook?*" he repeated

with no small amount of disbelief in his voice. "More likely I'll end up with a ruined hat."

Temple was incredulous. Connie had snared him, yet she was accusing *him* of fouling *her* line. She was the silliest girl he had ever known and no matter how he vowed to ignore her she kept managing to involve him in her foolishness.

"I narrowly avoided having that hook put in my eye—you could've blinded me with that blasted thing. The least you could do is apologize."

The fragrance of her sun-kissed hair wafted around his head. Each time she reached up to take hold of a knot, the front of her body softly collided with his. Her shiny hair, combined with the odor of fresh air and her own clean scent, made his vitals tighten.

Temple clamped his lips together. This was not the way he intended to behave around her. He fought to rein in his wild response while equal portions of shame and dread coursed through him. How on earth could his body be responding in such a way?

"I don't believe I heard you correctly. Apologize? To you?" She arched one brow. "I do believe you are in *my* tent. If apologies are due then I think you should be the one offering."

He opened his mouth to reply, then changed his mind. She had the damnedest habit of blaming him for her failings. And he was not about to explain his presence at her tent.

"Really, Temple, don't scowl at me like that." She slanted one disapproving glance at him. "I don't know what to make of you. First you leap upon me at the lake, now you skulk around, come uninvited into my tent where you snarl my fishing line, and you have the brass to accuse me of trying to disable you." She halted her efforts and peered up at him from behind her rectangle lenses. "Are you quite sure you've not gotten too much sun?"

Temple swallowed hard and tried not to notice the golden flecks around the irises of her eyes. "I did not leap upon you at the lake," he said sullenly. "I only grabbed you."

"Grabbed—leaped—what is the difference? What were you doing out there? You never did explain." She resumed her efforts to free him from the hook and continued speaking, not waiting to see if he offered any explanation. "As I recall, you did come upon me without warning. What possessed you to do such a thing?" she asked.

He was able to scan her face while she concentrated on the line. Her lashes were so long and thick they actually grazed the inside of her lenses.

"I...was...worried about you," he admitted grudgingly.

Once again she paused and stared at him in total disbelief. "Why on earth would you be worried about me?" She lifted one section of fishing line away from his hat and stared up at him intently. "There is no danger out here—there is only you and me for miles and miles."

A chill ran up his spine as the truth of her statement settled upon him like icy water. There was only the two of them—alone. And while he was fighting to ignore the sight and scent of her, a small voice in his head pointed out that Connie had come a long way from being a child.

He had to stay angry, he realized with a start. He had to keep his guard up. His future, his reputation—as sullied and tarnished as it was—depended upon his winning this prize.

"Temple?" Her voice wrenched his thoughts back. "Why on earth would you be worried about me?"

"Under the circumstances, Constance, it is a perfectly reasonable reaction. I couldn't find you in your tent—though Lord knows, as big as it is, it would be easy to lose a person inside here," Temple quipped. "As a sane and rational man, I was concerned that some harm had come to you out here in the wilderness." Temple realized with a jolt that he had said far more than he should have, far more than he'd intended, but as usual she caused his control to slip.

He observed a smile tickling the corners of her lips and her eyes crinkled slightly at the corners.

"I see," she said softly.

Temple wished he had the same clarity of vision she seemed to possess, because he did not see. Try as he might, he could find no reasonable explanation for his actions. The only thing he should be interested in was digging up bones, yet he was fretting over Connie at every turn.

"There." Constance removed the last of the fishing line and stepped back. "You are free."

She pushed the spectacles up on the bridge of her nose and smiled mischievously at him. "I am going to go catch a fish for my dinner, and while I am perfectly capable of taking care of myself, you are more than welcome to come along—if it will relieve you of any unnecessary worry."

Without waiting for a response, she put her huge hat on her head, gathered her pole and line and stepped outside the tent. Then she marched off toward the lake without so much as a backward glance. Temple stared at the voluminous outline of her day coat swaying from side to side while he tried to sort out his feelings. The bones were waiting for him—all he had to do was go dig them up. He could be out of here before Connie even broke ground.

"Damn and double damn," he swore. He kicked a nearby stone but all he accomplished by that action was making his toe hurt. He looked up and saw Connie growing smaller and smaller as she walked away in the direction of Lake Nowhere.

Damn it, he was concerned about her. Any number of possible calamities raced through his mind. Everything from snakebite to bear attack loomed before him. Images of little Connie in peril flitted through his head.

With one last string of oaths about his stupidity and her stubbornness, Temple started walking. He couldn't let her go wandering off alone—even if it meant losing an entire afternoon of digging.

By the time Temple reached the river, Connie was sitting comfortably on the bank. She had removed the canvas day coat. The ample folds of her dress were draped around her ankles and the pole was propped between her knees. Relentless sunshine beat down on the top of her hat. The long sleeves of her butter-colored dress had been rolled up. She looked quite snug—and very capable.

It annoyed him to the core of his soul.

"Connie…"

"Shhh…sit down and be quiet, before you scare the fish," she ordered without even looking in his direction.

That annoyed him more.

Temple fixed the most intimidating frown he could manage on his face and cleared his throat gruffly, but

Connie never even glanced his way. He realized she wasn't going to, so he grudgingly plopped down on the gravelly earth.

The spring wind blew across the surface of the lake and raised little ripples along the water. A blue-green dragonfly landed on the end of Connie's pole, but other than those natural occurrences it was silent. Temple could actually hear the sound of his own heartbeat and the cry of a hawk far, far away.

Once again the reminder of too many dark nights, alone and cold in the park, assaulted him. He needed to talk, needed to hear another voice.

"What ever happened to Herbert Pollock?" Temple blurted out in a voice that shattered the stillness.

Connie turned to glare at him over the top of her spectacles. Her dusky brown eyes were wide with displeasure.

"Shhh," she hissed. She turned back toward the pole. Just when Temple decided she had no intentions of answering his question, she spoke. "Do you mean Professor Andrew Pollock?"

"No. I mean young Herbert Pollock, the professor's son." Temple picked a stem of bear grass and started shredding it. Now that Connie had answered, he wished he had not asked the question he had carried for ten years. "Of course I suppose nobody calls him young Herbert now, do they?"

"I...don't know. I haven't heard his name mentioned for some time." Connie frowned. He could see her searching the recesses of her mind for information. "Let me think. Oh yes, I believe he came into some money—an inheritance or some sort of bequest, a while back. He is a prominent merchant with a string of stores in New York." Connie reached up and tweaked the line with one slender finger. Ripples appeared on the silvery water moving out in ever widening circles toward the shore.

Temple snorted. "I rather imagine that did not sit well with his father."

"Really?" Connie asked absently while she adjusted her pole. "Why would that be?"

Temple shrugged. "Professor Pollock had made no secret of the fact he was grooming his son to follow in his footsteps. I would've thought he would be the head of the scientific department by now."

Connie gazed at Temple as if he had lost all his powers of reason. He wished he was a clairvoyant so he might read what was going on beyond those inscrutable eyes of hers.

"Pollock? Are we talking about the same Herbert Pollock?" She searched her memory, but the only thing she could recall about Herbert Pollock was that he had rather narrow shoulders and a sallow complexion, and he stammered a lot. But then again he may have only appeared to be awkward and puny when measured against Temple's youthful brawn—something that Constance had done quite often.

"I didn't realize any of that. Where did you ever get such a notion?" She asked.

With Connie's velvety brown eyes gazing at him over the reflective surface of her lenses, he suddenly found himself tongue-tied. It was not a reaction he expected or liked. Temple turned away and looked out at the shimmering water. He swallowed hard and forced his voice to respond.

"Ten years ago Pollock made it plain he wasn't going to let a street rat like me stand in his way, or thwart his plan for his son's future."

"Why would he say such a thing? How could you have had any effect on Herbert?"

"Perhaps Andrew Pollock and Herbert saw me as a rival."

Constance's brow shot upward. The idea that Temple could ever have considered someone like Herbert Pollock a rival took her breath away. Poor Herbert was so outmatched by Temple in every way the entire notion was laughable. She was about to tell him how absurd she found the idea, when the sudden dip of her pole brought her gaze back to the lake.

"Oh—I've got one." She leaped to her feet. Herbert Pollock was completely forgotten while her attention was riveted on the fish thrashing at the end of her line.

Temple stood up and reached out for the pole only to have his hand unceremoniously slapped away by her smaller one.

"I know how to do this, Connie. Let me help you," he offered stiffly.

"I know how to do this as well." She raised one brow as if the gesture would emphasize her abilities. "Now stop interfering." She looked back at the churning water and focused on the fish.

"Connie, it is a big one—don't be silly, let me land him for you."

She did not look at Temple while she continued to direct the fish's course. "I am perfectly capable of landing my own fish, thank you." Her glasses had slid to the end of her nose again. She managed to shove them up with one finger while she precariously balanced the pole in her left hand, while maneuvering her skirt.

The fish leaped from the water leaving a spray of

jewel-like droplets in his efforts to pull free of the hook. Temple was sure the line would break. "He's a fighter, Connie, let me take the pole—" He paced beside her anxiously. He could hardly restrain himself from snatching the pole from her hands.

"No," she snapped before he could finish his request. "Now stand back before you foul my line." She held the pole aloft and stepped around Temple. When he turned, he found himself trapped between the water and her damnable full skirt. She grabbed the trailing line in her free hand and tried to steer past him again when the trout suddenly changed directions.

"Careful, Connie. Give him some play," Temple advised. The fish swam to and fro while Temple walked beside her, barking directions with each step he took.

"Stop ordering me about, Temple. I am quite proficient at this—if you would just kindly get out of my way." She turned away, refusing to listen to him.

Temple felt a tug on his boot and looked down. His foot had nearly become tangled in the end of Connie's line. It occurred to him that she would find some way of blaming the situation on him so he decided to act before that could happen. "Hold still, let me get free here first."

"What? What are you saying?" She cast one exasperated glance at him but the fish jumped, tugging on the pole.

Water churned while the fish began to fight in earnest. Connie sidestepped down the bank, while Temple tried to disengage himself from the line, but the loop continued to shrink around his boot top.

"Connie, give me the pole, I'll get him to shore," he offered. He stretched his arm toward her, shifting his center of gravity, compromising his balance in his attempt to reach the pole.

"Don't be ridiculous, Temple. Just grab the dratted fish when I bring him up to you." Connie deftly transferred the pole to her other hand. He closed his fingers around empty air.

Temple was certain the fish would break free, but to his astonishment, she neatly guided the great trout nearer the bank.

"Good work, Connie girl." Temple felt an unexpected burst of pride, followed by a renewed sense of frustration because she would not let him help her. "Just a little closer—a—little—closer."

Temple leaned toward the line but the fish made one last desperate run at freedom. Before he knew what was happening, the fish, or perhaps it was Connie, had somehow managed to tighten the line around his boot tops into a noose. He felt himself slipping on the pebbled shore.

"Connie, wait a minute, I seem to be—"

Temple's words were cut off by a splash. Constance turned to see his shapeless hat floating on the surface of the lake. Concentric circles rippled outward. Suddenly he came up sputtering, cursing a steady stream of obscenities. He shook water from his head like a great wet dog and glared at her.

"Temple, what on earth are you doing? You are going to make me lose my fish with all your foolishness," Constance said. "Do stop capering around and assist me."

He glowered at her through a clump of wet green moss clinging to his forehead. "I am *not* capering around. I think you are intentionally trying to drown me." He dragged his palm down his face to remove some of the water and moss. A small piece remained stuck on the bridge of his nose.

Constance rolled her eyes heavenward and continued to play the fish. "Don't be utterly ridiculous. Why on earth would I want to drown you?"

She took a step out into the water. The moisture quickly climbed up her full skirt and soaked the fabric until it clung suggestively to her thighs.

"You know, Temple, I think you have the mistaken notion that I am your enemy."

Temple's gaze kept skimming over the wet outline of her upper legs while his gut tightened painfully. He tried to stand but his boots kept slipping in the soft mire of the lake bottom.

"Aren't you my enemy?" he asked, finally managing to lurch into a standing position.

"Of course not. We are competitors—there is a difference." She glanced at him over the top of her glasses. "You don't seriously believe I wish to injure you in some way so you will be unable to dig for bones?" she inquired while she played the fish. "Do you?"

Hearing her put the concept into words made Temple feel like a dolt. "Don't be silly, Connie, just let me have the damned pole," He reached out but she jerked away from him. In the process of thwarting his attempt to take the pole she threw herself off balance. She disappeared in a splash of water that twinkled like jewels in the sunlight.

Temple reached beneath the water and grabbed her shoulders. He pulled her to the surface with one hand. Her hat was drooping down around her face. Water dripped from her spectacles, but she still had a firm grip on the pole.

"I hope you are satisfied, Temple Parish. Now we are both wet."

He started to give her a sharp retort but realized it was useless to try to reason with her. She took off her hat and neatly snagged the fat trout inside the saturated brim.

"There we are, my fine fellow. It's off to the frying pan for you." She turned and frowned at Temple over her water-spotted lenses. "If you are quite through frolicking and accusing me of trying to disable you, I *could* use some help." She stumbled in the mud and landed on her backside in the water again. The last pin holding her wet hair slipped out. Sodden strands came tumbling down upon her shoulders in a shimmering mass.

Temple could only stare at her in disbelief. He raised his palms heavenward in a gesture of frustrated supplication.

"What do you think I have been trying to do? I have offered to help, several times in fact, but you insist on doing everything by yourself." He dragged his hand down his face and sighed.

She shook her head as if to deny his words. A little spray of water from the ends of her hair hit him in one eye.

"I am quite sure I don't know *what* you have been doing—or what you are talking about." With one last indignant toss of her head, she regained her feet and trudged back toward the shore. "I am a reasonable person and would *never* refuse a legitimate offer of help."

Temple bit back a scathing reply about how reasonable she was. He tried to take a step but the line was still tangled up around his ankles. His backside ended up in the muck again. He was cursing steadily under his breath while he reached down and grasped the line with one hand. Too late he realized what was going to happen when he jerked. The pole snapped taut, pulling against Connie's unyielding grip. She disappeared beneath the water. She came up sputtering, with her hair hanging in her face like wet strings, blinking like a little owl finding itself in the bright sunshine.

"Oh drat," she gasped. "I seem to have lost my spectacles in the lake."

Temple managed to untangle himself, grasp Connie's hand and trudge to the shore. When he was at last on dry land, he made the mistake of really looking at her.

Her clothing was plastered to her flesh. She was not wearing a corset. The yellow material clung to her attributes. Temple swallowed hard and wished he were the one with the impaired vision.

His eyes skimmed over the fabric, rendered translucent from the water, while a sizable knot formed in his belly. The image of her in braids and pinafore evaporated forever—shattered by one afternoon of fishing and calamity.

He swallowed hard while his perception of her tilted, shifted and transformed.

He would never, could never think of her as a child again.

"Can you make it back to camp?" he managed to choke out.

Connie picked up the excess of her skirt and wrung a stream of water from it. "You'll have to guide me, Temple—I don't recall my way well enough to risk it without my spectacles." She squinted her eyes and looked toward the river. "Did we get the fish?"

"Yes, we got the fish." The trout flopped inside Connie's big hat, lying at the edge of the water.

She smiled brightly. As Temple's breath lodged in his throat he allowed himself to acknowledge how lovely she was without her glasses.

"If you will take my hand and show me the way to camp I will fix us dinner."

Temple nodded dumbly. He couldn't keep his disobedient eyes from her alluring form. Her waist nipped in and the clinging weight of the sodden skirt only served to emphasize the feminine flare of her hips and the outline of her long slender legs. The last thing he wanted to do was take hold of her hand and walk beside her. Each minute in her company was becoming torture.

"What about your spectacles?"

"I always pack an extra pair," she said airily. "It seems like the most unlikely accidents happen to me on these expeditions, so I have learned to plan for such possibilities."

"Somehow I am not surprised," Temple said with a sigh. He gulped down his dread and took hold of her small hand. The sensation that it somehow belonged in his nearly made him reel but he stoically placed one foot in front of the other and led her back to her camp.

"Have you got the fire going yet?" Constance's voice floated from behind the blanket she had had Temple stretch between her tent and the top of one tall crate. The contraption had created a makeshift dressing screen for her. Temple opened his mouth to answer her question but a sodden garment come flying over the top of the blanket and wrapped around his face with a wet slap. His reply was trapped by material that carried the scent of fish and lake water.

"Can you catch my chemise?" she asked. "I don't want it landing in the dirt."

Temple was already peeling the clammy chemise off his face. "I'd be happy to." He grumbled while he tossed it over one of the tent lines to dry.

"Oh, thank you. As soon as I get into some fresh clothes, I'll find my spare glasses and fix us dinner." There was a moment of silence, then a blur of cold sodden yellow cloth engulfed his entire head. He was blinded and swathed in Connie's dripping dress.

"Temple, can you hang my dress out to dry?"

He stripped the saturated material from his shoulders and neck. "I wouldn't have it any other way. Is there anything else I can do for you?"

"No, I can't think of anything."

If she heard the irritation in his voice, she didn't let it show. She stepped from behind the makeshift dressing screen in a fresh calico and smiled in his general direction in a sort of vague unfocused way. He realized she really couldn't see him—at least not clearly.

The dress had tiny buttons up the front and she was only half finished doing them up. All her concentration seemed to be focused on that task as she cautiously picked her way through the maze of crates.

Temple tried not to notice the soft bulge of her breasts while she pulled the material closed and fastened each closure, but of course it was a pointless attempt.

How could she have hidden such a figure in that shapeless costume? How in God's name had he failed to notice?

Connie disappeared back inside her tent. When

Temple heard a shout of glee he knew she had found her spectacles. She appeared at the entrance of her tent with the glasses, identical in shape and size to the others, now in place on her nose.

She blinked a couple of times as if just now fully aware of his presence. "My goodness, Temple, you should change clothes. You are still dripping wet." Connie shook her head. "What have you been doing—just sitting there? You will catch your death of cold and then blame it on me."

Temple didn't bother to answer as he slung the wet, yellow dress over a corner of her outside tent pole. There was no use in trying to explain anything to her. But as he stomped off toward his own camp he found himself wondering who was crazier—because no matter how hard he tried he couldn't ignore her appeal.

Constance paused to watch Temple kicking rocks as he walked across the meadow to his own camp. His voice rose and fell as if he were talking to someone. He threw his hands up in the air and gestured wildly and she realized that he was talking to himself. One moment he was playing in the water like a child and the next he was lost in solitary conversation, cursing a blue streak.

"I will simply never understand men." She grabbed the frying pan and prodded the hot coals into a blaze. "Not in a million years." But she found herself looking up once again, just to see the way the fabric of his shirt and trousers molded to his body as he walked. And she realized she didn't understand herself anymore either.

Chapter Seven

Constance packed away the last pan and firmly closed the lid on the crate. Leaving out cooking utensils and food invited vermin and she had no desire to wake up staring a bear in the face. Contrary to what Temple seemed to think, she did know about such things and took proper precautions.

A bird called somewhere out in the distance and she realized how relaxed she was. It was odd, but out here above the gully where Temple had started digging a massive hole she was almost able to forget he was her rival. In fact, when she looked at him now, with the breeze fluttering through his tawny hair and the kerosene lantern casting youthful shadows over his face, it was easy to forget he had been gone from her life for ten years.

"Temple?"

"Hmm?" He had been staring toward the rim of the canyon.

"Why did you ask about Herbert Pollock today?"

His head came up and his brows pinched together in a frown. Finally he shrugged and grinned, but Constance could see lingering tension in the set of his jaw.

"I just wondered what he had accomplished in the past ten years."

"Why?"

Temple leaned back on the crate he was using for a chair and studied his inquisitor. In this respect Connie had not changed. She was still as tenacious as a bull terrier when she had an idea in her head. If only her physical appearance had not altered so drastically.

"Why, Temple?" she asked again.

"I have my reasons." He laced his hands behind his head.

"Reasons you don't wish to share?" She wasn't going to let the subject drop.

Temple brought his hands down, and sat up. He seemed to stiffen under her steady gaze.

"Not now, Connie—perhaps when this dig is over—but now not."

She shrugged off his refusal and sat down on a large crate. She leaned forward and rested her chin in her palms as if to get a better view of the meadow below. She had the notion that the half-mile-wide expanse was an arena where she and Temple would be forced to oppose each other.

"What have you done for the past ten years besides break the hearts of women all over the world, Temple?"

Temple's brows arched in surprise at the question. The smooth seductive timbre of her voice had escaped his notice, until now.

"I am a heartbreaker?" He chuckled uncomfortably and looked away. "Where did you get such a notion?"

"I have kept up with you through the newspapers, of course. What was it really like—being on your own? Was it everything you hoped it would be when you left Papa—and me?''

His gaze returned to her face. She was still staring at him in that open honest way that unmanned him. Temple felt all the air rush from his lungs.

"What do you mean, Connie?''

"Has life been as exciting as you believed it would be? You left so quickly and never found the time to send a Christmas card or birthday greeting all these years. I assume you have been on one grand adventure after another.''

She convicted him with her guileless eyes. He did indeed feel as if he had deserted her that night. But it was foolish—the decision to go had not been his to make. And the reasons he had not contacted her were too complicated to put into words.

How could he explain to her the loneliness and hunger he felt the first few years? How could he put into words his utter disappointment when he discovered that a lovely face usually hid an empty head? There were no words to describe how he missed an atmosphere of intellectual stimulation.

"You are right, Connie, my life has been one long adventure.'' His voice lacked enthusiasm.

"The newspapers have printed accounts of your exploits over the years. You have made a name for yourself and become very successful. I know how much that meant to you.''

Temple felt a strange tug on his heart when she looked into his eyes. What would she say if he told her his only interest had been C.H.'s opinion of his skills? What would she say if he told her he was almost stone broke, and his future hinged on winning Montague's endowment?

"You've read the newspapers—what do you think?" Temple answered evasively. He prayed Connie would not see through him with her warm brown eyes.

She smiled innocently and tilted her head a bit.

His gut tightened.

"I'm glad to know you have done well, Temple. It will make things easier."

Temple narrowed his eyes and he felt a strange hollow void growing in his middle. "What do you mean?"

"When I find the bones and Mr. Montague awards the endowment to Dandridge, I will feel better now. It is important for me to know you will be all right—that you are successful and this will not matter so very much to you."

His anger flared like a lightning-ignited brush fire. She had unknowingly cut him to the quick. He couldn't tell her how those words bruised him without admitting what a disappointment the past ten years had been. So he took the only course left to a man who has only his pride to wear as armor against the world—he lashed out at her.

He stood and glared down at her. "Connie, I am going to win that prize. Then C.H. and all his pompous colleagues will finally have to—have to..."

"Have to what?" she asked.

Temple silently cursed himself. He didn't want Connie to know what had happened. That had been the reason he left without a fuss—to keep all of it secret.

"They will have to admit that my methods have merit," he finally bit out.

Constance sat a little straighter. Her eyes were no

longer soft and inquisitive. A new determination filled her face. "I see. Well, be that as it may, I can't let you win. I made Papa a promise to uphold the family honor. I promised him I would do my very best for Dandridge University." She brought her chin up an inch. "And I have never broken a promise." She stood and picked up one of the kerosene lanterns. "If you will excuse me, I need to get some sleep. I want to get an early start tomorrow." She turned and walked into her tent.

Temple sat there feeling a mixture of emotions while he watched her silhouette inside the canvas. One part of him admired her for her determination, while another part of him felt nothing but dread. He could not allow anything to get in the way of his goal.

"I am going to win Montague's endowment," he said loud enough for her to hear. "I have to," he added in a whisper.

He picked up his lantern and started back to his own camp. With each step he cursed himself for allowing Connie to get under his skin—again.

"How did the journalists find out Honoria went in my place?" C.H. crumpled the newspaper and flung it on the dust-covered hall table, narrowly missing Livingstone in the process. The bird hopped onto a tall wrought-iron stand and stared at the professor's guest with a baleful eye.

"I'm sure I don't know." Professor Andrew Pollock smoothed the thin strands of hair over his bald pate. "Just what are you implying?" His voice cracked slightly, reminding C.H. of Andrew's son, Herbert. Andrew opened and closed his palm several times before he thrust his hand into the pocket of his sweater. The moment C.H. saw Andrew's nervous gesture, he knew exactly where the gossip mill had received its latest grist.

Memories of what happened ten years ago came marching through his mind. "Andrew, I know how you feel about Temple, but subjecting Honoria and the university to this kind of yellow journalism is unconscionable."

Andrew paled a little but he held his ground. "A little publicity is good for the university. Temple Parish is a bounder—I won't rest until he is exposed for the fraud and schemer that he is."

"Bounder, bounder, awrk," Livingstone mimicked.

Professor Pollock started slightly and moved a few inches away from the perch where Livingstone stepped back and forth.

Livingstone flapped his wings and flew onto C.H.'s shoulder. "Temple Parish is a bounder...awrk." The bird chirped while he paced back and forth—doing a little dance—along C.H.'s shoulder.

"Yes, that's right—a bounder and a pirate," Andrew Pollock agreed with the mynah.

"Andrew, you are having a conversation with a bird," C.H. observed dryly.

Andrew looked up, his eyes widened. A stain of red entered his cheeks. "Yes, well, quite so." He rubbed his hand down his face. "What were we discussing?"

C.H. thumped across the room and picked up the discarded newspaper. His leg itched inside the cast, and he was damned uncomfortable—and more than a little annoyed with Andrew Pollock for stirring up the local press.

"We were discussing Temple," C.H. said. "You

shouldn't involve my daughter or the university in your effort to publicly discredit Temple.''

Professor Pollock stared at C.H. in disbelief. ''It amazes me, C.H., after all that happened you are still ready to defend that pirate.''

''Pirate,'' chimed Livingstone. He tilted his head to focus one beady black eye on his human perch. ''Pirate, Temple, awrk.''

''Be quiet bird,'' scolded C.H. He turned his attention back to his colleague.

''I am not defending him. He is a rogue, we all know that, but you and I both know none of the missing artifacts were ever found in his possession. You never should have threatened to contact the newspapers—it forced him to make a quick decision back then.''

Andrew speared C.H. with a milky-blue gaze. ''If he wasn't behind the thefts ten years ago, then who was? Everyone else who had access to that room was either on staff or family, including your daughter and my son. And if Temple Parish was innocent then why did he leave so easily?''

C.H. stared at Andrew and leaned heavily on his cane. He had asked himself the same questions a hundred times. As usual he had no answers. Temple Parish, the orphan from the streets, was the most likely suspect. But a part of C.H. still refused to believe the boy he loved like a son would betray him by stealing from the university. ''I don't know,'' C.H. mumbled while he shook his head. ''I just don't know.''

''Well, I know. He didn't even bother to defend himself before he stormed out of your house. Are those the actions of an innocent?''

C.H. well remembered the harsh words he and Temple had exchanged that night—words he could not call back or forgive.

"There were other reasons he left my house," C.H. challenged. In truth it had been Temple's stiff-necked pride that had allowed no other options.

"That is neither here nor there. The young scamp was quick enough to leave when the threat of exposure loomed over his head. You must agree or you wouldn't have sent Honoria to contest him." Andrew pointed out.

C.H.'s head snapped up and he swallowed hard. He had been very upset when he saw Temple's comments printed in the newspaper. "I admit I did get my hackles up over his disparaging remarks. He always was an arrogant scoundrel." C.H. could barely control the tickle of a smile that played at his lips. One of the things he admired about Temple was his fearless nature, and many other things he had never admitted to the lad.

"Arrogant? He is an ingrate—a bounder." Andrew began to pace the floor. His steps raised little motes of dust. They floated in the shaft of light coming through the tall narrow window of C.H.'s office.

"Temple is a pirate," Livingstone squawked. "Bounder, ingrate, awrk."

"Do be quiet, bird." C.H. turned to stare at the beady black eye scrutinizing him from his perch on C.H.'s shoulder.

"Really, C.H., why don't you get rid of that noisy fowl?" Andrew asked.

"I wish I could, but he is Honoria's pet." C.H. retrieved another seed from the dish. "I wish I had asked Honoria to make other arrangements for this confounded bird. His incessant chatter is playing hob with my nerves.''

"Then send the annoying beast to her. Let him entertain her with his senseless prattle!'' Andrew snapped.

"Send him to Honoria?,'' C.H. muttered absently while he paced the length of the small office. "Send him to Montana to keep Honoria company?'' C.H. looked at Livingstone. "That is a capital idea, Andrew, just capital.'' He reached out one finger and stroked the top of Livingstone's soft ebony feathers and the bright yellow wattles. "How would you like to go visit Honoria and the pirate, bird?''

"Temple is a pirate,'' squawked Livingstone. "Awrk, bounder, ingrate, awrk.''

"For once, Andrew, I think I am in complete agreement with you,'' C.H. said with a chuckle.

Peter sat in the chair beside the cracker barrel and listened to the citizens of Morgan Forks comment on the newspapers he had just brought from the train station. Most of the womenfolk from the surrounding ranches and outlying spreads had come in to buy their supplies. Even one of the small mine owners was standing nearby, listening while pretending not to.

It tickled him to see how much commotion Miss Cadwallender's presence was causing. Half the town was outraged that a woman would consider doing what she was doing. The other half—who coincidentally were the women—thought it was about time that a strong-willed female took a role in the academic and scientific world. Miss Cadwallender had stirred up so much interest the topic of Montana's pending statehood was hardly being mentioned at all lately. Tempers were flaring, opinions were flying and Peter was happy as a pig in a deep wallow. Some excitement had finally come to the sleepy town of Morgan Forks.

"It simply isn't proper," the wizened preacher pronounced.

Peter grinned and waited for an opposing comment. He didn't have to wait long before a familiar voice cut in. "Parson, I'd like for you to tell me what's not proper about it?" Bessie Morgan asked. Her spurs rang out on the wooden floor when she stepped forward and stared at the minister with a look cool and hard as jade.

"Surely, Sister Morgan, you can see where the impropriety is. Camping out there—alone—it just isn't proper." The minister's words were firm but he backed up a step in the face of Bessie's unrelenting scowl.

Peter stood and cleared his throat. The crowd shifted and turned toward him, ready for a new view. "Miss Cadwallender is about the most proper lady I have ever seen. Heck, she wouldn't even allow that scalawag Parish to set up his camp on the same side of the canyon." That piece of information went through the crowd and brought a murmur of approval and a few chuckles. Peter stared at the pinched-faced preacher, silently daring him to say more against the moral fabric of Miss Cadwallender.

"Parson, I have been out there on a regular basis. There isn't any patty-fingers going on. You have my word upon that."

"You don't say," the preacher said thoughtfully.

"I do say. She is a right smart woman, that Miss Cadwallender. You should be ashamed of yourself for thinking otherwise. The only thing that little lady is interested in is scientific exploration. Why, she told me so herself.'' Peter glanced down at the dome-shaped oilskin-covered article sitting between him and the pickle barrel. ''And as much as I would like to stand around here and jaw with you, I have to deliver those newspapers and this—other thing—to Miss Cadwallender.''

Peter reached down and picked up the object in his arms, then he strode out the front door of the mercantile to put it in the back of the wagon. He had to nudge his way back through the curious crowd in order to retrieve the bundled newspapers.

Bessie Morgan followed Peter to the wagon. ''What I want to know, Peter, is when I can come out and see the bones you claimed was going to make me famous.''

Peter set the bundled papers on the seat and turned to look at the owner of the Flying B. ''Don't know that they have actually found any bones yet.'' He rubbed his chin and allowed his appreciative gaze to skim over Bessie. Her thick hair, once fiery red, now shot with gray, hung in one heavy braid over her shoulder. Her eyes were the color of new grass. ''But when they do, you mark my words, you and the Flying B will be famous all right.''

''I hope you are right, Peter. I'd hate to think I was letting those easterners dig up my land for nothing.'' She tilted her head and narrowed her gaze at Peter. ''And I won't forget you are the one that talked me into this.''

''Those bones will put Morgan Forks on the map, I am sure of it. Tell me, Bessie, are you busy today?'' Peter asked with a flirty grin.

"Not any busier than usual. Why?" She tugged the leather vest into place over her sturdy plaid shirt.

"I'm headed out there now. Why don't you ride with me? We can visit on the way. It would help me pass the time." Peter grinned wider.

Bessie shoved back her hat until it fell from her head. The strings beneath her chin kept it resting at the nape of her slender neck. She squinted skeptically, and flecks of gold in the green irises winked at Peter.

"And me camping for the night with you would get the preacher's tongue wagging even more. No, I don't think so."

Peter winked at her. He had been trying, without success, to finagle a kiss from her for years. His repeated failure only made the chase more fun and his determination more steadfast.

"I'll tell you what I will do, Peter," Bessie continued. "Holt and I will ride over to the gorge tomorrow afternoon. You ought to be there by then, even in this bone-buster you call a wagon. That'll give you time to notify Miss Cadwallender that she's going to have company. Any woman, whether they are eastern-bred or not, likes a little warning before people come dropping by."

"Whatever you say, Bessie." Peter's mind was already moving ahead, wondering how Temple Parish would react to all the new stories in the newspapers and Miss Cadwallender's other gift. After he saw what was hidden under the oilskin cover, Peter was fairly certain Miss Cadwallender's reaction to visitors would likely pale in comparison to Temple Parish's reaction.

Chapter Eight

Temple leaned on the handle of his shovel. Against his better judgment he glanced back across at Connie's camp. No matter how much he willed himself to ignore her, it just wasn't possible. Even though they had managed to avoid speaking to each other he was too aware of her presence across the empty expanse of canyon that separated them.

A small dust devil swirled through the ravine and up over the edge of the canyon toward her location. She, as usual, was perched on an outcrop of rock, sketching. Her hat went flying from her head and spiraled upward for a second, caught in the vortex. Temple felt a bit like that hat, spiraling helplessly out of control.

She dropped her sketch pad and scampered after it—as much as her voluminous skirt would allow her to scamper, that is. Temple smiled in spite of himself.

The damnable costume that covered her body was part of the reason he couldn't keep his mind on his own dig. Each time he closed his eyes, the image of Connie's wet clothing plastered to her very womanly curves flashed through his mind.

Temple quit dawdling and rammed the nose of the shovel in the dirt. He picked up another spadeful of earth and tossed it aside. The sound of a bird drew his eyes heavenward. It was the first sound he had heard today, other than the scraping of his own shovel. It grated on his nerves, this damned quiet, and that, he told himself, had to be the reason he was so edgy—not Miss Constance Cadwallender.

While he stood there trying to convince himself of the obvious lie, a large cloud of dust appeared on the far horizon. He squinted at it for a full minute before he climbed out of the gorge. With his hat shading his eyes, he watched the approach of the dusky nimbus.

Peter Hughes was coming.

A smile curved his lips. Now he would be able to let the world know that he was already on the trail of a promising find—before Connie even finished sketching. The papers would do their usual amount of embellishing and by the time Filbert Montague read the article, it would appear that Temple had found several unknown species and was on his way back.

Temple glanced across the meadow at Connie. For some reason the thought that he was so far ahead of her in their quest didn't fill him with nearly as much happiness as he expected it would, but he pushed the notion aside. It had been years since he had been bothered by anything that remotely resembled a conscience. And he certainly didn't intend to start growing a new one now with his future—and a bit of his tarnished past—hanging in the balance.

From the distance of the far-off dust cloud, Temple knew it would be several hours before Hughes arrived. He slapped at the thick layer of dirt coating his trousers. A puff of dust went up his nostrils and a sneeze exploded from him. When he rubbed his hand over his face, grit caked on his jaws and scratched along the inside of his palm.

"It is definitely time to clean up." Temple entered his tent and dug out a change of clean clothes, a cake of strong soap and his shaving kit. He glanced over at Connie's camp once more. She was bent over her sketch pad with her oversize hat in place as an umbrella.

Would Connie notice he was not digging? Would she notice the change in his appearance? he wondered. Then he shook the silly ideas from his head and marched off toward the lake. He was doing this for Hughes's benefit and his own comfort, and most assuredly not in some vain attempt to impress little Connie.

Temple inhaled and dived under the cool water. His breath left him in one shuddering exhale as he slid through the long stems of underwater grass. The morning sun had yet to warm the depths of the lake but he enjoyed the feeling of the silken water sluicing over his naked limbs. He had not realized how stiff he had become, sleeping on the hard narrow cot each night, shoveling the packed earth all day. He kicked himself to the surface and floated motionless on his back, allowing the tension and strain to ebb from his muscles.

He opened one eye just enough to squint up at the periwinkle sky. The sun was quickly blazing a trail across the eastern sky. Temple swam to the shore and grabbed the hard milled soap he had brought. He stood up in the shallow water, and felt mud squeeze up between his toes. He rubbed the soap between his palms and raised a thick lather, then he slathered it across his face. With the ease of practice he swiped the razor over his jaws while he used his reflection in the lake as a somewhat ripply mirror. After he had removed the growth of beard he scrubbed at both his face and hair. When he was fairly covered in foam, he turned and dived back into the deeper water to rinse.

Constance flattened her body beside the large boulder and watched Temple cavorting in the lake like a sleek river otter. She shoved her spectacles up and angled her head to get a better view. Droplets of water shimmered on his hard lean form each time he surfaced. Time seemed to halt when he broke the water and her gaze held him for a heart-catching moment before he dived back under.

While she watched him a strange sort of heat began to uncoil in her middle. She swallowed hard and focused her gaze on Temple's sinewy form.

And then she knew.

"It's him. Watching him brings about a debilitating weakness of my limbs and a strange catch to my throat," Constance whispered to herself in wonder.

She was not sure which discovery was more remarkable, the fact that Temple had a body equal to any Greek statue she had ever admired while traveling with her father, or finally realizing that simply looking at him made her hot, weak and all fluttery inside. Her symptoms were not unlike those her father had experienced when bitten by a particularly virulent insect two years ago in Egypt. Except that in a strange manner they were not altogether unpleasant.

She turned and walked back toward her camp, totally absorbed in thought about the mystery that she had just discovered. "I must take some time and explore this further," she muttered to herself. Her newest breakthrough had obliterated any shame she might have had about spying on Temple or finding him naked. In fact, while she pondered his effect on her senses, she managed to shove both those concerns completely from her mind.

Temple spent another half hour swimming before he climbed out onto the pebble-strewed bank. He hobbled quickly to his clean clothes and sat on a flat smooth stone to dress. While he was in the lake he had had the strangest notion that he was being watched but when he'd scanned the area he'd seen nothing—heard nothing. Still, he found himself glancing over his shoulder from time to time, unable to shake the feeling of prying eyes upon him.

While he jerked his suspenders over his fresh white shirt, Temple mentally composed the message he wanted to send with Peter. Over the years he had learned the importance of what the papers printed.

"Temple Parish is hot on the trail of a new dinosaur...." He yanked on his socks and boots. "No... Temple Parish, world-renowned explorer, will unearth... No. Still not right." He stuffed his pants down inside the tall leather boots and laced them. "Temple Parish is confident he will be claiming Filbert Montague's endowment in record time."

Temple smiled. Day after tomorrow the New York papers should be carrying the news of his latest find.

"Wonder what C.H. and the faculty of Dandridge will say about that?" He snorted. But while he was pondering their reactions, the image of Connie ripped through his mind. Temple shook his wet head as if he could physically remove her from his thoughts. He reminded himself that this dig would secure his future. If he handled this right, he would no longer be forced to scrounge up investors for his expeditions. But Connie's image remained firmly lodged at the back of his mind.

Temple climbed the gentle rise near the gorge and saw with no small measure of annoyance that Peter Hughes had not driven the team to his side of the canyon. The cloud of dust was wending its way toward Connie's camp on the opposite side while Temple negotiated the last rock-strewn hillock toward the canyon.

"Damn that old fool—what is he up to?" Now if Temple wanted to speak to Hughes, he would have to walk across the ravine, or take a chance that Hughes would come by tomorrow.

Indecision gripped him.

He didn't want to have to see Connie. He glanced over at her tent. Each time he looked at her the image of clinging wet clothes and eyes no longer shielded by spectacles threatened to consume him. Temple realized with a jolt that this struggle was beginning to occupy more of his time than the quest to find bones.

"Temple Parish, you have become a besotted fool." But he started making his way down the ledge so he could cross the gully and enter Connie's camp while the curse was still fresh on his lips.

Constance tugged the brim of her hat down and tried to pretend she was not watching Temple walk into her camp. The same extraordinary symptoms were rushing through her with each step he took, but this time she was determined to analyze them and discover why looking at him caused such profound reactions.

Her father had made sure she thought like a scientist, behaved in an analytical and detached manner at all times, but each time she gazed at Temple a kind of hunger seemed to grow inside of her.

Her curious gaze started at the top of his bare head. The shiny mass was still a tiny bit damp. It lay smooth and flat against his head, making it appear darker than it was. Tawny curls that had completely dried now brushed his nape and tickled the lobes of his ears above the neck of his collarless white shirt. Constance narrowed her eyes and adjusted her spectacles.

There really was nothing unusual about Temple's hair, she decided. It was quite ordinary, except for the million tiny sparkles the morning sun deposited in each silky gold strand.

She shook herself and swallowed. "Clinical, Constance, you must remain clinical," she reminded herself.

Her eyes traveled down his face. His cheeks were ruddy, freshly shaved, full of good health. She focused on the slightly asymmetrical bump on the bridge of his nose. Constance knew it had been broken the night before her father brought him home, but she had never noticed how it gave his face a rugged manly look. Or how the raised white scar on his cheek kept the length of his thick lashes from making him look soft or effeminate. Temple was blessed—or cursed—with the face of a rake, an adventurer, a seducer of women.

The bright sun caused him to squint against its rays until the flesh at the corners of his eyes crinkled handsomely. Constance forced herself to examine the shadows that capered beneath his deep-set mahogany eyes.

A tiny shiver coursed through her body. Whether

his face was perfectly normal or not, it elicited a decidedly profound effect from her body.

Just as Professor Eisley had shown her, Constance placed her index finger at the juncture of her jaw. Her pulse was accelerated as if she had been taking a brisk constitutional instead of observing Temple from beneath the protective camouflage of her hat.

"Astonishing," she gasped under her breath. "Dr. Barton would be most intrigued by my reactions." With a new sense of purpose Constance focused on Temple's body.

She told herself it was all for science as she examined his chest. Smooth skin where he had left the top four buttons of his shirt undone was exposed to both her view and the sun. His braces hugged the width of his muscular shoulders and skimmed over the flat trim planes of his belly where they attached to the waist of his trousers by buttons on either side.

As if on a quest of their own purpose, her eyes traveled lower still. It took little deductive reasoning to see why he used suspenders to keep his trousers up. Nothing but hard lean muscle rode those hips and yet the bulk of his thighs bunched and contracted with each step he took over the uneven rocky terrain.

Her gaze snapped back to Temple's face and slowly surveyed every inch of him between forehead and boots once again as if to confirm her original findings.

"Oh, my." Constance was shocked to hear the breathy timbre of her own voice. Her mouth had gone dry and her pulse was racing. She couldn't seem to think clearly, but watching him was satisfying to her in a way that defied explanation. There was nothing clinical, detached or remote about her reaction to Temple Parish—nothing at all.

Suddenly, as if she had been prodded by an invisible hand, she glanced down at her own clothing. For the first time in her memory she found herself wishing that she looked *different*. Constance had no idea why she should suddenly become susceptible to feminine vanity, but she surely did in the space of time it took for her to really look at Temple.

The sound of horses plodding and the jingle of harness drew her head around. Her cheeks filled with heat when she realized that Temple had walked right by her and was waiting for Mr. Hughes.

"Where is Miss Cadwallender?" Mr. Hughes's voice rang out as he maneuvered the team closer. She tugged the brim of her hat lower over her face and stumbled out into the open, embarrassed by both her recent thoughts and her appearance.

"I am here, Mr. Hughes. How nice of you to come out to see us." She tried not to notice Temple's newly discovered attributes while she walked beyond him toward the wagon.

Mr. Hughes smiled and jumped down from the seat. "I have some things for you, Miss Cadwallender." He walked to the back of the buckboard and removed a large stack of newspaper that was tightly bound with brown twine.

"For me?" Constance wondered who would be sending her newspapers. "Are they from my father?" She could not imagine anybody else sending her anything.

"No—I don't think so, miss." Mr. Hughes brushed by her as he carried the papers to the front of her tent. He stooped over and set them on the ground. "I think the conductor said they were sent by a Professor Pollock."

"Pollock? Professor Andrew Pollock?" Temple's indignant bark made Constance start. She turned and looked at him. This time his lovely deep-set eyes glowed like fiery agates. "Why in thunder would Professor Pollock be sending Connie newspapers?"

Peter Hughes stared at Temple with a stone-faced expression, then he shrugged. "I couldn't rightly say, but maybe there is something in them he would like her to read." A taunting grin flickered across Peter's lips.

Temple was already striding toward the bundle while he snapped open his pocket knife. He crouched and cut the string with a plop of sound. He yanked the first paper out and scanned the front page while he folded and slid the knife back into his front pocket. Within minutes his expression darkened, but he remained where he was, crouched beside the stack, while he picked up paper after paper and scanned the front pages.

"What is it? What do they say?" Constance stepped closer and bent near in order to read over Temple's shoulder.

The clean fresh smell of him washed over her. Her pulse quickened and her belly knotted in response. She was relieved when Mr. Hughes turned and walked back toward the wagon leaving her alone with Temple. It was disconcerting enough that she felt the way she did, without worrying that Mr. Hughes might detect her discomfort.

"Tell me what they say." Constance struggled to slow the thrumming of her heart. "Is it bad news? Has something dreadful happened?"

"I suppose that depends on your point of view. The general consensus seems to be that I am about to be bested by a woman. There is widespread speculation that a certain Miss Constance Honoria Cadwallender will put Temple Parish in his place.''

He tilted his head and slanted a look up at her. Their faces were only inches apart. Once again Constance felt the strange tug at her heart.

"It is also reported that Mr. Montague has increased the endowment to include a personal reward to the winning digger.''

"Oh.'' Constance didn't know what else to say. She uttered a silent prayer of thanks when Mr. Hughes reappeared and saved her from having to say anything.

Temple stared at Connie while a myriad of emotions rippled through him. He was furious to see her being called the victor in every headline. But a part of him, the part that felt strangely like his long-lost-missing conscience, reminded him that he had intended to do the very same thing. If Hughes had shown up as scheduled, and Temple had sent word by way of the telegraph, then it would have been his name splashed in ink prematurely declaring him the winner.

A new internal struggle began inside him. He wanted to be furious with Connie, but how could he be when none of the news had come from her? And he had been more than ready to use the same tool for his own personal gain.

A wave of frustrated anger swelled inside him, but his anger was directed at himself. He couldn't help but wonder when he'd become so damned *fair*.

The crunch of Peter's boots on the rocks drew Temple's attention. The old coot had an oilskin-covered object in his hands and a foxy smirk on his face.

"I do have something for you from your father, miss.''

Temple's belly tightened. If things continued as they had begun, he was sure he was going to be less than happy about the new "present" from C.H.

"Whatever it is, it is bound to be better than these damned yellow rags." Temple tossed the paper he'd been reading back into the pile while Peter unloaded the three-foot-tall cloaked dome.

"What is this thing, Hughes?" Temple asked, leaning down to get a closer look.

"According to the card tied to the cage, this is Miss Cadwallender's pet, Livingstone." Peter pulled the oilcloth off the cage.

"Awrk," the bird squawked.

Temple jerked back in surprise. The bird flapped his shiny black wings and squawked when the afternoon sunshine flooded the cage. His bright yellow wattles seemed to absorb the sun and reflect it back. He stretched his ebony wings and made a few more unintelligible sounds.

After his initial shock Temple's curiosity drew him back toward the cage. He bent at the waist and peered at the fowl. "What in Sam Hill?"

"How wonderful." Connie stepped closer to the cage and bent over as well. "It's Livingstone."

Her face was no more than two inches from Temple's—and she had taken off that damnable hat. He swallowed hard and tried to ignore her creamy skin and twinkling eyes.

"Livingstone, how are you?" She extended one finger through the sturdy wire.

"Do you expect him to answer?" Temple wasn't sure what bothered him most—the bird, or noticing the pleasing shape of Connie's lips when she spoke to the creature. He frowned and forced himself to look only at the beady black eyes that studied him from inside the cage.

"Yes, Temple. He does talk. Not well, but he can manage a few words." Connie looked up at Temple and smiled. "Livingstone the mynah—meet Temple Parish—the—uh—digger."

"Temple is a pirate!" Livingstone said loudly and quite clearly.

Temple snapped upright as if he had been hit in his very tightly clenched jaw.

"What did that damned bird say?" Temple's voice was taut.

"Why, I believe he called you a pirate." Constance's brows were arched. "How extraordinary. I wonder where he learned that?"

"Where indeed." Temple narrowed his eyes at the bird, then he glanced at Connie in silent speculation.

Peter Hughes erupted into a throaty gale of laughter. He whacked his knee with an open palm and hopped on one foot. Tears of mirth welled in his eyes.

"Surely you don't think I taught him to say that?" Connie glanced at him with a look of indignant denial on her face.

Temple wanted to deliver a cutting response, but the sunlight caught her eyes and filled the soft brown depths with a dozen subtle shades of dusky gold. He crossed his arms at his chest and forced himself to look only at Livingstone.

"All aboard, all aboard," the bird chattered on. "Temple is a pirate. Pirate."

Chapter Nine

As Temple watched the bird flap its wings and insult him, he felt his brows knitting more tightly together.

"He's a real mimic, isn't he? I wonder where he heard all those colorful descriptions?"

"He was learning one or two new words when I left New York." She unlatched the cage door and stuck her hand inside.

"Careful, the brute will pierce you with that beak." Temple extended his arm as if he might physically restrain her but she just avoided his touch and continued.

"Nonsense. He is perfectly tame. At home he rides upon my shoulder."

Just as she predicted the bird hopped onto her hand and walked up her arm. He nuzzled his smooth sharp beak against her cheek in an awkward caress.

Connie giggled at the bird's affectionate touch while Temple's insides flip-flopped. The sound of her laughter brought a frisson of chills down his arms. He didn't want to respond to her.

Livingstone pulled a lock of her hair from the tight coil on top of her head. He played with the tendril until he became bored and let it fall from his beak. The loose strand caught the sunlight and made Temple too aware of the delicate structure of her jawline.

"You better keep him in a cage or some hawk will make short work of him." Temple tried to deny what he was feeling while he made one last attempt to resurrect his dying anger.

"He will be fine, Temple, I'll watch him. But I do thank you for worrying about his safety." She stroked the top of the bird's head with one finger while she slanted a grateful glance at him.

Temple started to tell her he couldn't care less about the bird's welfare, but he was mesmerized by the picture of her soft finger stroking on the ebony feathers and gently chucking the butter-colored wattles.

He would love to feel her touch on his own skin—would like to know the pleasure of her caress. Temple started at his thoughts.

He did not desire Connie.

He couldn't.

He forced himself to focus on the fact she was his competition, but each time he looked at her, in that ridiculous oversize dress with the bird on her shoulder, a strange burst of heat twined through him.

"I'm going back to work," Temple choked out.

"Wait—I have another bit o' news for you." Peter was still grinning like a fox.

"Oh, and what would that be, Mr. Hughes?" Temple was ready to wring the old bandit's neck.

"You are going to have company today."

Temple's brows furrowed together. "Company? Today? Who?"

"The owner of the Flying B is coming over to see you." Peter's eyes twinkled mischievously.

In view of his short association with Hughes, Temple found himself wondering how much Peter was leaving unsaid.

"Enough for now, Livingstone." Constance urged the bird back onto her hand. Sunlight glinted on his blue-black feathers when he returned to his cage. She glanced at Temple. "Just in case your prediction of hawks and eagles should come true."

Peter tactfully looked up at the sky but Temple knew he was about to bust out laughing again. "As I was sayin', you'll probably get company in about an hour or so."

Constance brushed at the soil clinging to her dress and a new thought popped into her head. The owner of this land was coming to see them. Peter's announcement could work to her advantage. She could take a bath and change without Temple thinking she had taken leave of her senses. He would never realize he was the reason she had suddenly become aware of her own sad wardrobe and bedraggled appearance.

"How long did you say it would be before he arrives?" Constance asked while she latched Livingstone's cage.

"'Bout an hour, I'd guess. But it's not a he, it's a she. Bessie Morgan is the richest widow in Montana."

Temple's head snapped up. He could swear he heard a tone of admiration in Peter's voice.

"In that case, I have time to make myself more presentable before she arrives."

Temple stared at her in horror. "What for?" he blurted out. "What's wrong with the way you look?" A little voice in his head laughed at the absurdity of his statement. Her costume was utterly hideous, and anybody with any sense at all could see it. "I think you look just fine,'' Temple lied desperately. If Connie peeled away the layers of dirty cloth that now covered her, then he would be looking at the lovely form that had magically appeared at the lake.

He swallowed hard while fear gripped him. God, could he stand it? Could he ignore that siren?

''Temple, I certainly cannot allow the local people to think that Dandridge is being represented by someone who is…'' Constance stopped short. She could not think of a proper word to describe what she was feeling.

Dowdy? Absolutely.

Plain? Undoubtedly, for each time she looked at Temple she felt plainer than rice pudding.

Unattractive? A heaviness entered her heart. Temple could not possibly think of her in any other terms, and that made her unbearably sad.

Constance could have used any of those words to describe how she felt, but that would have allowed Temple a deep glimpse into a heart she was only just discovering for herself.

She knew he still thought of her as a little girl in braids and pinafore. For the life of her she could not fathom why she should suddenly be experiencing so many new and inexplicable feelings, and all of them involving Temple Parish.

''We're diggers, Connie. Why should you care about how you look?'' Temple felt extremely proud of his argument. By acknowledging her as a digger, he was sure he could manipulate her.

''You took a bath. You washed your hair and put on clean clothes,'' she pointed out. ''I don't know of any reason I shouldn't do the same.'' She smiled at him and he felt a little of his resolve dwindle away. "But it is nice to hear you call me a digger, Temple."

Temple clamped his lips together in a taut line. His eyes slid over her from head to toe. He was losing the battle—and he knew it.

"I guess you have a point," he said softly while his gaze skimmed over her.

Constance felt every inch of her flesh respond to his intense scrutiny. She feared she was going to blush so she turned hurriedly away, seeking shelter from his eyes. When she was inside, she closed her eyes and inhaled deeply. Her breathing had become rapid under that steady mahogany gaze.

"Remarkable," she muttered while she went to her trunk and opened the lid.

Peter cleared his throat in an exaggerated manner causing Temple to turn and glare at him. "I am happy I came by. This looks like it might shape up to be a real celebration."

Temple saw the taunting sparkle in the older man's blue eyes. He wished Peter Hughes were twenty years younger because he had the overwhelming urge to throttle him.

Constance used the long-toothed comb to work the tangles from her freshly washed hair. She had scrubbed and soaked until her fingers were puckered from the tepid water of the lake. Each time she thought of putting on her serge skirt and the softly gathered lawn shirt, a knot formed in her belly. Every season she purchased clothing in the latest styles, more out of a sense that she should do as other young women did, than any real desire to wear them, but now she wanted to look...*pretty*.

The notion somewhat surprised her.

She had never dressed with the intention of drawing a man's notice. Her life had been spent around aging professors and strangers, none of whom had ever shown the slightest interest in getting to know her, or to speak to her beyond the most Spartan greeting. She pulled the comb through the last damp strand of her hair.

"Except for Temple."

From the time he came into her father's household he had given her notice. He had taken the time to talk to her—to ask her questions—to tease her until she laughed shyly at his antics—or to tug playfully on her braids.

"And he still thinks of me as that same little girl." She thought once again of the small wooden statue. That was what Temple saw when he looked at her. "He will never take me seriously as a competitor if he continues to believe I am still a child."

Constance set the comb aside and looked at the new frock draped over the large boulder. It was not what she was accustomed to wearing. But while she stared at the pretty blue-and-white-striped fabric a new thought came into her mind. Perhaps that was exactly what this occasion called for; to be something different, to be *somebody* different.

She had persuaded her father to send her on this dig in small measure to prove herself. This change in her appearance could be the first step in that quest.

The thud of galloping horses' hooves could be felt through the earth long before the riders could be seen.

Temple let the brim of his hat shield his eyes while he scanned the horizon. Two riders on horseback finally appeared, tiny silhouettes between the dusky-gray earth and the slash of cloudless sky.

"I thought perhaps it was the buggy bringing Mrs. Morgan. But apparently not." Temple had hung around Connie's camp, partly to keep an eye on Hughes and partly because his curiosity about the predicted company would not allow him leave.

He glanced at Peter and saw the telltale smile tickling the corners of his mouth. He counted to ten, while he waited for Peter to dissolve into his annoying habit of sidesplitting laughter, but the old man only cleared his throat in his exaggerated manner and turned away.

"All right, Hughes, what is the secret—this time?" Temple had been the brunt of Peter's jokes since his arrival. "Tell me what's going on," Temple demanded.

"I don't know what you mean," Peter schooled his features and looked innocent while he answered evasively.

"Oh, yes, you do. I saw that twinkle in your eye. It usually means I am about to look like the north end of a southbound jackass. Now, what is the secret about Mrs. Morgan that you are busting to tell me?"

"There is no secret—really." Peter grinned. "You just sort of jumped to the conclusion that Bessie Morgan is the kind of woman who would be coming to visit in a buggy. Strictly speaking, that ain't exactly the case." Peter chuckled. "Not exactly that is."

Temple shifted his gaze back to the pair of riders. They were a little closer now and more details were becoming visible. One rider was small, and while Temple would not have described the person as frail, there was a certain hint of femininity about the way the rider sat in the saddle.

"Do you mean to tell me one of those riders is Mrs. Morgan?" Temple rubbed his palm down his face in annoyance. He was having enough trouble managing the unconventional Miss Constance Cadwallender. He certainly didn't want to have to deal with another eccentric female. Temple started to tell Peter Hughes that very thing, but when he looked up he found the old man staring beyond him in slack-jawed silence. His mouth was hanging open and his eyes were wide. Temple followed his line of vision and found himself stunned to motionlessness as well.

The bright sunlight made it impossible to identify the exact shade of the ribbon that held the glistening fall of heavy hair, but Temple thought it might have been pale blue. A modern creation of cream flowed softly from a seductively full bosom. Leg-of-mutton sleeves emphasized well-formed shoulders and drew his gaze to the tiny waist nipped in by a diamond-shaped cloth cummerbund. The navy skirt with a narrow white stripe running through it skimmed over the swell of her hips and belled slightly before it halted slightly above shiny lace-up shoes that showed off a pair of extremely well-turned ankles.

Temple swallowed hard and allowed himself to blink—but only once. A hot flush filled his face. He had seen calves and ankles artfully exposed by women on several continents when they had stepped from carriages, or climbed stairs—but never in his life had a pair of ankles affected him as Connie's were doing right now.

"My God!" Temple gulped down his surprise. The last hope of ever envisioning Constance as a little girl crumbled beneath his feet and something like the first dawn blazed across the horizon of his brain.

She was beautiful.

Temple's face was like an open page. For a moment Peter actually felt a measure of pity for him. The way Temple stared at Miss Cadwallender brought back memories of what it had been like to be young—to be ruled by raw emotion and almost no sense. Hunger, need and unabashed devotion filled Temple's eyes. Peter wondered if the damned young fool even knew that he was smitten with Miss Cadwallender.

He might have just come out and asked, but the opportunity was lost when Bessie and Holt Morgan rode up at the same moment Miss Cadwallender sashayed back into her camp. Peter took one look at the four people staring at one another in narrow-eyed speculation. He decided that Montana was about to get a whole lot more exciting than it had ever been.

Chapter Ten

"Howdy. I'm Bessie Morgan and this is my middle son, Holt." Bessie dismounted with the grace of a woman who had spent years straddling a saddle, wearing men's trousers and making her own decisions.

Just as Temple feared, she was very unconventional. He tipped his hat to Mrs. Morgan and glanced at Holt, but the new arrival was staring at Connie as if he might eat her up in one bite. Temple stepped forward and placed his body in Holt's line of vision as if his bulk could shield Connie from the newcomers' obvious interest. "I am Temple Parish."

"Pleased to meet you, Mr. Parish." Holt smiled absently, touched the brim of his hat and stepped down from the brown gelding. The reins slipped from his hand to the ground while he yanked off his hat. He took two long determined steps in Constance's direction before Temple could react.

"And you must be Miss Cadwallender." Holt's voice hummed with interest. "We—I—have heard a lot about you. The newspapers wrote about what you are doin' for the university—but golldang, miss, I didn't have no idea you'd be so…so…pretty."

The word hung in the air above Temple's head like a sharpened sword. He stood there, torn between his need to deny his own reaction to her transformed appearance and the unreasoning urge to somehow silence Holt Morgan.

"I am Constance Cadwallender." Roses bloomed in her cheeks under Holt's scrutiny. "I haven't read the papers yet—so I don't know what they have said about me."

"They don't do you justice," Holt said while he rotated his hat in his hands. "Not by a long shot."

"Thank you, Mr. Morgan." Constance smiled shyly and looked over the upper edge of her spectacles.

Temple grated his teeth. Connie was a grown woman, damn—but she was a grown woman. If this cowboy chose to give her compliments, it was none of his business. After all, she had been around men most of her life. But the timid way she allowed her lovely long lashes to flutter over her brown eyes told Temple that she had never been around a man with wide lean shoulders and narrow hips who stared at her as if she were a Grecian goddess.

Some part of Temple that had been dormant suddenly sprang to life. He felt his feet moving before his brain even registered the intent. He found himself wedging his body between Constance and Holt even while he told himself he was acting like a jealous ass.

He wanted to remove the spectacles from her nose. He wanted to be the man telling her she was the prettiest thing he had ever seen. But if she had noticed his reaction to her she was doing a good job of hiding it while she smiled at Holt over Temple's rigid shoulder.

"Miss Cadwallender, Ma and I brought a box lunch. Would—you, that is—aw golldang, would you like to eat?" Holt sidestepped and left Temple a least a yard out of the conversation. "Miss, it would be a pleasure if you'd let me sit by you."

Connie's eyes widened for a moment but she remained composed. "I would be honored, Mr. Morgan."

"I wish I had brought a blanket to put on the ground—for you to sit on. You look so fine, it would be a shame for you to get dirt on your purty dress." Holt's gaze never left Connie's face.

She smiled and a thousand fists pummeled Temple's heart. He should have been the one to comment on her appearance. Lord knew he was far more aware of her transformation than this cowboy could ever be.

Constance's cheeks flushed slightly. "I have a blanket in my tent. I'll just be a minute." She glanced at Temple and his heart leaped into his throat, but before he could get his feet or his voice to work, she disappeared inside the tent. He was left standing there with a thousand unsaid compliments choking him.

"Well now, wasn't that a neighborly thing to do?" Peter said behind Temple. "Bringing a picnic lunch and all?"

Temple wheeled around. Both Peter Hughes and Mrs. Morgan were staring at him with the hint of a grin playing about their lips.

"Most neighborly." Temple swallowed the strange mixture of feelings. He realized he was acting like a dolt. "Mrs. Morgan, forgive my rudeness. I am pleased to meet you." He offered her his hand. He was surprised by the firmness of her grip when she shook it. "And I want to thank you for allowing us to dig on your property. It was a generous thing for you to do."

"I don't know how generous it was, Mr. Parish. Peter promised me it would do our bid for statehood and Morgan Forks a heap of good if you find anything." She speared him with wise green eyes. "I don't suppose you'd be spendin' all your time socializin'—not with the amount of money that is at stake, would you?"

The reminder of the endowment shrouded Temple in a cold gray gloom. "No, I would not. Connie and I have both been—uh—staying busy. It seems we are both equally determined to secure the prize."

Temple found his gaze sliding to the opening of Constance's tent where Holt waited impatiently. Bessie took a step nearer.

"A little healthy competition is good for the soul—if you don't let it consume you, of course. After lunch perhaps you will consent to show me where you are diggin'. I'd really like to get a look at one of those bones Peter has been talkin' about—if you have found anything."

"I would be happy to take both you and Holt on a tour." Temple glanced up to see if Holt had heard the emphasis placed on his name.

"Maybe Miss Cadwallender could show me around." Holt tilted his head and beamed at Temple from beneath the wide-brimmed hat.

Temple was about to offer a dozen reasons why she could not show him around when she stepped out of the tent with a bright red-and-black-plaid blanket over her arm.

"I would be happy to show you where I plan on digging, Mr. Morgan."

Temple grated his teeth together.

"Let me help you with that, Miss Cadwallender."

Holt swept the blanket from her grip and slid his arm around her waist.

The contact was casual, yet Temple felt his brows knitting together. For the life of him he could not seem to control the rampant tide of feelings.

"Peter, don't stand around grinnin'. Grab that basket off the back of my horse. I'll walk down with Mr. Parish."

"Glad to see you haven't lost your ability to give orders, Bessie," Peter observed dryly. "All this talking has made me work up an appetite. How about you, Temple? You sure look like you could take a bite outta somebody." Peter had the good grace to turn away before he broke into hearty peals of laughter.

"If you were just twenty years younger," Temple threatened under his breath, but then a sobering thought hit him. If Peter were a young buck then he would probably be panting after Connie just like Holt Morgan was.

It was not a comforting thought.

Butterflies had taken up residence in Constance's middle. She wasn't sure if it was due to Temple's scowl or because Holt Morgan had looped his arm around her waist. She was not comfortable with such attention. He looked at her in a way that was not unpleasant, but it didn't seem to have the same effect on her that looking at Temple did. At the bottom of the path, Holt stopped and turned around to face her.

"Here, let me help you." Wide hands locked around her waist and before she could think of any response, she was airborne and then deposited gently on her feet just beyond the rock that had lain in her path. "Why, you don't weigh as much as a feather, Miss Constance. I could carry you around all day."

Constance didn't remember ever being picked up by anyone other than her father. It was a singular experience. A surprised giggle escaped her lips.

Something hot and raw coursed through Temple. If Bessie Morgan had not been walking on his arm he would have sprinted down the rocky path and demanded an explanation for Holt Morgan's actions.

The realization rocked him.

What would he say? Would he demand to know if his intentions were *honorable?* Holt seized yet another opportunity to put his hands around Connie's tiny waist when he lifted her over a small scatter of boulders. She had been climbing over them without assistance since her arrival—or couldn't Holt figure that out?

Didn't the man know how foolish he looked? Temple wondered. But even while he discounted every action, scorned every deed, he quickened his pace in order to stay right behind the young couple. He couldn't let her out of his sight with this—this—interloper.

By the time they reached the bottom of the flat ravine a wide slice of shade lay along the western floor, cast by the deep sides of the canyon wall. In that cool wedge, Holt unfolded the red-and-black-plaid blanket and spread it out over the small pebbles and short stiff grass.

"There now, Miss Cadwallender." Holt took her hand and guided her to the blanket. "You just make yourself comfortable. Ma and I had Cook pack up a nice lunch. You are probably plumb sick of camp food."

"That was extremely thoughtful of you—and your mother. Thank you." No man had ever treated Constance as if she were going to break, but Holt Morgan's attention seemed to indicate he thought she would. He stood above her and watched her every action until she had settled herself and smoothed the serge skirt. With a detached and clinical eye, she allowed her gaze to skim over Holt—strictly for scientific purposes, of course.

He had wide muscular shoulders and arms that looked strong enough to carry her all day, as he had suggested. His hair was lighter than Temple's, a little shorter and burnished with red highlights. When he smiled at her, deep dimples appeared in his tanned cheeks to complement the spring green color of his eyes. He and Temple were of a similar height and build; health and vigor emanated from both. Holt Morgan was a handsome man, but looking at him did not cause a knot to form in her middle.

Constance looked away frowning. This simply made no sense at all. Why did she feel as if her knees were turning liquid when she looked at Temple? How could her cheeks flood with heat each time she saw him smile?

Unless she were developing feelings for Temple.

The thought made Constance shudder involuntarily. She had made a pledge to her father and a promise to herself. And she knew the risk of falling victim to the well-publicized charms of Temple Parish.

The arrival of Temple and Bessie Morgan interrupted Constance's thoughts. She glanced up and saw Mr. Hughes following a few paces behind them, a huge wicker basket in his arms. There was a flurry of activity while the newcomers found a place to sit on the large wool blanket. Constance allowed herself one surreptitious glance at Temple.

The result was immediate.

Her pulse quickened, her mouth dried out and her stomach fluttered as if a field of butterflies had taken wing. Despair folded over her. How could she have allowed herself to become another conquest in a long line of simpering females? She nearly moaned aloud in disappointment.

It wasn't as if she had not known what kind of a charming cad Temple could be. Lord knew, the newspapers carried just as many tidbits about his assignations as they did about his flamboyant scientific career. How could she have been so silly?

While the lunch basket was opened and Bessie dolloped food onto metal plates, Constance mulled over her predicament. Finally she came to a decision. Just because she had been smitten by Temple Parish, she did not have to lose her head, or her heart to him. She was not a green girl. In fact, by New York standards she was pushing spinsterhood to a dangerous limit. After all, she was the daughter of C. H. Cadwallender, and surely she was capable of withstanding the dubious enchantment of Temple Parish. She would simply have to exercise a little *control.*

Temple chewed and swallowed mechanically. He knew he was eating fried chicken, but he could have been chewing sawdust for all the pleasure it gave him. His eyes and ears were trained on Constance and Holt Morgan. The more Temple watched them, the more his appetite deserted him.

"Tell me, Mr. Parish, what do you think of our pendin' statehood?" Bessie Morgan asked abruptly. She sipped her lemonade and watched Temple over the rim of her cup.

"What?" Temple blinked and turned his attention toward the widow.

"I was askin' what you thought about Montana becomin' a state," Bessie explained.

"It's a big hunk of country," Temple said noncommittally. He couldn't think about politics, or geography—not with Holt Morgan leering at Connie. Hell, the man was practically drooling over her bosom.

"We should be the forty-first state by the time you and Miss Cadwallender find that critter you're lookin' for," Bessie continued, as if Temple were really paying attention.

He didn't bother to try and formulate an answer. He couldn't think about pleasant conversation—not while Connie was smiling at Holt.

"How about you, Miss Cadwallender? Do you follow politics?" Bessie had evidently given up on Temple and was resigned to try and get a conversation going in another area.

"Please, Mrs. Morgan, call me Constance," Connie suggested. "I spend most of my time cataloging my father's recent finds—so I am afraid I have little time for other pursuits."

"Constance—what a purty name—for a purty lady." Holt poured some lemonade into a cup and offered it to her. He seemed even less inclined than Temple to discuss Montana's possible statehood.

"This has been a lovely lunch. I can't remember when I last went on a picnic." Constance pushed her glasses up on her nose. She smiled shyly at Holt.

An inexplicable fire flared to life in Temple's gut while a raw throbbing ache grew in his chest. Connie's voice had turned to warmed honey. It sluiced through him and left a hot trail of longing behind.

"How did a little thing like you start digging in the dirt?" Holt asked politely.

As Holt stared into Constance's eyes, Temple had the urge to grab him by the nape of the neck and bodily eject him from the circle of people on the plaid blanket. Just who did Holt Morgan think he was?

"My mother died when I was an infant, so I spent a great deal of time with my father," Constance replied. "I simply grew up going on expeditions. I find it fascinating."

"Miss Constance, you are a wonder." Undisguised admiration rang in Holt's voice.

"And you, Mr. Parish?" Mrs. Morgan lifted her brows and looked at Temple. "How did you come to this?"

Temple felt the cold seep into his bones. This was a subject he tried not to think about, much less discuss with strangers. "Not much to tell." He set his half-full plate aside, no longer interested in eating.

"Nonsense, Temple," Constance challenged. She looked at him over the edge of her spectacles and Temple felt a ripple of satisfaction at having her attention. "Tell them the story, Temple." Her voice was soft. He could not deny her no matter how much he wanted to.

"All right, Connie, if you want." His voice lowered to a husky whisper and he felt his throat tighten at the memories. "I was orphaned. My mother died after one of the worst blizzards of the century swept through New York. After that most of my days were spent carrying baggage, messages or whatever else I could do to earn a crust. My nights were spent in Central Park."

"Central Park?" Peter was suddenly alert and listening.

Temple glanced at him. "Yes, like a lot of other homeless children." He heard the defensive tone in his own voice and wished these old memories were not as raw as a fresh wound. "Benjamin Waterhouse-Hawkins had begun work on some models of dinosaurs. I guess that was where my fascination really started. I bedded down near them most of the time. It gave me a sense of comfort. I suppose because of their size, to a small boy they appeared indestructible."

Bessie Morgan cut several slices from a tall layered cake. "I have a feelin' there is more to this story than you are tellin'."

"Temple is leaving out the best parts." Connie smiled at Bessie and then looked back at him. Temple didn't want to dredge up all the old memories, but how could he refuse Connie when she gazed at him like that?

"I was sleeping near the sculptures on a particularly dark night. It was quiet. I don't mean peaceful—I mean silent—unnaturally so. I hate that kind of quiet. It means something awful is coming. It is always like that before a terrible storm—or someone dies. Anyway, a gang of thugs with torches came out of the trees—they started smashing the statues with sledgehammers and fire axes." Temple shivered involuntarily as if the memory still had the power to buffet him.

"Go on, Mr. Parish," Bessie urged. "This is startin' to get interestin'."

"There's not much else to tell. I tried to stop them, but I was just a skinny kid. One thug saw me and started pummeling me. Another fellow stopped him.

He actually saved my life that night. He shoved me into the bushes where I watched while they destroyed those wonderful statues. Word of the vandalism hit the streets next morning. Professor Cadwallender was one of the people who came to look. He found me there. I was kind of a mess." Temple glanced away.

"His nose was broken and both his eyes were black," Constance explained. "He had taken quite a beating while he tried to save the statues. Papa was certain he had some cracked ribs as well, but Temple refused to see a doctor."

Temple's head snapped up. When their gazes locked across the plaid blanket she was no longer his adversary. For half a heartbeat they were simply Connie and Temple—old friends—new companions. Something lodged in Temple's chest just below his heart at the futility of this discovery.

"So what happened then?" Holt's eyes were wide with interest. It gave Temple some satisfaction to know his story had diverted Holt's attention from Constance for a few moments.

"C.H. took me under his wing and started to train me. For eight years I studied with him—I learned enough to become his assistant."

"And then?" Bessie prodded gently.

"And then things happened and I went my own way." Temple smiled crookedly. "I told you—nothing interesting at all."

"You are bein' modest, Mr. Parish." Bessie smiled and the skin around her eyes created a fine network of lines. "I find this story very interestin'. What I can't figure out is how Constance came to be out here—in Montana—challengin' you for that endowment."

Everyone turned to stare at Constance. She

squirmed and shoved her spectacles up and for the first time Temple realized she used them as a shield against the world. That insight filled him with mixed emotions. The more he learned about her, the harder it was going to be to do what he had to do. He clamped his lips shut and vowed to put a halt to this ridiculous infatuation—if that was what he was feeling.

"I...have come up with a...theory," she said hesitantly, and shifted uncomfortably. "But it is silly."

"Oh no, Miss Constance. Don't stop. Please tell us," Holt pleaded.

Constance fidgeted under Temple's steady gaze. He made her feel awkward. Another small realization that caused a strange conflict of emotion to well up inside his chest.

"It really is nothing. I'm sure you would not find it interesting."

"Tell us," Temple said softly. "I told the story you wished to hear, now tell us about your theory."

She stared at the cake in front of her and sighed heavily as if she were giving up her last shred of resistance. "I have noticed that the earth is layered—much like this cake is between the icing. Look at the sides of this canyon—each one of those stripes you see contains little bits of the past."

"That makes sense," Holt agreed.

"But I have a theory that goes a bit farther. I believe there are only one or two of those layers that ever contain dinosaur bones." Constance glanced at Temple as if she expected him to denounce her idea.

"Your father must be so proud." Bessie put a large piece of cake on a plate and passed it to Temple. He took it without thinking while he focused on Connie.

"Actually Papa and his colleagues feel my theory

is in error. That is one reason I came out here. I need this opportunity to prove I'm right.'' She glanced at Temple. "And to help Dandridge, of course."

Her words settled in his mind and understanding sizzled through him. She hadn't come to challenge him but to prove herself and her theory.

He had believed she was part of the group at Dandridge who lived to see him discredited. Now he saw that she was not so very different than he was. They were both oddities—unique among the academics who discounted their opinions and skills. She was ignored because she was female and he was discounted because in their eyes he would always be no more than an orphaned street urchin.

Disquiet seeped into Temple's mind. It was almost impossible to see her as his adversary, yet even though her motivations were different than he had originally thought, it meant the same thing.

Both of them needed to win Montague's endowment—but only one of them could claim the prize.

Chapter Eleven

Temple read the last newspaper in the stack despite his mounting rage. Someone at Dandridge University had gone out of their way to dredge up the shadows of his past. He was fairly sure he knew who that person was.

"Damn you, C.H." Temple growled. "Why can't you just let the past stay buried?"

A grimace curved his lips. C.H. had made a career out of digging up antiquity. Why should Temple's saga be any different than the burial ground of long-dead dinosaurs?

Temple put the various editions of New York papers back into a stack and tied the twine around them. Every paper had carried tidbits about the ten-year-old mystery—the lingering and still unsolved mystery. Each editorial left the question of his guilt open-ended—not one reporter had entertained the possibility of his innocence. Temple shook his head in disgust. As usual, people would look for the easiest target, and they would find him.

It wouldn't be long until Ashmont University started to squirm under this kind of scrutiny. It would not matter to the wagging tongues that there was no proof—never had been. It would not matter that all the clues had led in an entirely different direction. They would look at Temple Parish and see a thief—a street rat. Then he would be an outcast again, struggling to find a place to work in the profession he loved. His gaze fell upon the top paper.

The bold headline announced Montague's additional twenty-thousand-dollar bonus.

"With that kind of money, I wouldn't have to worry," Temple murmured. "I could finance my own expedition—I could be independent and the ghosts from the past couldn't touch me."

He closed his eyes and a weary sigh escaped his lips. Now that Montague had announced his intention of awarding the winning digger a cash bonus separate from the university endowment, Temple could not allow himself one more minute of sentimentality. His very survival was at stake.

"I have to win," he said aloud. "And I cannot allow Connie to stand in my way."

He stepped outside into the blazing sunlight. It was quiet again. Two days had gone by without a glimpse of Holt Morgan. Temple grimaced at his continued jealousy. If he did not get his wayward feelings about Connie under control, the rugged Montana silence would truly be the harbinger of his professional destruction.

Temple snagged his shovel and a canteen of water. He did not even allow himself so much as a single furtive glance in the direction of Connie's camp. He kept his eyes on the stubby grass as he walked to the area he had been inspecting. Now was the time to stop this crazy preoccupation before he lost all pretense of control.

Constance stood and stretched the kinks from her back and shoulders. She had finished the last of her sketches and fulfilled half of her promise to her father by ensuring that Dandridge's archives would benefit from her expedition. Now she could begin to put her theory to the real test.

If she could document that all dinosaur bones were in the layer she believed them to be, and nowhere else, then her father and his colleagues would be forced to acknowledge her abilities. Each time one of them dismissed her with an indulgent smile or condescending word, she wanted to scream. It simply was not right that her possible contribution to the scientific community should be overlooked because of her gender.

"Papa will have a fit if I succeed," she muttered. But even as she said it, she knew it was not true. Her father would support her theory if she provided proof. He was a hard man in many ways, but one of the fairest she had ever known. That was one of the reasons she could not fathom what had happened between him and Temple, and why he refused to discuss it with her. It was one of the few incidents in her memory where he absolutely refused to satisfy her natural and abundant curiosity.

Temple could be overbearing and infuriating, she would be the first to admit. It was easy to see how he could drive the most patient person to distraction, but that did not explain her father's uncharacteristic behavior. It was as if Temple and C.H. shared a secret, one they would not allow her to be part of. Perhaps that was what really disturbed her. Even though

Temple had been out of their household for ten years, there were still areas that he shared with C.H. that she was not privy to.

"But after I prove my theory, then I will be in a position to find out why everyone at Dandridge whispers about Temple and why his leaving is still such a guarded mystery."

Constance picked up the sketch pad and returned to her tent. She wrapped an oilskin around the charcoal and paper to ensure it would remain clean and dry, before she packed it away into a crate and replaced the flat wooden lid. Then she prepared to begin her own dig.

Sunlight blinded her when she emerged from the tent. Papa's sand-colored trousers and shirt of the same color allowed a slight breeze to waft around her body in a way that her voluminous dress and corset never could. Papa would not be happy if he knew she had taken some of his field clothes, she thought. But then again, how would he ever know?

Constance plopped the huge hat, minus the netting, atop her knotted hair and adjusted the brim against the rays. She was ready to begin digging in earnest.

"Blast and stuff!" Livingstone called out from his iron cage. His screechy bird voice froze her at the mouth of the tent.

"You frightened the life out of me, you silly bird." She leaned back into the dim cool confines of the canvas and watched the fowl flutt his feathers.

"Silly bird, awrk," he agreed while he paced to and fro on the thick dowel that served as a perch.

"I suppose you want to go?" Constance focused on the round ebony eye studying her intently.

"Awrk. Go, go."

She suppressed the urge to laugh. "Temple is right, you are a bother and a nuisance, but I would welcome some company."

"Blast and stuff—Temple is a pirate," Livingstone sang out.

Constance wondered what kind of conversations her father had been having in her absence—and with whom. Or had the professors at Dandridge stopped whispering and begun to gossip openly about the black-hearted pirate named Temple Parish?

Temple crouched beside the pile of dirt. Disappointment folded over him in a suffocating wave. The vertebra that had held so much promise had led him to nothing. What he had envisioned as the beginning of a great find had turned out to be one solitary isolated bone—not the entire skeleton he had been banking on—perhaps the vertebra had not even been a dinosaur bone.

"Probably one of Holt's damn stray cows," he grumbled dismally.

Temple squinted against the sun and unleashed a string of epithets. He had believed he was ahead of Connie—that he had all the time in the world. Now an invisible clock started to tick inside his head. He had to find another area before she finished her sketches and started to search.

He turned and looked across the grassy meadow toward Connie's camp. Temple's breath lodged in his throat. The same outlandish hat he had been looking at for weeks met his eyes, but Connie the chameleon had once again altered her appearance. Just when he'd managed to steel himself against her transformation from child in braids to water-soaked siren, and then once again to a blooming beauty in the latest New York fashions, she had yet again thrown him off balance.

She was garbed in masculine trousers and shirt. The outfit displayed her long legs and small waist, but it also left no doubt in his mind that she was every inch a capable competitor and adversary. Sunlight glinted off the rainbow iridescence and bright yellow throat of the bird perched on her shoulder. Another flash of light drew Temple's eyes to her hand. She was methodically digging with a small spade.

Hard-edged resolution settled in Temple's gut. He was going to have to work his tail off if he hoped to be victorious. He had no time to waste moaning over a single backbone that had disappointed him. These things happened all the time. The sooner he found another site, the better off he would be. With that thought propelling him he set off down the canyon at a rapid walk, in search of the area where the Morgans' cowhand had come across the first bones.

For hours Temple looked at the earth with the practiced eye of a digger. Finally, when frustration weighed in his gut like a stone, his gaze focused on something—elusive and difficult to define—but something that made his pulse quicken with hope.

"This looks interesting," he mused aloud. He knelt and rubbed his dry dusty hands across the rocky surface where a slab of sandstone had broken away. A tiny sliver of pale beige caught his eye.

"It is petrified bone."

A cautious grin blossomed across his face. He had found his new location.

He looked up to get his bearings. Surprise brought his brows shooting upward. The canyon was a giant wedge, much like a huge slice of pie with his and Connie's camps at roughly the center. But now he found himself standing at the narrowest point of that wide wedge. And when he looked toward the site of his camp he found it was nowhere in sight. There was no sign of Connie's tent either. In his quest he had walked the entire length of the grassy meadow, many miles from his starting point if the sun and his aching feet were any indication.

Now when he stood and looked from one edge of the canyon to the other, no more than a few yards separated "his side" of the canyon from the opposite slope.

"Good thing we didn't set camp here," he muttered. The thought of having to stare at Connie across this narrow space filled him with dread. It was bad enough when half a mile blurred the details of her face and form. It would be sheer torture to look up and be able to count the freckles on her pretty nose.

The man inside him tingled at the sensual prospect, but the weary digger who wanted to clear his reputation once and for all breathed a sigh of relief.

He glanced once more at the subtle indications in the dirt at his feet, then he turned and climbed out of the canyon and headed back toward his camp along the ridge. Temple decided he might as well get a look at the area from the top of the cut to see if he had missed any other good clues. Comforted by the promise of his new site, he strode toward the lowering sun, whistling a tune.

Constance frowned at the striations along the canyon wall. None of these was what she was looking for—had hoped for. She glanced at Livingstone, perched upon her shoulder. His head was tucked beneath his wing. She glanced up at the sun and realized she had been at her task for many hours.

"Are you ready for a nap?" His feathers ruffled slightly at the sound of her voice. He roused himself enough to stare at her with one black eye. "I'll take you back to the tent, you sleepyhead."

Constance glanced once again at the slices of earth in the canyon walls. If there was nothing promising at this location, then perhaps she should simply follow the striations down the grade and see where they led her. She was convinced her theory was correct, and if so, then she need not worry about digging anywhere but in that band of color along the canyon walls.

When Constance reached her tent she put Livingstone in his cage, and filled a canteen with water. She glanced over at Temple's camp, but saw no sign of him.

"He's probably dug halfway to China by now," she muttered. With that thought spurring her on, she turned and started walking down the center of the gorge. Time inched along while Constance examined the striations without success. Sweat dampened her clothing and her feet started to ache. And then when she had almost given up hope, her eyes fastened on the thick band of color in the dirt. She touched it with her fingers, then she started to break away small clumps of dirt.

The telltale signs she had been praying for began to emerge from the dusty soil. This was the first promising section she had come upon, miles from where she had first looked. Still, it was not unusual for things to get moved around by floods and redeposited elsewhere during the centuries. She thought about the long walk back to her camp and a weary sigh escaped her lips. If she made this trek twice a day it would leave little time for digging.

"Temple will have found his specimen and be out of here while I am still strolling through the bottom of the canyon," she grumbled. "Well, there is only one thing for it." Constance pulled her hat down on her head and starting walking back the way she had come. "I'll just move my camp."

Peter used the leathers to direct the horses toward Miss Cadwallender's side of the canyon. He was going to her side first to irritate Temple, but if he forced himself to be completely honest, it was also because of Temple's revelation about those damned models in Central Park.

He shook his head and pondered the whimsy of fate. Out of the whole of Montana, and the dozens of men who could have been hired by Montague's agent, Peter had ended up being the one to accept the job.

So far Temple had not recognized him, just as he would not have known Temple if he had not heard the story he told. No wonder, after eighteen years. Temple was a foot taller and filled out in hard corded muscle. And Peter had become an old man since Boss Tweed had sent him and his thugs to destroy the dinosaur models that night. Peter had come to Montana to get away from his memories of that life and all the terrible things he had done in his youth. And the plucky boy who had tried to save the statues had been the catalyst for that decision.

The team followed the faint trail from his last trip. He had little to do but let his mind wander and recount all the wasted days he had spent in New York. He was paying little attention when the team negotiated the last turn. To his surprise, Miss Cadwallender—or he thought it was Miss Cadwallender—was walking along the same path, in the same direction, toward her camp.

"Whoa." He gathered the reins and slowed the team. He swallowed his surprise and tried not to gawk at her clothes. After spending years around Bessie Morgan he should have been used to a woman in trousers, but when his cheeks grew hot, he realized that he was not.

She stopped and waited until the wagon was parallel with her, then she raised her hand in greeting. "Hello, Mr. Hughes."

"Miss Cadwallender, what are you doing out here?" Peter pulled harder on the reins. The wagon clattered to a lumbering stop.

"I have been at the other end of the canyon. I waited in the bottom for a while, but then I decided I would follow your wagon trail back to my camp—it made the walking easier, even if it was a bit longer."

"I see." He didn't see, of course, but he didn't want to sound ignorant.

"May I ride with you?" she asked.

"Pardon my manners, miss, I should've offered." Peter wrapped the reins around the foot brake and leaned across the seat so he could grab her outstretched hand. She climbed up and flopped on the hard wooden seat with a weary sigh.

"I have some fresh supplies, and more newspapers for you that came in on the train." He forced himself to look away from the long slender legs ending in the tops of tall laced-up boots.

"Good, I do look forward to reading a bit in the evenings by my fire. And I—I need your help."

Peter's brow furrowed. Up to this moment he had never heard Miss Cadwallender ask for anybody's help about anything. A prickly feeling of premonition crawled up his spine. "I'd be happy to help. What can I do for you?"

She pulled the hat off her head. Sweat plastered her hair to her forehead. High color stained her cheeks. "I want to move my camp."

"I don't believe I heard you correctly."

She cleared her throat. "I—I—want to move my camp—to this end of the Devil's Spur. I have found where I want to dig, but it is too far to walk twice a day. And I'd like to get moved before nightfall."

Peter gathered the reins and the team moved forward. There had been a tone of determination in Miss Cadwallender's words that required no more discussion about her decision. She had made up her mind, that was plain enough to see, but a nagging question crowded the edge of Peter's mind.

"What does Mr. Parish think about this idea—if you don't mind me asking?"

"What do you mean?"

"Well, I just wondered what he said when you mentioned your idea."

"He didn't say anything because I have not discussed it with him." Her brows bunched together at the middle. A tiny furrow appeared above the bridge of her nose. "Mr. Hughes, as I told you in the beginning, Temple Parish can be unorthodox in his methods. It is important that I don't lose sight of my goal. I feel my theory can best be tested at this end of the canyon—far away from Temple's dig."

Constance did not tell Mr. Hughes the rest of her reason for wanting to move. Quiet contemplation while she hiked had finally made her realize that she was skirting disaster by remaining near Temple. He *affected* her. And given her lack of experience she was no match for him. The wisest thing she could do would be to move away from him—far away before circumstance spun out of control.

"Then I better get this team moving so we can get your camp set up before dark." Peter gave her a side-long glance, but he didn't ask any more questions.

Temple yanked the suspenders up onto his shoulders. A long twilight swim had allowed him to clear his head and gather his thoughts. Now he knew exactly what he was going to do—and why.

His preoccupation with Connie had cost him enough time. If he intended to find the bones and collect Montague's prize, and by God he did, then he had no more time to waste on sentimental foolishness.

Tomorrow he was going to pack up his bedroll and a few basic supplies and move to this end of the canyon. If he worked from sunup to dark each day, then he could not help but find some bones. He was determined to unearth the prize and be back in New York within two weeks. Temple glanced up at the twilight sky and realized he was walking near Connie's camp. He abruptly changed direction, taking a different path down into the gorge and across the flat to his own camp. The last thing he needed or wanted was to see Connie and have to explain what he planned to do.

"It is time to stop thinking about her and start thinking about myself."

Chapter Twelve

Constance released a sigh of contentment. The campfire Mr. Hughes had built before he left cast a comforting glow over her newly erected tent. From her current camp she looked out at the unfamiliar purple and gray evening landscape, and the shadows dancing over the treeless earth.

Now she was truly alone. Her first night in her new camp—her first night away from Temple. Now he and the temptation he represented were several miles away up the cut. Her only distractions were Livingstone and the stack of fresh papers from home.

With her hands wrapped around a reassuring cup of warm tea, she entered her tent and surveyed her home. It was too large, just as Temple accused, but it was well stocked with everything she needed close at hand.

She perched on the edge of her narrow cot and picked up one of the newspapers Mr. Hughes had left. The headlines referred to New York politics and a terrible fire that had swept through another tenement.

Constance turned the pages several times before she found mention of her or Temple. She set the cup on the dirt floor of her tent and read the article.

Mr. Montague's offer to reward the digger apart from the endowment was the main topic of the piece. There was little mention of what she or Temple hoped to find—or why. Constance wondered if the public had already tired of hearing about the quest. She had learned at an early age how important it was for any institution of higher learning to be popular. Publicity brought in students, which in turn brought in money for projects such as this dig. It was vital for Dandridge to keep its name in the public eye.

Constance retrieved the cup and took a sip of warm tea. Worry tickled the corners of her mind. The longer it took for her to find the bones and return to New York, the less impact it would have for the university.

"Or for me," she muttered. If she was going to benefit from the cascade of interest the find would bring, she needed to hurry.

"All I have to do is beat Temple to the prize," she mumbled.

All? a voice inside her head questioned. To speak of the deed was simple, but the doing was a bit more complicated. In spite of all his annoying faults, Temple was good—perhaps the best digger around, and Constance was bright enough to know it.

"Temple is a pirate," Livingstone squawked as though he could read her thoughts.

Constance frowned at the ebony feathers reflecting the lantern light. "He is a talented pirate, and a man like Temple should not be underestimated."

She rose from the cot and walked to Livingstone's cage. Constance wrapped a shawl around the wire to keep the talkative bird warm through the night—and to silence him. "Now be quiet and get some sleep."

After tugging off her boots she slipped out of her

trousers and shirt. The thin fabric of her gown settled over her body with a whisper of sound. She tied the tent flap tightly from the inside and blew out the lantern.

She needed a good night's sleep—there was no time to waste.

The morning wind whispered through the canyon like a lover's call. Constance stared up at the overcast sky of dawn. The blue-gray bowl was cloudless, but the color put her in mind of a storm. She sniffed and the attar of rain floated to her on the first morning breeze. The usual flocks of birds were absent from the Montana sky.

"Livingstone, my fine friend, you are going to have to stay inside in case a storm does blow up while I am off digging."

The bird ruffled his feathers and glared at her as if he understood the notion of his confinement. While she chided herself for attaching human qualities to the mynah, she secured the flaps from the outside of her tent. Then she filled a canteen with water from one of the barrels Mr. Hughes had left and gathered the rest of her supplies. When Constance was sure she had all of her equipment, she started examining the strip of color in the canyon side once again.

At her first site, the canyon walls had risen twenty or thirty feet, but here at the point of the canyon only about four feet of canyon wall separated the rim from the bottom of the ravine. The only disadvantage was the fact that on this end there were no natural stairs. The grade was steep and treacherous and it took her complete concentration to descend into the gorge.

She made her way carefully to the point of the huge

pie-shaped wedge of earth. She was not more than fifty yards from the mouth of her tent, but she was six to seven feet below the rim of the canyon on which she was camped, when a dark bank of clouds began to gather.

"Today I will find out if I have any real talent for this work." She took a deep breath to fortify her courage and began to search the canyon walls. And while the morning sun tried to burn off the scudding clouds, Constance took a pick and began to knock away centuries of dirt and soil.

Temple grabbed an empty gunnysack and shoved some leftover biscuits and a slab of bacon into the opening. He never allowed himself a single glance toward Connie's camp. He told himself it was because he did not wish to explain why he was going to the far end of the cut, but he knew there were other reasons. The simple truth was that he had become a coward. His cowardice was born of his growing awareness of Connie. Temple could not deny his reaction to her but neither could he control it. Like it or not, he wanted her.

But on the heels of that sobering admission, he had to come to grips with the fact that he could not allow himself to risk his future because of his attraction to her.

Peter Hughes had mentioned in his vague I've-got-a-secret way that he had been to Connie's camp before he arrived at Temple's last night. Temple had been able to resist the temptation to pry information from him for the simple reason he did not want to slip up and let Hughes know he was relocating this morning. It was enough to know that Peter had seen Connie, that she was fine, she had fresh supplies and Peter would be back in two days to check on her. That was as far as he was going to allow his concern for her to extend.

He had bones to dig up—and a past to overcome. And God willing, he was going to begin doing both today. But if that was true, why did he have a lump in his throat and a pain in his gut when he started walking down the meadow away from Connie?

Temple shoved the question to the back of his mind. Then he shifted the weight of the shovel, bedroll and gunnysack full of supplies higher on his shoulder and trudged off. He had started to take along a rain slicker, but his stubborn nature wouldn't let him. If he did that then he would be admitting that Peter was right, and he was loath to do that. Still, he glanced at the early-morning sky in apprehension within a matter of minutes. The air was thick and heavy.

"It is not going to rain," Temple muttered to himself. "It is *not* going to rain." Temple challenged the heavens as if he could hold back the storm with the strength of his own willpower.

He looked away from the sky and focused on other matters. As much as Peter Hughes had annoyed him with his sly glances and secret smiles, Temple had at least been able to get him to take the new dispatches for Montague and Ashmont. Temple doubted he could do much to quell the present gossip, but some news about his progress would make the people at Ashmont happier—and give the wagging tongues at Dandridge something fresh to focus on besides his past.

Sweat beaded beneath the band on Temple's hat while he hiked. The sun, which had been playing hide-and-seek with him all morning, now vanished behind a dense gray veil. He quickened his pace, determined to get to the end of the canyon and set up his temporary camp. He placed one boot in front of the other with dogged determination and forced himself to ignore the ominous black thunderhead rolling toward him from the north.

The sound of metal striking stone rang out. He frowned and climbed up the rocky incline to get a better view of the landscape—and find out who was in the canyon. Holt had spoken of the mines. Perhaps they were near here—perhaps it was Morgan himself. When Temple reached the top, he turned and scanned the area.

His breath caught in his throat.

At the very end of the cut, at the narrow tip where the two steep sides met, was an unexpected sight.

"Connie!" Amazement rang in his words.

How had she beaten him here? How had she known he was coming?

Anger and suspicion seeped into his mind. Her cunning and perseverance shocked him. He had underestimated her drive, and possibly the extent she would go to in order to receive the endowment. As he stared at her, he began to wonder if she had been observing him, spying on him all the time he had assumed she was sketching.

"That little vixen will not stop me," Temple grumbled.

As if in agreement with his angry vow, a deep boom of thunder rolled across the prairie and echoed through the canyon. It shook the earth through the bottoms of Temple's boots. Even though he was seething with suspicion, a thousand worries about Connie's safety vibrated through him with the ominous sound.

She stopped digging, as if she felt his concerned eyes upon her back. Across the narrow space that now separated them, he saw shock in her gaze. Was that guilt he saw in her sienna eyes—or was his mind playing tricks on him?

Then she stood and he realized what she was wearing. He swallowed and felt his weak and traitorous body harden with interest. Just then she looked up and Temple knew...

Questions nipped at the corners of Constance's mind. Had Temple followed her? She had not wanted to believe the whispers she heard in the hallways of Dandridge, but seeing him standing on the rocky ledge above her brought doubt cresting through her mind. Was Temple willing to steal another digger's finds rather than work for his own?

Her breath caught in her throat.

Could he? Would he? She didn't want to believe it. But what other explanation could there be?

While she stood staring at him her stomach twisted into a hard knot. But as if God himself had tired of the silent argument going on inside her heart, the heavens cracked like a teamster's whip. Heavy droplets pelted her hat and shoulders, soaking deep into her father's purloined shirt and trousers. She had no more time to worry about Temple or his motives as she scrambled up the steep and difficult path toward her tent.

Rain soaked her clothing and plastered the fabric to her skin. Her boots slipped and several times she lost purchase in the slick muddying earth. Her feet became heavy with the dusty-gray muck and only through dogged determination, sometimes by more crawling than climbing the incline, Constance finally stood at the mouth of her tent.

The canvas ties were already soaked, making the knots nearly impossible to undo. Her fingers were cold and her hat brim had collapsed from the weight of the rain. Rivulets ran over her spectacles and down her cheeks, blinding her.

"Let me do it." Temple's deep voice rumbled behind her. She spun around and found him no more than a hand's span from her, glaring so fiercely that for a moment she wondered if his stormy expression had brought the torrent.

"I—I can—manage," she stammered.

"Yes, I know how capable you are, Connie. I concede that you are the most capable woman alive. Now kindly move aside and let me do this before you catch your death of cold."

His sensible words penetrated her suspicions about why he was here. She jerkily nodded her approval and moved half a step.

She stood there dripping like a wet mop. Because of the gray torrent, all she could see was Temple's wide shoulders. His clothing was wetter than her own, if that was possible. The pale collarless shirt clung to his skin, so translucent from the water it nearly disappeared against the lean expanse of his back. She was reminded of his swim and the way his magnificent bare body had glistened in the sunshine. She swallowed hard and looked away into the gray veil of rain.

"There, now get inside and change those clothes." Temple stood aside and gestured toward the dry shadowy confines of the tent.

"Aren't—you c-c-coming?" Connie was shivering from head to toe.

Lines of tension bracketed his lean mouth as he stared at her. "No."

"You c-can't be s-s-serious."

"I brought my bedroll. This won't last long, I'll find a sheltered overhang down there somewhere." He inclined his head toward the canyon and told himself he had been a prize fool to have left his slicker at the other camp.

Constance was unable to stop staring into the deep agate depths of his eyes. He was a lodestone and she the iron—unable to resist his magnetic allure.

"Temple..." Constance felt herself swaying toward him as if in a dream. Her body had no strength—no substance.

He narrowed his eyes. His fierce gaze flicked to her mouth and back again. A low growl seemed to bubble up from inside him, and then miraculously, his hard arms were around her.

The heady masculine taste of his lips mingled with that of the sweet spring rain. Sensation jolted through Constance, causing her to wonder if she might have been hit by a bolt of lightning, but then Temple broke the kiss. He held her away from him and she knew that the frisson of heat blazing through her trunk and limbs was caused only by his searing kiss.

"Connie—just—get inside." His voice was husky and low. The sound of it sent a new set of chills skipping up her arms.

"I—I will—if you—c-come inside." She blinked and pushed her rain-dotted lenses up on her nose, but they were no barrier against the licking heat caused by Temple's stare.

Constance swallowed hard and turned. Only then,

when she looked down at her damp hands, did she realize that she was shaking like a leaf.

She stepped inside the dark tent and made her way toward her bed as a finger of lightning drew a jagged line across the sky. She grabbed a blanket off the narrow cot and tossed it to Temple as the lightning died and darkness engulfed them. A muffled curse brought her spinning around just as a rumble of thunder shook the earth beneath their feet.

Another flash of blue-white illuminated the shelter. For half a heartbeat she was once again able to see her surroundings clearly. The blanket had landed squarely across Temple's nose, mouth and shoulders. His brown eyes blazed above the material like bronze fires. His hat was askew on his head, allowing droplets of water that had been caught in the brim to trickle down into the front of his shirt.

"Thanks," he grated out while he untangled the blanket from his upper body. Another flash of lightning charged the air as if to emphasize the anger she saw burning in his eyes.

"You are w-wel—welcome..." Constance took off her glasses and wiped them on the edge of the shawl covering Livingstone's cage. The movement pulled the fabric free, allowing it to slip down from the top.

A white arc flashed outside the tent and Constance slipped her spectacles back onto her face.

"Awrk, wake up, wake up." Livingstone fluffed his feathers and blinked in startled response to the violent storm. "Awrk, blast and stuff."

"Where is your lantern? I'll get us some more light in here." Temple's disembodied voice came from somewhere behind her back. But speech seemed to have abandoned Constance. She felt, more than saw,

Temple moving through the tent. The small hairs along her arms stood on end when he was near. And as she stood in the tent a peculiar thing started to happen.

The tent had seemed overlarge before, but now with Temple groping through its gloomy confines Constance fancied it was shrinking around her. The charged air was too thick to breathe, yet the cloaking darkness was not concealing enough to keep her from seeing with a sharpened sixth sense.

A spark flared as Temple lit the lamp, and her pulse quickened.

The golden glow of light drove the gloom to the edges of the tent. Constance took a deep breath and found herself staring into Temple's eyes. She hoped he would kiss her again—prayed he would not—while the tension between them, like the storm outside, gathered force.

"Th-this is quite a storm." Her throat was tight with anxiety. She had shared a thousand private conversations with him when they were younger, but now the act of putting together a few coherent words required all her concentration.

Temple swallowed hard and she watched his Adam's apple bob up and down in his throat. Could he perceive even a tiny fraction of what she was feeling? Was it possible he might be feeling the same thing?

"It will blow over soon. Springtime gales blow in and out quickly." His words were clipped and tight.

Constance felt as if they had been seized by some curious malady that constricted breathing and lowered their voices into seductive whispers.

"Yes, I suppose you're right." She couldn't seem

to stop twisting the shawl in her hands. Temple's gaze held her, transfixed. They stood staring at each other like statues, frozen together in awkward silence.

He cleared his throat and Constance found herself able to release the breath she had been unconsciously holding. His expression was taut—controlled. Lines of tension bracketed his stern mouth.

"Awrk, blast and stuff," Livingstone chirped.

Temple took a step closer to Constance, and her nostrils filled with the heady smell of rain and him.

"Take off your clothes," he commanded in a husky whisper as thunder boomed to emphasize his request. "Take your clothes off now."

Chapter Thirteen

"I beg your pardon?" Her voice squeaked and broke.

Did the merest hint of a satyric grin touch his lips, or was it a trick of the lantern light?

"Take those things off and put on some dry clothes, or you'll be nursing a fever tomorrow instead of digging."

"Oh," Constance whispered. Relief—or was it disappointment?—coursed through her at the familiar mocking tone in his voice. Whatever strained enchantment had bound them with invisible cords was gone now, banished by Temple's taunting remark. The illusion of attraction between them wafted away like smoke. Clarity of purpose brought the reality of their situation into sharp focus. Her reason returned.

"Take off your clothes, take off your clothes, awrk," Livingstone chattered above the din of the storm.

The bird's voice helped her to regain her composure. She and Temple had shared one mad impulsive kiss but that was all it could ever be. They were rivals—adversaries—trapped together for a short time because of the whims of weather. No more—no less.

"Yes." She looked at the trunks and then at Temple. "I do need to change, but I..."

This time his full bottom lip curled upward without restraint or repentance. Constance felt her cheeks flush with embarrassment at the gleam in his flinty eyes.

"Regardless of what you may have read in the newspapers, or heard whispered in the halls of Dandridge, I am not a total bounder. I'll turn my back. I have no intention of molesting you."

More heat filled her cheeks. Had he read her mind? Or did he instinctively know a part of her wanted him to sweep her into those strong lean arms and kiss her once again? Kiss her until she could no longer focus on career or promises or far-fetched theories.

While she pondered the possibilities, Temple simply turned his back on her. She found herself staring at wide shoulders encased in clinging wet cloth. An unbidden sigh of appreciation escaped her lips.

Stop! she chided herself silently. Remember your pledge, remember the bones.

Constance swallowed her confusion and forced herself to turn toward her trunks, but indecision continued to keep her rooted to the spot. One trunk contained all her digging clothes—while the other was filled with the fashionable frocks. She knew she must be mad to even consider putting on a pretty dress, but the thought flitted through her mind on butterfly wings.

"Hurry up, Connie, you'll end up with pneumonia—and find a way to say it was my fault."

Temple's hard impatient voice washed over her. Before the thought had truly congealed into a solid idea, she felt her feet moving. Constance tore at the sodden clothing with sudden furious intent. No matter how capable she was, he insisted on treating her like a child. No matter what the situation, he barked orders at her as if she had not a single brain in her head. Disappointment and fury rippled through her.

"Hurry up, hurry, awrk." Livingstone chimed the order and made her more determined to silence Temple.

Temple heard the sound of wet clothing being peeled away from rain-damp skin. A tight coil began to unwind deep inside his loins. The image of Connie in wet breeches was burned into his memory like a flash of lightning that comes with no warning. But that picture was nothing compared to the certainty that she was now removing those formfitting, too-flattering, all-revealing gentleman's trousers.

"Temple, why are you here?" Her voice floated to him.

"What do you mean, why am I here?" He heard each sigh, each flutter of material even while he answered. She was peeling away layers of fabric, layers of protection. Soon she would be standing behind him as naked as the truth—a truth he wanted to deny.

"I mean that you are miles from your camp. Why?"

"I could ask you the same thing, except that your entire camp seems to be miles from where I last saw it."

There was a moment of silence. Only the sound of the storm could be heard. "I asked Mr. Hughes to help me move it," she finally answered.

"Why?"

"I asked you first."

He swallowed hard while the image of Connie undressing gnawed at his insides. "I thought the digging would be better here. And you? Why did you move?"

Again a moment of silence where the patter of rain on the tent seemed to grow louder with each passing minute.

"I arrived at the same conclusion."

"How curious that we both decided to move at the same time." His voice was a husky purr, full of innuendo and promise, ripe with possibility.

"Yes, isn't it?" Connie said softly. "Very curious, indeed."

Temple closed his eyes. He tried to focus on the fact they were both here to dig in the same place, but the portrait of damp pliant flesh would not release its grip on his imagination. His mind was sluggish, as if he had been drugged by Connie's potent kiss. He tried to focus on the fact that the damnable rain was keeping him from digging.

It didn't work. He grimaced as he peeked through the flap of Connie's tent and saw his bedroll getting soaked. He had dropped it in fear for Connie's safety. That same fear had driven him across the ravine without thought. But even anger at himself for being so damned impulsive failed to take his mind off the woman behind him.

His skin itched where his own wet clothing chafed at his shoulders and waist. Heat mingled with an intense restlessness while his mind painted pictures of her flesh, of her eyes—of *her*. No matter what he tried to concentrate on, all he could really think about was Connie...beautiful Connie stripping away her men's clothing until her lovely woman's body was bare.

A soft sigh behind his back sent a frisson of passion clawing its way up his spine. He swallowed hard and prayed the rain would stop soon. He wasn't sure he was man enough to weather a long storm. Not inside Connie's tent, where temptation stood only a few feet away.

"All right, Temple, you can turn around now."

He heard her words but his legs refused to respond. He knew he was acting like a frightened schoolboy, but he dreaded having to look at Connie all the while he longed to stare at every inch of her. What if she had put on another pair of men's breeches? Could he look at those long elegant legs without moaning with physical need?

Or if she had covered herself in that hideous costume that she traveled in, could he look upon her without wishing he could peel away the layers until he found her form hidden inside like the flesh of a sweet and very much forbidden fruit?

"Temple? Did you hear me?"

"Yes, Connie, I heard you." He dredged up the last of his courage and spun around on one boot heel.

She had chosen neither of the modes of dress he had thought about. Regret and appreciation flowed through him in equal measures.

Her hair fell in dark rippling waves, still heavy from the rinsing of rainwater. The baby-pink dress brought a pale Montana sunrise sweeping across her cheeks. She looked fresh and dewy and entirely kissable from head to dainty bare feet.

"Connie—you are…"

"I am what?" Her breath lodged beneath her breast while she waited for him to finish. She didn't want Temple's opinion to matter, but it did, oh dear Lord, it did matter.

Lovely, he wanted to say, but he held the word

back, clinging valiantly to the last shred of his resolve. "Finally dressed," he said gruffly.

"Yes, I am. Thank you for noticing." Constance pushed her glasses up on her nose.

He swallowed hard. Her nervous little gesture should have made him feel less awkward, but it only made her appear more vulnerable.

"I may not have said anything but I have noticed all the things you wear." The admission tumbled from his mouth before he could stop the words.

Her eyes widened and she took a step forward. His body thrummed, just knowing that she was within arms reach. But then his gaze focused on her ears. His eyes were riveted to the cameos hanging from her delicate lobes.

"Connie, are those the same pearl and cameo earrings?"

"Yes, they are."

He reached out, halting his hand only inches from actually lifting the dainty gold filigree with his fingertips.

"You kept them." Amazement sizzled through him. "All these years."

"Of course I kept them. It was the only present you ever gave me."

Temple stared at the jewelry while a mixture of feelings washed over him. He had worked like a dog to earn the money to buy those earrings and a new pipe for C.H. And in the end those presents had led to his ruin. He could never reveal how he had earned the money, that he had broken his word to C.H. and associated with criminals. He didn't have the courage to disappoint C.H., but by keeping his silence he had given Professor Andrew Pollock and his son, Herbert, all the ammunition needed to blow Temple's fragile world apart.

"They look lovely on you."

"Lovely, lovely on you, awrk," Livingstone agreed and gave Temple a moment in which to gather his tumultuous thoughts. He glanced outside, searching in vain for an avenue of escape. Rain pelted the earth without slackening. There was no place for him to go, nowhere for him to hide. He was trapped with Connie and his own conflicting feelings. He couldn't leave and he couldn't allow her to know how she affected him, because if she ever knew how hard it was for him to be here, she might use his weakness against him.

He stepped away from her and forced his hands to his wet thighs. Frustration nipped at his heels, compelling him to pace the width of the tent like a caged animal. He tried to ignore Connie and all the old feelings she had unintentionally prodded while he stared out the slit in the tent opening. And he fought to keep his thoughts and his hands off her while the storm grew worse.

Constance sat on the edge of her bed and counted the seconds between the blue-white flashes and the subsequent rumbling thunder. She had tried desperately to find something to engage her mind, but Temple's presence tossed her thoughts willy-nilly.

"The storm is getting closer," she commented when the rolling thunder vibrated through her tent.

Temple paused in his pacing to study her in silence, then his frown deepened and he resumed his strides in tense silence.

"Why don't you sit down on one of those crates? You are wearing me out with your pacing, Temple."

"Temple is a pirate." Livingstone said quite clearly. "A bounder, an ingrate, pirate...pirate, awrk."

Constance cringed when Temple's scowling gaze slid to the bird.

"I wonder how he would taste boiled up with dumplings?" His eyes narrowed down to predatory slits and he tilted his head as if speculating on Livingstone's taste.

"Temple!" She stiffened on the edge of her cot. "You wouldn't. Would you?"

"Why wouldn't I? That feathered chatterbox has done nothing but insult me since he arrived." Temple's gaze slid to her. "Well, perhaps not...." He graced her with a lopsided grin that softened his expression. She was reminded of the boy he used to be. "I won't wring the beast's scrawny neck. At least not right now. Besides, I shouldn't blame him. He is only repeating what he has heard."

"What do you mean?" she challenged defensively.

Temple's smile slipped. In the uneven glow of the lantern light his predatory eyes glittered like polished agate. "The mynah bird is only aping what he has heard. Livingstone did not form his opinion of me all by himself, even if he is an extraordinarily bright creature."

Heat filled Constance's cheeks. The same thought had occurred to her. Since she and her father were the only people who lived with Livingstone, the implication was obvious.

"Do you think I taught him to say those things?" Constance asked in a small voice.

Temple gave her another twisted smile. "No, Connie, I do not."

She could not avoid the unmistakable truth. And for the first time in her memory she was embarrassed by her father's actions. If she had not taught Livingstone, then C.H. must have. "I—I'm sorry, Temple." she said softly.

He peered at her from beneath his furrowed brows. "You have nothing to apologize for, unless you *are* the one who taught him to say that."

"Oh, no." Constance averted her gaze. "I wouldn't repeat things I didn't think were true."

Temple told himself that Connie's opinion of him didn't matter. He told himself to turn away from her, to stare out at the rain-ravaged badlands. He silently said all these things but he did not listen to his own voice of reason.

"Would you say them if you thought they were the truth?"

Her head snapped up and she found their gazes locked in another silent tug-of-war. Something hot and almost as brilliant as a bolt of lightning arced across the tent between them.

"Temple—I...." Constance felt the invisible pull as if he held cords that had been bound securely around her heart.

She knew she was losing the battle and a part of her would have been happy to surrender to the compelling force that seemed to cocoon her tent, but she could not. Constance had given her word to her father, and a Cadwallender never ever went back on their word. But as she stared into Temple's bottomless eyes a deep raw hollow of need seemed to open up inside her heart. The sound of thunder mingled with her pulse while she wondered what her father was doing—and what he would say if he knew her traitorous thoughts.

C.H. wiggled his toes. Relief at finally having the confounded heavy cast off his foot surged through him.

"How does that feel?" Dr. Lambkin asked.

"Much better." C.H. reached for the stocking and boot he had carried to the physician's office. "Now maybe I can move around without knocking over tables. Honoria is going to be peeved when she finds out I broke her favorite lamp."

Dr. Lambkin shook his head and chuckled. "Why don't you take a walk and see if some fresh air will improve your outlook, C.H.?" The stricken look on C.H.'s face nearly brought a burst of laughter from Dr. Lambkin, but he managed to restrain himself.

"There is nothing wrong with my outlook." C.H. bristled. "How dare you imply I am not even-tempered."

"Really?" Dr. Lambkin raised his brows in doubt. He had known C.H. long enough to risk such familiarity. "Even-tempered, are you?"

"Yes." C.H. bent over his lean middle and jerked on the sock and boot. Years of digging and hiking had kept him thin and his confinement had worn on his patience. "Everyone who knows me would say so."

"Then why have you been wearing a hangdog look since you came in here?" Dr. Lambkin folded his arms across his chest.

"Well, I have been a little preoccupied lately. You know that Honoria has gone to Montana to dig, of course?"

Dr. Lambkin rolled his eyes. "How could I *not*

know it? Every newspaper in town has been following the expedition. How are things proceeding?''

"Fine. Honoria sends regular messages. She is a capable girl and I have faith in her—that is not the reason I have been muddled in my thinking." C.H. stared at the wall with an unfocused expression.

"Then what is?"

"It is all this old business being stirred up. No good will come of resurrecting the past." C.H. shook his head from side to side. "No good at all."

"How is he?" Lambkin asked softly.

C.H. snapped to attention and his brows knit together. "How is who?"

"Don't play the innocent with me, Charles Herbert Cadwallender. You know very well who I mean. How is Temple?"

"Temple is—" C.H. sighed and lifted his palms into the air. "Well, he is Temple." C.H. allowed his hands to drop onto his thighs as if further explanation eluded him. "He is a rascal—he'll never change."

"I see. And how is Honoria handling him?"

C.H. expelled a heavy sigh. "I wish I knew—I just wish I knew what she was doing about him. And I wish I didn't feel I had made a grave error by allowing her to go in my stead."

"Things going as well as that, eh?" Dr. Lambkin asked gently.

"Oh, I don't know. I think you are right, though, I need to take a walk and clear my thoughts."

"Good idea, get some air and some exercise, I am sure once you stretch your muscles all of this will seem much better."

C.H. took his physician's advice when he left the office. The afternoon sun was warm on his face and his feet picked an old familiar path without his even being aware of it. Before he realized it, he was standing in Central Park. The sunlight mottled the leaf-strewn grass into dappled patterns of shadows. A sense of peace swept over him while he strolled the old grounds.

Within the hour his newly healed foot began to cramp from overuse after weeks of immobility, and cried out for a rest. He glanced around and found an empty park bench near a lovely fountain. His cane was a helpful anchor while he gingerly levered himself down to the cool iron bench and stretched out his foot. Birds gathered at his boots, unaware he had no bread or seeds to give them. They bobbed and pecked, coming within inches of his boots, reminding him of Livingstone, which in turn brought his thoughts to Honoria.

"Nice day, isn't it?" A man's voice caused the birds to take flight in a flurry of wings.

C.H. looked up, but all he saw was a slender silhouette haloed against the brilliant orb of the sun.

"Yes, yes—nice day," C.H. muttered absently while he squinted against the brightness.

"May I sit with you?"

"Of course." C.H. looked away and blinked. He was blinded by the lingering effects of the sunlight—helpless as a baby, while white and black spots danced in front of his eyes. Slowly his vision returned to normal. The first thing he saw was a pair of adventurous pigeons waddling near his feet once again.

"How is your daughter doing, Professor?" The voice brought C.H.'s head around. This time he could see his bench companion clearly. A well-dressed young man with sharp intelligent eyes searched his face.

"You're a reporter," C.H. declared without preamble.

"Yes, I am. My name is Thaddeus Ball. I interviewed Temple Parish before he left." The young man pulled a stubby pencil and pad of paper from his pocket. "I wanted to ask you a couple of questions."

"Leave me alone." C.H. started to rise from the bench.

The reporter snapped the pad closed and replaced it in his vest pocket with amazing alacrity. "If you don't want to be interviewed, that's fine." Thaddeus smiled and revealed a wide gap between his two front teeth. "I only thought you might like to set the record straight about what happened ten years ago." The young man shrugged and looked away as if the subject had little appeal to him one way or the other.

C.H. studied the reporter's profile while a myriad of emotions flowed over him. "Why are you interested?" he finally asked, unable to resist the bait the young man so artfully dangled in front of him. "You couldn't have been much more than a toddler at the time."

The reporter turned and smiled wider. It was a friendly smile, without guile or pretense. "I hate loose ends—all those things happened ten years ago but there is one *big* loose end."

"But what does it matter to you?" C.H. gripped the head of his cane a little tighter while he waited for the reporter's answer.

"Call it professional curiosity. I have been doing a little discreet digging of my own, if you will excuse the pun. What I am finding just doesn't add up. Tell me, Professor, why wasn't there a formal inquiry?

Why did Temple just leave and let all the wagging tongues draw their own conclusions?"

C.H. suddenly felt every one of his sixty-plus years. "I wish I knew. That question has nagged at me since the first."

"All right, let me ask this, why didn't *you* speak out?"

C.H. turned to look Mr. Ball straight in the eye. "I didn't want to do anything that would put Temple under more suspicion. My colleagues kept insisting that if I pushed for an investigation and brought more scrutiny to Temple, his past associations and activities would be held against him. They seemed to think he might end up behind bars." C.H. was silent for a moment. "I couldn't do that to the lad. I could not be the reason Temple lost his freedom. Temple is not the kind of person that could stand being confined."

"You like him, don't you?" Wonder rang in the reporter's voice.

A melancholy wave of loss swept through C.H. "I love him like a son, though he'd never believe it. Now, if you will excuse me, I really must get home."

Thaddeus Ball watched the old man limp away while a hundred new questions danced through his head. This mystery was getting more interesting with each passing day.

He stood and started walking. There was a story here—a big story—the kind of story that could make a career. Thaddeus intended to do some digging of a different kind, right here in New York City. It was about time someone unearthed the truth about Temple Parish, exactly what had happened at Dandridge University and why it remained such a well-guarded secret.

* * *

Memories buffeted C.H. while he slowly walked home. Thaddeus Ball's questions had unlocked a Pandora's box and now all the old feelings that C.H. had ignored came pouring out. He opened the door to his silent house and stepped inside. Late-afternoon shadows were capering across the floor of the library when he entered the room.

C.H. took a meerschaum pipe from the gutta-percha box on a dusty shelf. He wrapped his fingers around the bowl and closed his eyes. He had never used the pipe. Not because he didn't like the gift from Temple, or because he didn't favor pipe smoking, because he did on both accounts. He just couldn't stand to be reminded of what had happened.

"Ah, Temple. Why did you have to do it, boy?" C.H. whispered. His head snapped up, shocked by the hollow echo of his own voice in the too-large, too-empty brownstone. He shook his head at his foolishness and replaced the pipe in the gutta-percha box and closed the lid. His blunt fingers lingered for a moment on the ornate design pressed into the top.

He pulled his hand away. What was done was done and no amount of wishing would undo or change anything. Temple was gone from his life. Now the only thing left was Honoria and his work.

That was what he needed to concentrate on, not the past, not his failure to keep Temple from larceny, just his beloved daughter and the work.

Chapter Fourteen

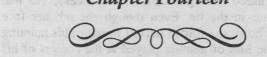

"Blast and stuff." Livingstone's screechy outburst made Constance jump. She felt like a clock that had been wound too tight.

"It hasn't let up a bit," Temple observed sourly in between long agitated strides, continuing to glare at the tent opening as if he could will the rain away.

Constance neatly folded the paper she had been reading. "There are some bits you might find interesting." Temple turned and met her gaze with one brow arched and she nearly regretted her words.

"Hmmm, which newspaper do you recommend for my afternoon reading?"

"They are all much the same." She avoided his eyes while a hungry hollow feeling invaded her middle. "Although the *Banner* seems to do the most thorough reporting."

"Yes, I quite agree, but I myself am a bit partial to the wagging-tongue section of the *Sentinel*—I believe it is in the piece you are holding now. In fact, I think I saw my name in print on that very page." He nodded toward the folded paper still in her hand.

Constance immediately shoved it deep into the stack

at her feet. "You may find this hard to believe, Temple, but I do not follow your exploits in the papers."

He crossed his arms at his chest while a knowing grin spread across his face. "Really? I could have sworn you mentioned reading something about my South American dig...."

Heat flared through Constance's cheeks. He had caught her in the lie. Even though she felt her face coloring hotly she forced herself to return his taunting stare. The hint of a smile played at the corners of his mouth while he studied her.

"Admit it, Connie. You have been reading the gossip just now, and you have read it before. Tell me, am I accused of defiling a lady or have I been implicated in some act of grand larceny?"

Constance was horrified that Temple could be so flip about her deceit and his reputation. "How can you joke about the slurs against your character?" She twisted her fingers together but she managed to meet his gaze without flinching.

One side of his mouth jerked into a wry cynical expression.

"Never having had a good reputation to guard or display, I find it less than tragic when the papers embellish the truth or invent some preposterous lie just to improve their circulation." He uncrossed his arms at his wide chest and defied Constance to correct him.

While she stared at him, the scandalous account she had just read took on new meaning. "Temple, I..." A strange tangle of emotions swept through her. She wanted to believe that most of what she read and heard about him was false. But she told herself that she was foolish beyond belief.

He gave her a sadly wicked grin. There was something cloudy and unreadable in his eyes. "Little Connie, you will mar your lovely brow if you keep frowning at me like that."

Constance unconsciously touched the spot above the bridge of her glasses with one fingertip. As he said, a deep furrow did crease her flesh.

Suddenly Temple took in a great breath and curled his hands into fists at his sides. "Enough of this melancholy nonsense." He plastered a bright, if somewhat false smile on his face. "We are stuck until the rain stops and that is that. Now what can we do to pass the time besides moan about my wasted youth and the veracity of New York's reporters?"

"I don't know." Constance was surprised by the mercurial change in his mood. "I have a chessboard." She looked up and met Temple's eyes.

He took a step toward the cot where she sat. Then he reached down to clasp her hands inside his rough warm palms. His smile blossomed into a genuine expression of happiness. Her heart constricted at the sight of it. "A chessboard? A real chessboard?" A hot tingle crept from her fingers to her torso while Temple gently held her hands.

"I try to be prepared. I carry a chess set and my fishing rod and one or two other things."

"Yes, I remember the fishing rod." Temple grimaced and wondered if he would continue to be soaked at regular intervals throughout this dig.

"Would you like to play?" Constance asked.

"It would take our minds off the storm and keep us occupied until it clears." Temple released her hands abruptly. He shouldn't have touched her. He shouldn't have allowed himself that pleasure. Already his thoughts were straying to the pulse spot in Connie's throat. He fought to control the powerful desire surging through him. "Break out the chess set, and we will attempt to lose ourselves in a good game." He smiled at Connie and hoped she would not detect the lustful tension coursing through him.

Temple's sudden ebullience filled the tent. She was smiling when she rose from the cot and crossed the floor. Even Livingstone quit pacing along his perch and began to clean and fluff his feathers as if he'd been calmed. Constance opened the rounded lid of one of her trunks and burrowed deep inside. She felt Temple's eyes upon her while she searched for the chessboard.

Temple watched fabric flutter into the air like doves as Connie tossed out discarded items. She nearly climbed inside the huge trunk in her effort to locate the promised chess set.

"What shall we play for?" Her muffled voice wafted from the trunk.

"What?" Temple moved a little closer, not sure he had heard her correctly over the din of the storm.

"I asked what stakes we will play for," she said in a louder voice. "It makes the game much more interesting when you have something to lose, don't you think?" She levered herself out of the trunk enough to look at him from beneath her outstretched arm.

Her words penetrated Temple's brain like an arrow. "Yes, the game is always more important when the ante is high." He wondered if she had any idea just how high the stakes in this contest had become.

The storm continued while crates were shifted and the board set up. Now Constance was bent over the chess set, concentrating on her next move. Suddenly her forehead met Temple's with a thud. They had both been leaning forward over the board, unaware of how close they were.

"Oops." She pulled back and sat up straight on the edge of her cot, which served as her seat during the game. The spot where Temple's forehead had touched her flesh seemed to burn with electric fire.

"It was my fault." Temple ripped his eyes from Constance's face. Instead of the game taking his mind off her, he had only become more focused on her. Each breath, every little sigh while she played sizzled through him.

"I should have been paying more attention." He shifted his weight on the camp stool and frowned at the board, willing himself to ignore her. She had already taken several of his pawns; now his queen was in dire jeopardy—right along with his wayward heart.

He wanted to kiss Connie again. It would be his greatest pleasure to take her in his arms and make love to her while the rain relentlessly pelted the tent. He shook his head and tried to banish the lustful thoughts from his mind.

It didn't work.

"Bishop and rook...queen. Temple is a pirate," Livingstone squawked. "Bishop and rook, bishop and rook. Blast and stuff...Temple is a pirate, awrk."

Temple turned and glared at the offensive bird. When he looked back he found Connie was trying not to smile. He felt his own mouth twitching at the corners in spite of himself.

"I think it might be in my best interest to teach that creature some new phrases." Temple winked at Constance and some of the latent tension between them vanished.

She giggled. Whether it was because of his silly comment or the fact he was openly flirting with her he didn't know, but her soft laughter sent his pulse racing like a runaway team.

"And what, exactly, would you teach him to say?" There was just the barest hint of a dimple in her cheek as she tried not to grin.

"Oh, I don't know. 'Temple is a prince,' would be nice, or how about 'Temple is the best'? Anything but being called a pirate." He watched her deftly remove one of his knights from the board. Her quick mind had remained on the game while his had meandered down the proverbial garden path.

"Connie, you little minx." He sat back on the camp stool and stared at her in wide-eyed shock. "You distracted me. And I think you did it on purpose."

"Me? How can you say such a thing?" Her brown eyes twinkled with playful mischief while she toyed with him.

"I am wounded. All this time I thought you were honorable, Miss Constance Honoria, but I find you are a devious and scheming woman." He chuckled and allowed the feeling of frisky camaraderie to steal over him. Suppressed memories of playing board games by a crackling fire in C.H.'s snug brownstone invaded his mind.

"What are you thinking about, Temple?" Her voice was so soft, for a moment he wondered if he had really heard her or if his mind had conjured up the question.

"Old times. Remember that winter it snowed so much and we had to stay indoors because some friend of C.H.'s had decided that breathing cold air weakened the constitution?"

"I remember." Constance rolled her eyes toward

the top of the tent. "But it was lovely to look at, wasn't it? The snow billowing down outside while we drew pictures in the frost on the windowpanes. And I remember Cook making cider and gingerbread." Her eyes took on a faraway look and her smile slowly faded. "I was so happy that winter."

"So was I." He admitted the truth even though it made him squirm on the camp stool to do so. "Even though the snow reminded me of my mother's death. I think that was the first and last time I ever actually enjoyed looking at it."

"Remember that Christmas morning?" Constance's brown eyes were bright with feeling behind the barrier of her spectacles.

"Uh-hum." The memory took root in his mind. "C.H. was a good sport—wasn't he?"

"I suppose you could call him that." Constance leaned forward toward Temple. One strand of her brunette hair fell forward to rest on the chessboard. "You were the best snowball launcher I have ever known, Temple Parish. Better even than Papa." Her sweet breath fanned across his face when she whispered the compliment as if it were still a secret shared only between them.

Without thinking, he reached out and picked up the dangling lock of hair. He rubbed its silken strands between thumb and fingers absently for a moment.

"It is nice to hear you say I was good at something, Connie." When he realized what he was doing, he abruptly placed the dark strand behind her ear.

"I thought you were good at a great many things, Temple. I never understood why you didn't know it yourself."

"Maybe I believed the opinions expressed so often

by those Dandridge professors.'' It was madness, but he reached out with both hands and grasped the corners of her spectacles to gently slide them from her face. She blinked, whether from surprise or because she was trying to focus, he couldn't say.

"I've been wanting to do that for a long, long time.''

"Why?''

"To have you look at me without them as a shield—I don't know, I just had the urge to take off your glasses.'' Temple could not give her answers when he had none for himself. He simply wanted to remove the glass as if it symbolized all the barriers that stood between them.

A quick succession of lightning brought low rumbling thunder sweeping through the tent. The sound was like drums being beaten.

"Do you always give in to your impulses, Temple?'' She stared at him openly, not pulling away but making no effort to come closer as her heart matched the tempo of the thunder.

Temple knew he was standing on the edge of a crumbling cliff. He could retreat and continue to deny this emotion that clawed at his insides. He could pretend that Connie was still a little girl and he did not want her so badly it made him ache.

Or—he could take a leap of faith and hope Connie would not mock him for the torrent of feelings he had discovered lying dormant within him.

He swallowed hard and studied her face. Her lashes were long and wildly curly. Flecks of pale green and gold glowed within her chocolate eyes. Another growl of thunder shook the tent and vibrated through the soles of his boots.

"Sometimes I do not give in to my impulses. I have been wanting to do a particular thing for a long time but I have not allowed myself."

"What?" she whispered. "What have you been wanting to do?"

"This." He leaned farther over the board and touched his lips to hers. Hunger bubbled to the surface, but he held himself tightly in check while he tentatively tasted her sweetness. By degrees the intimate caress matured. The kiss unfolded, changed and evolved into something seductive and powerful. It became a tempting promise of what could be—and what should not ever be.

Temple pulled back and looked into her eyes while the sound of renewed rain beat a steady tattoo on the canvas over their heads.

Constance was shocked by the roar of her own pulse which threatened to drown out the crackling lightning and booming thunder. The touch of Temple's lips had ignited something strange and wonderful within her. Some unfamiliar voice inside her head hinted there was more beyond kissing. Instinct promised this was just the beginning and that Temple could lead her— teach her.

And that frightened her.

She was torn between wanting to feel the electric touch of his lips and jerking away before she made a complete fool of herself. Indecision warred with desire while the minutes ticked silently by and thunder shook the tent and drowned out the sound of the storm. Then while she was staring into his eyes, contemplating her own ruin, the unmistakable sound of a horse's hooves splashing through mud right outside her tent broke the spell.

The tent flap flew open and rain blew inside. The lantern guttered when the cold Montana wind whipped through the opening and more chills marched up Constance's back and arms while reason returned to her. Her cheeks flamed when she realized what she had been about to do. She groped for her glasses among the chess pieces. She was aware of Temple moving around the chess table and placing his body between her and the opening of the tent as if to protect her from some unknown threat.

"Miss Cadwallender?" Holt Morgan called from beyond the loose tent flap. "Miss, are you in there?"

"Mr. Morgan?" Constance shoved the spectacles onto her face and blinked in surprise.

A wide-brimmed hat popped inside the tent. Rain dripped off a yellow slicker and made a puddle at the doorway. "I thought this tent looked like yours." He stood half-inside, his gaze lingering upon Temple. "Mr. Parish."

"Mr. Morgan." Temple's greeting was clipped and gruff. "What brings you out here?"

"I was goin' to ask you and Miss Constance the same thing." Holt slid his gaze back to her. "Are you all right, miss?"

"Yes, quite all right." It was a lie but she could not put into words what Temple's kiss had done to her.

"Why did you move your camp, miss? Is there anything wrong?" Holt's eyes went to Temple in a gesture almost of silent accusation. "Do you need help with—anythin'?"

The two men visibly bristled as they stared at each other in silent challenge.

"I'm fine. Why don't you come inside before we

are all soaked through." Constance felt Temple's disapproving gaze upon her. "What on earth brings you out in this storm, Mr. Morgan?"

"I thought you were goin' to call me Holt." He allowed the tent flap to fall back into place behind him as he stepped inside, shrugged off his wet slicker and dropped it near the door of the tent.

"Isn't it a bit wet to be out riding, Holt?"

He smiled and the deep grooves appeared in his cheeks. "Ranch work don't care about sunshine, miss. I had some things to check at the mine. On my way back I spotted the new camp and thought I should come and see if you were havin' any trouble."

"That was very considerate of you, Holt." Constance felt the heat rising in her cheeks. "But I am fine."

"What made you move, miss?"

"The digging appears to be more promising in this area so I asked Mr. Hughes to help me relocate my camp." She saw Temple's eyes narrow at the mention of the dig.

"I see." Holt raised one brow and gazed at Temple. "And you, Mr. Parish? I only saw one tent when I was ridin' in. I guess that means yours is still in the same place. How did you come to be out here so far from your camp?" Holt's question was spiced with a touch of sarcasm.

Temple's fingers curled into a fist, but he tamped down his anger. He couldn't very well start a brawl in the middle of Connie's tent, but how he wanted to wipe that smug look off Holt Morgan's face. And just who the hell did Holt think he was, staring at Connie as if he had a right to look at her in that sort of way?

"Not that it is any of your business, but I also decided the digging might be better at this end of the cut. I didn't have a chance to move anything but my bedroll before the storm hit.''

"I've seen city slickers do worse, I guess." A slow smile crept across Holt's face. "Well, now that I know you've moved closer to the Flyin' B ranch house Miss Constance, I'll be sure to stop by more often.''

Something hot and bitter gripped Temple. He absolutely refused to think what he was feeling could be jealousy. "Just how close?"

"About two miles or so." Holt grinned. "I expect I'll be seein' you several times a week.''

"That would be delightful, Holt," Connie said. "Wouldn't it, Temple?"

"Yeah, sure, I'll be looking forward to it," Temple grumbled.

"The way you act, Parish, a body would think you were tryin' to keep this purty little filly all to yourself," Holt said with a teasing grin.

Temple took a half step toward the interloper but suddenly Connie was in front of him. She placed her palms flat on his chest. Liquid fire blossomed around her fingers. Temple found himself glancing down at her hands just to see if his shirt was ablaze beneath them. Her touch caused his flesh to tingle with excitement.

"Temple." She looked up at him. When their eyes met a strange kind of unspoken communication passed between them.

"All right, Connie, I'll be nice. For you." Temple allowed himself the pleasure of casting one more menacing look at Holt, but all it did was make the Montana cowboy chuckle.

"Blast and stuff!" Livingstone shrieked as Constance removed her hands.

Holt's attention shifted from her to Livingstone. Temple found himself appreciating the black chatterbox a bit more than he had before.

"I never, a talking bird."

"A gift from my father. I would offer you some refreshment, Holt, but because of the rain..." Connie apologized.

Holt rose from Livingstone's cage. "Well, if Mr. Parish can stand getting a little wet, we can stretch out a canvas on a couple of poles in front of your tent to make a coverin'. I bet we can get a fire goin'."

"I think I can tolerate a little moisture, for Connie's sake." Temple sneered.

"Didn't you bring a slicker?" Holt asked as he nodded toward his.

"No," Temple snapped.

"Wait. I have one in my trunk." Connie scurried to the trunk and once again a flurry of bright cloth filled the tent. When she found the slicker, she stood. "Here you go, Temple."

He tried to avoid her hands when he took it from her in case the same blazing fire accompanied her touch again. When he was covered with the bright yellow slicker he turned to Holt.

"Glad to see you're ready, Parish."

"I could've managed without it. Only sugar melts in the rain." Temple winked at Connie and waited to see if she would grace him with another smile but Holt gave a derisive snort that drew her attention.

Holt pulled on his yellow slicker. "Maybe in the city, but out here one or two other things melt in the rain and they sure ain't sugar." He disappeared out the tent flap with his laughter ringing over the rat-a-tat of rain.

"Now, Temple, remember you said you would be nice..." Connie reminded.

"Yes, I know," Temple grumbled. Thinking about what Holt had interrupted made it difficult even to be civil.

"Be nice, be nice, be nice," Livingstone intoned while Temple stepped into the rain.

Chapter Fifteen

Temple wrapped his fingers around the cup of coffee and glared at Holt Morgan over the campfire. A gust of wind blew under the canvas causing the flames to gutter before they rallied and flared blue-white.

"It will smoke like the dickens, but at least you can dry out a bit." Holt handed Constance a cup of fresh hot coffee.

"How very ingenious of you." She accepted the brew with a shy smile.

It made Temple even more grumpy to see that Holt had won Connie's gratitude and the smile he had been working so hard to see.

"Sorry about the slicker, miss." Holt apologized but he didn't look very contrite.

"Oh, think nothing of it. I am confused as to how it got ruined though." Connie glanced at Temple as if she were waiting for him to explain.

"Dangedest thing I ever saw—Mr. Parish seemed to get all tangled up in the canvas and rope somehow. Slicker ripped to shreds when he went sailing down that ravine." Holt chuckled and took a sip of coffee.

"How soon will you be heading to your ranch?"

Temple stared over the fire and inquired bluntly, refusing to be baited any further.

Mock seriousness creased Holt's face. "I was thinking about leaving soon—but if you'd like me to hang around..." He shrugged and gestured helpless compliance with his hands.

"Don't stay on my account." Temple knew Holt was having fun with him, but try as he might, he wasn't able to join in the joke. "I'm sure you have important things to attend to."

"Right now this diggin' is about the most important thing going on at the Flyin' B. Ma is really countin' on this to get our bid for statehood some attention. In fact, I can bring over some of the boys to help you dig. There won't be much we can do until the mud dries up a bit."

Temple and Connie exchanged glances. Having more diggers was always a tempting offer.

"As long as we both have equal help, I guess that would be fair," Connie said diplomatically before Temple could refuse.

Temple was pained to admit it, but Holt Morgan had just done him a favor. He had been agonizing about Connie doing her own digging—torn by his need to succeed and his unshakable habit of protecting her.

"Good. Tomorrow I'll send some of my men. And I'll send over a couple of cases of dynamite from the mine—that'll hurry things along."

"*No!*" Both Temple and Constance shouted in chorus. They looked at each other in wide-eyed amazement.

"Your offer is very generous, but dynamite is too destructive," Constance said tactfully.

"Do you feel that way too, Parish?" Holt was frowning.

"Yes. Dynamite destroys more than it reveals. Digging by hand is slower, but in the end it's the best way." Temple took another sip of coffee. He stared into the dark liquid. He was not happy to find out he and Connie agreed on the controversial issue.

"There are some experts who don't concur with my opinion, of course." Connie's brows knit together above her spectacles as if she were thinking the same thing.

Temple snorted. "Most of the professors at Dandridge University have disagreed with me about one thing or another, but in this case they are supported by just about all of the scientific community," Temple quipped bitterly.

"But you two agree," Holt observed while a small frown creased his brow.

"So it seems." Temple rubbed his palm over his day's growth of beard. To learn that Connie supported his opinion was just another chip in his crumbling resolve.

Holt suddenly stood up. He tossed the contents of his cup out into the drizzling rain. "I'm headed home. The rain will probably peter out during the night. I'll send over a few men in the morning. Then you two can get back to your competition." Holt flashed Temple one last taunting grin. "And I will be sure to have somebody pack up your camp and bring it over tomorrow. Knowing you are bedded down on the hard earth here at Miss Constance's camp would keep me from sleeping."

Temple raised one brow. "I just bet it would."

Holt Morgan laughed heartily while he shrugged

back into his rain slicker. Temple wondered why the men in this state always seemed to be laughing at some private joke, as Holt mounted his horse and disappeared into the gloomy dampness.

Temple thrashed inside the borrowed blankets and heavy canvas that covered his bedroll. He dreamed of snow falling silently over a frozen city. In the dream he struggled to find Connie, but she was lost in the white wasteland. Lost and alone just as he was without her...

The jingling of harness brought his eyes open with a start. He levered himself up and peered into the fog that shrouded him. The sky, what he could see of it, was a thick gray blanket.

"Is that Mr. Hughes?" Connie stuck her head out of her tent opening and looked down at Temple.

She was drowsy and her thick hair tumbled around her slender neck and shoulders in charming disarray. When she yawned, Temple had the overpowering urge to pull her into the cocoon of his bedroll.

He looked away, focusing instead on the sound of the approaching wagon. Squinting he tried to make out the shape in the foggy morning.

"No, I don't think so. It's hard to tell, but I think it might be the men Holt promised."

"Oh, how wonderful." Connie yawned once again before she disappeared inside her tent.

Temple climbed out of his blankets and pulled on his boots. During the long cold night he had come to a sobering realization. Unless he won the endowment and Montague's support he would continue to be nothing more than an upstart without consequence or worth to the scientific community. No matter how he felt about her, he could not allow C.H.'s daughter to stand between him and that goal. The only hope he had for any kind of future was to defeat her without mercy.

As he greeted the new day, he made sure his thoughts were only on claiming the prize.

Thaddeus Ball leaned back and rubbed his palms over his tired eyes. The table in the main branch of the New York City Public Library was strewn with old newspapers and yellowed clippings. He had read every word the *Sentinel* and the other New York papers had printed about Temple Parish over the years. Thaddeus leaned forward once again and trained his gaze at the man's lean face staring back at him from a blurry photograph.

Thaddeus had learned Temple's preference on everything from women to wine, even knew the brand of suspenders he bought, but he still lacked the knowledge of one important detail. And it had to be the key to solving the puzzle of Temple Parish's life.

It was apparent that Temple had never had any kind of monetary windfall after leaving Professor Cadwallender's home. Rumors abounded about the missing artifacts and relics. Speculation and innuendo about a billionaire collector who had enticed the young man to steal had shown up repeatedly in each news account for years, but there was nothing solid. And there never had been.

If Temple Parish had pilfered artifacts and sold them to some nameless collector, then he had chosen to live like a pauper.

"And that I do not believe," Thaddeus grumbled.

Why would any man struggle as hard as Temple had done, to build a career and a reputation in this new science, if he had sold relics for a small fortune ten years ago?

There had to be a logical explanation. "And I think C. H. Cadwallender has the missing piece of this puzzle."

He skimmed over the page in front of him once again. Faded pictures of the magnificent models of dinosaurs that had once stood in Central Park caught his eye. Temple Parish had been taken into Cadwallender's home at about the same time they were destroyed.

"Coincidence?" Thaddeus wondered aloud. Or was there some connection between Temple and the destruction of those models?

Questions layered upon questions while Thaddeus flipped open his pad and began to scribble quick dates and notes from the articles in front of him. He grinned while he wrote and spun a fantasy about his own future. It would be quite a feather in his cap if he solved the mystery of Temple Parish and Dandridge's ten-year-old unsolved larceny in one fell swoop.

"So, Temple Parish, it would seem both our futures rest upon me digging up your past," Thaddeus told the aging photograph as he gathered the clippings and stuffed them back into the dusty box.

Temple stood up straight on the small promontory and tried to stretch the kinks from his spine. He had been bent over, grubbing in the wet soil, all morning and he felt the weight of every grain of sand he had moved. He glanced upward at the sun still trying to find its way from behind the layer of clouds.

He scowled at the bank, silently cursing the rain. Suddenly a flash of movement caught his eye. One of the men Holt had sent over stood up and waved his hat in the air while shouting a wild Indian war whoop.

"Have you found something?" Temple loped to his location and skidded down into the muddy, slick depression beside the cowboy.

"You said to give a holler, if'n I found sump'en," the cowboy drawled.

Temple squinted at the dusty-gray earth while excitement gripped him like a tight band. He forced himself to be calm, shoving aside all hopes, refusing to allow himself to be pulled into false confidence like the last time.

He ran his fingers over the rough limestone surface and brushed away the thin layer of dirt that had fallen back into the hole while he and the cowboy were talking. The tips of his fingers tingled and he closed his eyes to utter a silent prayer of thanks.

It was bone. But was it old bone?

He knelt closer and used the tip of his finger to clean the edges. One eye socket, large as a melon, took shape while he brushed and blew aside dirt from the ages. With more haste than he should have risked, Temple scooped up more dirt until he could see the sinuses and yet the huge skull did not end. It tapered forward and as he cleared away enough dirt to examine the upper jaw, a constriction formed in his chest.

The skull was magnificent. Rows of long recurved teeth lined the upper jaw. Temple felt the grin break across his face while he wiped away the remaining mud to reveal the entire nose.

The skull was huge. From eye socket to tip it was well over four feet long—and Temple had never seen anything like it in his life.

"Is this it?" the cowboy asked.

"This is it," he whispered more to himself than the anxious cowboys who stood in a half circle around him. "You are looking at the head of a dinosaur."

"Would you look at them teeth?" one man whispered in awe. "I'd rather dance with a griz than meet somethin' with teeth like that."

Temple rubbed his palm down his face and tried to calm his growing exhilaration. "Now the real work begins. We need to free it from the limestone and dirt—and pray there is more. Be careful and call me if you have any questions." Temple took one step up out of the hole, then he turned back grinning from ear to ear. "This is what we've been looking for—this is the prize."

Constance heard the low rumble of voices from Temple's area. She could almost feel the zeal emanating from them. The feeling was solid and unmistakable. Nobody needed to tell her what it meant, she already knew.

Temple had found something.

A sharp current of envy and joy swirled through her. The competitor inside her was disappointed that she had not made a find first. Whatever had been unearthed at Temple's camp had the normally stoic cattle drovers thrumming with excitement.

She looked away, feeling a bit ashamed of her streak of jealousy. Perhaps she was overtired. Maybe a cup of tea would bring her back into sorts.

Constance started to climb out of the muck she and the cowboys had created in the muddy earth. Her boot slid in the sludge and she stumbled to her knees, hampered by the voluminous skirt of her utility dress. Constance had been too shy to wear her father's pilfered trousers around the cowboys, but now annoyance nipped at her while she struggled to regain her footing. The more she tried to climb out, the more the sodden fabric pulled her down. She was puffing with exertion, ready to call out for help, when she saw something in a shallow puddle of muddy water.

It was the outline of a large vertebra.

Constance dropped to her hands and knees. The more water her clothing absorbed, the more of the vertebra was exposed. She glanced up to find several cowboys staring at her with stricken expressions.

"Right here, we need to begin digging right here." She didn't care that her clothing was filthy and soaked with silt and water. All she cared about at the particular moment was freeing the bone from its cocoon of earth and stone.

By midday the sun had barely managed to unfold itself from the bank of clouds, but the attempt to remove the bone from its prison had not been quite so successful.

Constance had worked steadily shoulder to shoulder with the shocked men. She was down on her knees with a brush in her hand, when she felt the rhythmic tattoo of galloping horses telegraph through the soggy ground. She looked up to see two mud-spattered riders pulling their mounts to a stop.

"I told Holt we'd find you digging." Bessie Morgan chuckled when she dismounted the strawberry roan.

"How nice to see you, Bessie—Holt," Constance wiped at her face. The cold clammy feel of mud on her face made her glance down at her grime-caked hands. "You'll have to forgive me, I look a sight."

"Nonsense, I've seen dirt on a woman before. We

brought you lunch. Holt told me that you probably wouldn't take time to feed yourself—I see he was right. I can't have two famous scientists droppin' over dead on my ranch, now can I?'' Bessie's smile was warm as summer sunshine.

Holt swung out of the saddle. He climbed down into the gully until he was no more than a foot from Constance. Without warning he wrapped his hands around her waist and began to lift her from the damp hole.

''Have you found somethin'?'' Bessie squinted at the mound of earth Constance and the men had removed from the hole.

''Yes. It's a little early, but I think it is wonderful.'' Constance heard the excitement in her voice. She cast a surreptitious glance at Temple's camp. He was only a few feet away and scowling at her without restraint.

''That's great news, now come and eat. You look all done in.'' Bessie smiled indulgently. ''Mr. Parish, we brought lunch, come join us.''

''I don't have time to eat,'' he called back.

''Nonsense, I insist you come have a bite with me. Besides, I also have a letter for you. One of my men brought it out from Morgan Forks at Peter's request.'' Bessie withdrew a paper from her shirt pocket. She waved it in the air as if to show Temple that it really did exist and was not just some ruse to get him to leave his excavation. ''And it wouldn't be fair for Miss Cadwallender to stop digging if you don't.''

Temple glanced at the emerging dinosaur skull. Indecision warred within him. The sooner he released the bones from their stone prison, the sooner he could be on a train back to New York. He glanced up at Connie once again. A glob of mud clung to her cheek and the heavy cloth of her dress was soaked and muddy to the level of her knees. While he was watching, Holt Morgan reached out and wiped a smudge of grime from Connie's cheek with his fingers.

That was all the incentive Temple needed. With one blistering expletive, he climbed out of the hole.

"I think we came on just the right day." Bessie held out the letter to Temple. "You had a letter waitin' in town. Peter thought it might be important."

He took the paper and glanced at the address then stuffed it inside his shirt.

"Aren't you going to open it?" Bessie asked.

Constance shoved her spectacles up and peered at Temple. She was trying to hide her curiosity, but he knew her too well to be fooled. He stifled a grin and decided to let her remain curious.

Temple nodded at the basket Holt was carrying. "I'll read it later. What's in the basket?"

Bessie motioned for Holt to set it down, then she bent over and opened the hamper. As soon as the wire lid on a heavy crock popped open the smell of hearty stew filled the air. Temple's belly growled. He had only been feigning interest to vex Connie, but now he realized he was starving.

"I guess I am hungry." He shrugged when Bessie looked at him with a speculative arch of one brow.

"How are things goin'?" she asked while she unloaded baskets and crocks.

"Well enough," Temple hedged.

"Miss Constance has already found something," Holt supplied while he gazed at Constance in open admiration.

"Is that so?" Temple glanced at her. "Does your find look good?"

"Yes, it looks very favorable. And yours?" She

shrugged. "I could not help but notice the excitement at your camp this morning. I knew you'd found something. Do you think it will prove to be an unknown?"

He frowned and tried not to notice her eyes. The cloudy weather made them look a rich mahogany. He couldn't decide if the flecks of color around her irises were green or perhaps gold. The question nipped at the edges of his mind while he struggled to keep his thoughts on their conversation.

"Perhaps it is too early to say. And your bones? Do they appear at all familiar?"

She shook her head and the combs holding her heavy hair in place shifted. One strand fell down and curved beneath her chin with a springy bounce. Temple felt his fingers flex while he fought the urge to put it back into place—or take it down completely—he wasn't sure which he wanted to do.

"Well, this is all mighty fascinatin', and I do hope you both have found somethin' but the food is gettin' cold." Bessie shattered the enchantment around Temple. "We rode a long way to bring you this, so dig in."

Temple blinked and glanced around, suddenly embarrassed and a little angry that he had allowed himself to lapse yet again.

Constance picked up the edge of her sodden skirt and moved toward her tent with as much grace as if she were walking on polished marble.

"It smells wonderful, Bessie," she said. Even in her outlandish muddy costume, in the middle of the Montana badlands, Constance was a lady. She brought out her two camp stools and opened them up. "Please, have a seat."

"Thank you, Miss Constance."

While the women settled themselves, Temple looked around for a rock to sit upon but found nothing but muddy slick earth and short stiff grass.

"There are some empty crates just on the other side of my tent," Constance offered.

Temple realized she had been watching him. It filled him with an odd satisfaction. A warm feeling rushed through him as he dragged up a crate and seated himself, trying to ignore the way Holt looked at Connie.

The foursome ate and talked about nothing in particular. The hot stew and steaming coffee had driven some of the dampness from Temple's bones and he found himself relaxing a bit.

"I do hope Mr. Hughes doesn't have any trouble getting out here." Connie's comment drew Temple's attention and he realized he had missed part of the conversation.

"Oh, Miss Constance, I hate to tell you this, but Peter Hughes won't be comin' for several days." Holt looked truly disappointed and that made suspicion blossom inside Temple's head.

Holt would be happy as a whitewashed pig to have any excuse to come and see Connie. If he had been jealous—which he wasn't—the idea would have made Temple angry.

"Oh, I hope no harm has befallen Mr. Hughes." The concern in Connie's voice tugged at Temple's heart.

"No, he's as ornery as ever, but he doesn't ride, refused to even try and learn, and the washes are runnin' with water. He won't be able to get through for a couple of days. If the rain doesn't stop, it could be a week or more. But don't you worry, I'll come and check on you."

"Oh, thank you." Connie ducked her head and stared at her coffee cup. Temple couldn't tell if she was pleased with Holt's offer.

"Was there somethin' special you needed, Miss Constance?" Holt trained his attention on Connie. "I'd be happy to ride in or send one of the men."

"No, that won't be necessary. I was just..." Connie glanced at Temple as if she didn't wish to speak in front of him. "That is, I try to communicate regularly with my father."

Knowledge illuminated the borders of Temple's mind. "You've been sending telegrams back to New York, haven't you, Connie?"

She met his gaze and flushed a bit. "Yes, I have been sending telegrams to Papa."

"And of course C.H. has been sharing that information with Dandridge and the *Sentinel*." Temple narrowed his gaze and allowed the questions to advance unchecked.

How much information had gone back and forth between Connie and C.H.? And how much of the new interest in his past had been generated right here in Montana? He didn't want to think it of her, but she wanted to win as badly as he did—perhaps even more.

Feelings of betrayal flooded through him. "Thanks for the lunch, but I have to get back to work." Temple stood and tossed the dregs of his coffee into the saturated earth.

Bessie stood also and brushed at her trousers. She glanced at Holt. "I need to get back too. Will you be stayin' awhile, Holt?"

"That depends on Miss Constance." Holt left the hint for an invitation hanging in the damp air.

Temple flashed one dark gaze at Constance, then he

stalked off down the slope toward his site. He couldn't allow himself to get all tangled up worrying about how she felt about Holt. Especially not if she had been feeding information to those bloodthirsty reporters in New York.

Constance glanced up at the darkening sky. "It's going to start raining again and I have to cover my bones with canvas before they get soaked." Apprehension gripped her as she bolted to her feet. She had to safeguard her find.

"May I offer my assistance?" Holt was beside her, matching his long stride to her short quick one.

Constance glanced at Temple's wide back one more time as he climbed onto the hillock he and Holt's men had created. A spurt of anger coursed through her. "Yes, Holt, I'd be pleased to have you help me."

Temple reached the mound of dirt beside his new find and paused. He glanced back over his shoulder and found Bessie had already mounted her horse and was riding west. Once again Holt Morgan seemed to be using any excuse to put his hands around Connie's waist as they maneuvered by cowboys and boulders.

Possessiveness flared in Temple's gut. He turned away and told himself to focus on the bones. Connie was a big girl—and most important, she was his rival in this quest.

He bent down on his knees and carefully started chipping at the sandstone encasing the lower jaw on the magnificent skull. The teeth on the top jaw were longer and thicker than his index finger with beautifully serrated edges. Just looking at the fossil made his pulse quicken. He had found a predator—a hunter—and something previously undiscovered.

Constance giggled and the sound of her laughter

floated through the humid gray air toward Temple. He could not stop himself from rising in order to see over the hillock of dirt. It took all his willpower to keep from leaping out of the hole and marching over to see just what was going on between Holt and Connie.

"I never knew digging could be so damned entertaining," he snarled aloud. "Hell, I wish we knew the joke so we could all be laughing over here." He commented to himself but a nearby cowboy stopped digging and listened as if Temple had been carrying on a conversation with him.

A deep chuckle from the man brought him back to his senses with a jolt. He was making a fool of himself over his competitor.

Chapter Sixteen

Temple stretched the canvas tight over the skull and weighted down the edges with heavy rocks. The last cowboy from the Flying B had ridden away more than an hour ago and now silence hung as heavy in the air as the threat of rain.

He glanced at Connie's tent and then back to his own. Holt had made sure his tent had been retrieved from the old camp and erected before he left. Now there was no possibility of Temple needing to sleep on Connie's side of the canyon. That should have made him happy, but as the oppressive silence bore down on him he found himself wishing for an excuse to speak with her.

The discovery of the skull made him realize his time in Montana was rapidly drawing to a close. After he returned to New York and claimed the prize he would finally be able to settle the old score with C.H. and Dandridge. Then Connie would never speak to him again.

That made him ache with sadness.

A soft thud and a yelp of surprise brought Temple spinning around. His boots bogged down in the soft wet soil as he climbed up to peer over the hillock of dirt. He was not prepared for what he saw.

Connie was sprawled on her backside on top of folds of heavy canvas tarpaulin, with her knees in the air. She had evidently slid down the muddy embankment and landed on her newly covered find.

Temple chuckled and shoved his hat back on his head while he stared at her. ''Do you need some help?'' He carefully made his way down the slippery incline toward her. Mud clung to the sides of his boots, making them heavier and more clumsy with each step. The rocky slope was tricky when dry, but the added hazard of water made it treacherous.

''I lost my footing,'' she said self-consciously. While he stood there trying not to laugh, she pushed her spectacles up and unconsciously did her owl impersonation. A dollop of mud was drying on her cheek.

Temple stood over her, torn between his impulse of wanting to kiss her and wishing she would just go home before she broke his heart, or the other way around. If she would quit before he humiliated her then at least there might be a chance she wouldn't hate him.

She started to rise but her feet slipped again. The jolt made her hair tumble down on one side again. The yellow dress was coated with so much mud its original color was no longer discernible. And yet with all the mud and grime she was still as pretty as a Montana sunrise. Temple was tempted to stand there and just admire her, but the sudden sizzle and crack of lightning galvanized him into action.

He hopped down beside her and grabbed her arm.

"We'd better hurry or we'll be soaked again." The husky timbre of his voice made him grimace.

When she gripped his hand and pulled herself up, they were inches apart, her nose nearly touching his chin. It would be so easy to lean down and kiss her. He wanted to taste her lips. He wanted to hold her close and feel her heartbeat.

The first raindrop landed on her spectacles. Connie did not seem to notice as she motionlessly stared at Temple.

"Connie, we are going to—" There was no need for his warning because the sky simply opened up and cold droplets pelted down upon them.

"Oh, no. The water will flood my site." Connie yanked at the loose edge of the tarpaulin, determined to securely cover her find.

Temple's admiration for her rose another notch. No matter how she looked on the outside, she was all business and duty on the inside. Her serious expression and frantic tugs on the canvas cut a swath straight to his heart.

"Here, let me do it." Temple stepped around her body and grasped the edges.

"Thank you, Temple, but I can manage," she protested, squeezing in beside him to secure the tarp at the edges. The sky darkened into shades of purple and indigo.

"Stand back, Connie, I almost have it." Temple took a step, but she stubbornly blocked his path on the small hillock. The soil was soft and unstable, turning to mud as quickly as the rain soaked into it.

"Temple, you are in my way."

Before he could correct her on who was actually the one in the way, Temple found himself tangled up in a flurry of legs, mud and skirt. He knew he was going down and flailed his arms futilely. Then he found himself in the muddy pit beside the tarp-covered bones. Connie was right on top of him, her legs straddling his hips and her nose only inches from his chin.

"You knocked me down." Connie swiped at her cheek and left a thick smear of mud on her face.

"I did no such thing." He stared at her in disbelief. His mind and body were at war. The pleasing weight of her brought his manhood to attention while his mind wanted to challenge her statement. No matter what the situation, she seemed bent on blaming him for their predicament. "You were the one in the way," he managed to point out.

She glared at him through the trickles of water coursing off her hair and down into her face. "This is no time to argue about it. I suggest we get out of this hole before we are struck by lightning, or drown."

He wondered if she had struck her head during their fall, because she was sounding completely addled. He tried to clear away the swarming confusion that conversing with Connie always brought him while he savored the way it felt to have her legs around his body. Several forbidden images of entwined limbs flashed through his mind, but then a blue-white burst snapped him out of his lethargy.

"Come on, we don't have time to argue about it now." He lifted her off him and leaped to his feet. When he started to move his feet came free of their muddy prison with a sucking sound. Connie slipped on the wet canvas and lurched into him with a thud. Her elbow found a tender place in his ribs, causing his breath to escape in a painful grunt.

"Hang on to me, Connie." Temple ducked his head

against the deluge and bounded up the hill of earth as fast as the muck would allow with Connie in tow.

A silver arc of lightning struck frighteningly close to Connie's tent. Temple glanced back and saw fear written on her face. A burst of protective instinct made him quicken his pace. He was nearly running now as she clung to his hand.

The air crackled with power, but Constance could not tell if it was due to the lightning or Temple's strong fingers wrapped around hers. Her heart beat a rapid tattoo while Temple ran, pulling her behind him until her muddy shoes barely skimmed across the rain-slicked earth.

Thunder vibrated across the badlands. Temple jerked her forward and she found herself inside the dry dim tent. Their breathing was labored and harsh. She was just barely able to make out the shape of her cot, and Livingstone's cage still snug beneath its cover. Temple was standing near the opening of her tent, and she saw his silhouette when he yanked the hat off his head. A shower of water droplets sprayed from his trousers and sprinkled her face when he slapped it against his thigh.

"Damn it all to hell—not again." He cursed. "I am going to grow webs between my toes if this keeps up."

Constance's senses were unnaturally heightened. She could hear her own pulse in her ears and Temple's harsh raspy breathing could feel the blood coursing through her veins. She twisted her fingers together and tried to slow her rapid heart, telling herself she was being foolish.

There was something hot, palpable and wild within the canvas tent. It hung between the two of them like a gauzy veil. Each agonizing moment that passed brought a thrum of anticipation surging through her. She had the feeling something was about to happen—something she had been waiting for.

Rain continued to drum upon the canvas overhead, insistent and rhythmic, like the beat of her heart. Their situation was so similar to the last time, yet this time her rebellious heart prayed for a different outcome.

A crimson flame sparked and drove back a tiny portion of darkness while the smell of sulfur filled the tent. Constance instinctively looked toward the light and saw Temple's strong fingers wrapped around the match. He touched the flame to the wick, then he lowered the glass into position. A glowing arc fanned out across the tent. He pursed his lips and blew out the sulfur stick. Her breath caught in her throat as she focused on his pursed lips.

Water dripped from his ink-black hair onto the raw wooden top of the crate. One touched the chimney of the lantern, hissing as it evaporated. Her gaze was drawn to the fabric of his sodden trousers, molded to the muscles of his thighs and calves in such a way that looking made her mouth dry.

She glanced down at her muddy boots, embarrassed by her thoughts. Her gaze traveled to his feet where she saw an edge of red-brown clay clinging to the soles of his boots. She drew in a shuddering breath and tried to compose herself.

''We make quite a pair, don't we, Connie?''

Her eyes snapped back to his face, wreathed in flickering light. A cynical grin twisted one side of his mouth.

She glanced down at her own clothes and suddenly

became aware of the weight of the mud-covered skirt. "I—I—suppose."

"Water is running like a stream outside. There is no way to build a fire this time, no matter what Holt Morgan might think." There was sarcasm in his words.

"You will have to stay." Her voice was barely audible above the din of rain.

"What?"

"You will have to stay, until the rain stops."

"I can make it to my own tent. I have dry clothes there."

She took a step toward him, her boots squishing as she moved. "It would be foolish to risk crossing the wash."

Temple's eyes darted to the tent flap and she was reminded of an animal caught in a trap.

"It will let up soon." He peered outside. He swallowed hard. "Connie, I can't stay."

He appeared reluctant to step from behind the crate between them.

"See for yourself, Temple."

He edged past Constance and raised the tent flap. Droplets of water hit his face and dripped off his determined chin. "I have to leave—now."

She tried to follow him but as her shoes tangled up with her skirt the cloth tightened around her ankles and she lurched forward. Constance put her arms out in front of her to break her fall, but she suddenly found herself with Temple's arms wrapped protectively around her. Her bosom was crushed tightly against his chest as he peered down into her face. A few raindrops still meandered down his cheeks and dropped off his chin.

Constance swallowed while time slowed. She wanted to speak but could not find her voice. Temple's arms were warm against her back and that contact, and the spot where she was touching his chest, were the only things that seemed real.

The smell of rain clung to him and she sucked in great gulps of air, making the space between their bodies more intimate with each breath.

"Are you all right?" His voice was deep like the purr of a house cat and his warm breath fogged her glasses.

"I—I must have tripped." She stared into his brown eyes and experienced the sensation of falling from a great height. "I can't imagine how it happened.... "

"You mean you aren't going to blame me?" He loosened his arms and leaned away from her. His new position only made her more aware of his grip upon her—more aware of his strength and power. A crack of lightning drew their attention to the deluge outside the tent.

Temple turned and Constance rose on tiptoes to see. A torrent of rushing water foamed down the gully only a few feet beyond her tent. It plunged over the areas where she and Temple had been digging. Instead of the formerly dry riverbed fifty feet away, there was now an active creek running in the ravine not more than a yard from the opening of the tent.

"Now you have to stay," she said softly. "Unless you want to swim."

Temple dropped the flap and she found her gaze returning to the hard planes of his face.

"Connie, you had better get that wet dress off," Temple said gruffly. He let her go so abruptly she pitched forward and almost lost her balance again. He frowned at her in a way that was both expectant and questioning, and she found her breath lodging in her throat.

"You are wetter than I am." She swallowed hard and tried to keep her thoughts logical and under control.

"Wetter, but certainly not muddier." He laughed but it was a nervous sound. "Please, for once—don't argue with me."

"All right." She started to take a step but the sodden fabric dragging on the tent floor got in her way again. Temple caught her waist with his hands.

"Just tell me where your dry clothes are and I'll get them." He seemed anxious to move away from her. She wondered if he had felt the same molten attraction when they touched each other. But surely a man with Temple's romantic expertise would not be so shaken.

"In there." She gestured to the large trunk. Connie felt her pulse thrumming in her ears. She licked her dry lips, suddenly feeling hot and chilled at the same time.

Temple's eyes roved up and down her face from her eyes to her mouth and back. It seemed as if he were surveying every inch of her, memorizing every nuance of her expression. A hunger started deep within her belly and every nerve in her body seemed to take on a will of its own.

He turned away and opened the lid of the trunk and she heard him swear softly under his breath. She watched the wet material of his shirt strain across the width of his shoulders and her breath caught again. There was something so pleasing about the way his clothing hugged his form. Constance licked her lips again and wondered what it would feel like to peel the wet shirt from his body.

Temple dug into the pile of clothes blindly. He could not think with Connie standing so near. Each time he glanced at her his belly tightened into a knot. He wanted to touch her. He wanted things between them to be different.

He moved aside a pair of C.H.'s standard khaki-colored trousers while he ignored the hot desire coiling within him. As he grasped a fold of fabric, Temple felt something hard inside his palm. He opened his hand and looked at what it was.

The small honey-colored carving lay in his hand. He stared at the childish figure in braids and pinafore and nearly laughed aloud at his stupidity.

Had he really thought of Connie this way? Had he been so blind that he did not see the sensual woman beneath the layers of cloth and netting? Was he such a dolt that he had believed her to be a child, the image of the tiny piece of wood in his hands?

Every nerve along his body sprang to life and he knew she was kneeling beside him. The hair along his nape prickled while his body became instantly attuned to her—ravenously hungry for her.

He knew it was a mistake, but he turned toward her. Their lips were only inches apart. He stared at her lush mouth. "When did you find this carving?"

"After I bandaged your hand." She touched it with her fingertips and as they grazed along his palm an involuntary shudder pulsed through him. "The likeness is striking."

"It might've been, ten years ago." He watched her smile uncomfortably and wondered how long it would be before she shoved the spectacles up from the tip of her nose. "Connie, I have to tell you something."

"What, Temple?" A droplet of water dripped from her disheveled hair and landed on his outstretched palm.

"In case I don't get another chance, I want you to know that I—well, I admire you." The words nearly stuck in his throat before he managed to get them said.

"You do?" Her eyes widened and he saw the flecks of gold. "You admire...me?"

"In more ways than you can imagine. You have shown a lot of grit and skill." He gave her a twisted grin that was an expression of unease and amazement. "You have grown up, Connie." He closed his fingers over the small carving in his hand and drew in a shuddering breath.

His words swept over her like a warm wind. He had acknowledged the fact she was no longer a child. The carving was concealed in his wide palm, but the truth was revealed in his eyes. A lock of wet hair dangled over his damp forehead, nearly touching his long water-spiked black lashes. Without thought she swept the strand of hair back with her fingertips.

He shuddered.

"Thank you for finally noticing."

"Oh, I've noticed." His nervous bark of laughter sent a shudder through her body.

Her knees turned to liquid and she would have collapsed in a heap at his boots if she had not been gripping the lid of the trunk for support. She gulped down her astonishment. "You did?

"Uh-huh."

"When?"

"When you fell into the lake. The way that ridiculous dress clung to your body, I would have had to be dead and buried not to notice."

His eyes flicked toward her bosom and heat rushed into her cheeks. Warm tendrils of satisfaction began to grow inside her.

"Temple, I'm glad that I came. No matter who wins, no matter how this turns out, I'm glad that we had this time together."

He let out a little groan while his gaze slid over her face. "Connie, I have to leave now...I don't want—I can't let—I must go."

She reached out and stroked his beard-roughened cheek with her fingers. "If you leave now we'll both be sorry. I—I want you to stay with me—all night."

His deep moan escaped his mouth. The sound of it wrenched her heart.

"Connie, you don't know what you're asking."

"Yes, I do." She smiled and started undoing the buttons on the front of her mud-slicked dress.

Temple licked his lips and glanced once more at the opening of the tent. Then he sighed as if he had finally lost a great struggle. He reached out and took Connie's fingers from the buttons. Then, with agonizingly slow precision, he began to undo them himself.

Constance's flesh warmed and tingled beneath the dress. Each time a button slipped free of the cloth she shuddered. He pulled the bodice open by small degrees, until finally she was standing before him in nothing more than her drawers.

He narrowed his eyes and flicked a hot hungry look down to her booted feet.

"Connie, you are a beautiful lady," he whispered. Then he bent down on his knees and lifted one foot. He placed it on top of his knee, smearing mud on his trousers. "And a lady should have a man to do this for her."

Constance swallowed hard and stared at the top of Temple's damp head. A million unfamiliar and wonderful emotions were exploding inside her. She felt a moment of light-headedness and found herself gripping the tops of his shoulders for support. He gazed at her with a look of smoldering desire.

"I promise you, Connie, I will be gentle, I will make it as good for you as I can."

He placed her bare foot on the ground and picked up her other boot, then he repeated the process. Each minute he spent unlacing the mud-caked boot seemed like an eternity while Constance watched the lantern light shimmer on his dark head. Her palms burned where she touched his shoulders and butterflies filled her middle.

When he was finished, he stood up and kissed her until she felt all her bones turn to gelatin. Then he scooped her up and she melted into his solid muscular chest. He strode across the dirt floor with her in his arms.

Constance wasn't quite sure of the sequence of events after Temple deposited her on shaky feet. First her spectacles vanished. Then she had a vague recollection of him running his fingers through her dark hair. She seemed feverish and their familiar surroundings of her tent took on a dreamlike feel as images of Temple's magnificent form being freed from his muddy shirt and wet trousers filled her mind. And then she was lying in the protective circle of his arms on the narrow cot.

"Connie, you are the most lovely creature I have ever seen," Temple said while he nuzzled her earlobe. "I want to taste every inch of your body."

And to Connie's shocked delight, he began to do just that.

Chapter Seventeen

Temple told himself that he had lost his mind, but his arms remained locked around Connie in a protective embrace. He knew he was not worthy of her—knew she would hate him when he claimed Montague's money, but suddenly all those concerns seemed small and insignificant compared to the pleasure he felt.

She had asked him to stay. She wanted him. The impact of her words settled over him like a warm blanket and that simple request had enabled him to block out the voices from his past and bury himself in their shared passion.

"You are so beautiful." Her hair had begun to dry and it lay in wild ringlets around her lovely face. The flickering lamp cast shadows across her soft doe's eyes.

She looked younger without her glasses, more vulnerable. He bent his head and grazed her mouth lightly. The fresh taste of rainwater lingered on her skin like fine perfume and he hardened even more while he explored her wondrous body.

"Temple, I hope you will not be disappointed. I

have no experience.'' There was insecurity and apology in her voice.

He laughed and hugged her. Then he nipped the soft flesh near her throat. ''Dearest, only you would think such a thing was a deficiency.'' He levered himself up on one elbow so he could get a better view of her face. ''Believe it or not, Constance Honoria, I do not expect you to be skilled in everything. There are some men who prefer to teach a woman certain things. I happen to be one of them.''

He touched a hidden part of her body and ribbons of liquid fire coursed through her. Her breath came in shuddering gasps. ''Oh my, that was unique.'' Her eyes fluttered shut and she sighed while he caressed her neck. ''I like it when you call me Connie. Please don't ever call me anything else.''

''What?'' Temple raised his head and stared at her.

''You call me Connie. Nobody else has ever called me that but you, Temple.'' She opened her eyes and stared at him with a drowsy heavy-lidded expression. ''And you made me laugh when I was a little girl.''

He caught a rare glimpse of the inner woman who had been forced to grow up around a collection of aging academics and old bones. She had never been allowed to laugh. It would be his greatest pleasure to take Connie around the world and see that she laughed—often.

He wished things could be different.

''I thought you hated that nickname.'' He watched emotion play across her face. She had no guile, no deceit within her. He felt a sharp pang of guilt knowing that he was going to defeat her. They could have this one night, but when the sun came up they would go back to being competitors.

He had to win the prize.

"I thought I hated the name, but I have come to realize it is really very special to me." She moved slightly and her nipples grazed against the hair on his chest.

His pulse quickened at the gentle friction. "Connie, sweet, sweet Connie." He kissed her again, but this time it was not a gentle touch of lips. He allowed himself to drink deeply—to taste her while he moved his body over her. He was ready to fill her.

Constance could not focus on any part of herself. There was too much sensation, too much pleasure springing to life. Temple put his rough hand upon her breast and kneaded her flesh with an expert's touch. She sighed in contentment, but then he moved that warm and magical hand to a new location. It was as if he were restless, hungry, and each new touch brought a thousand sleeping nerves to life.

While she lay beneath him and feeling a new world of sensation being born she forgot about her awkward lack of knowledge. Temple kissed her and she tentatively explored the inside of his warm mouth with her tongue. And then, miraculously, as if she somehow did know what to do, her body was arching toward him.

Something hot and silken nudged against her throbbing body and she felt herself moving toward it with a natural rhythm that seemed to match Temple's movements perfectly. He kissed her once again and she felt a growing sensation of heat and need deep within her. It was a burning, a yearning that was impossible to describe.

"Oh, Connie, why did we wait so long?" Temple's breath had grown hot. His tongue flicked across her earlobe. "We have wasted so much time,"

"I didn't know it was like this," she murmured thickly.

"It never has been like this with anyone, before," Temple mumbled more to himself than to her. That truth sent a searing wave rolling over him. He had been with many women, but he had never felt this intensity—this desire to bring satisfaction to his partner. Confusion and a little fear crept into Temple's mind, but he shoved it away and explored the hollow of Connie's throat with his lips. He wanted to hold her—to worship her with his body until the sun came up.

To Constance, it seemed as if the canvas walls of the tent had disappeared. She was floating somewhere weightless, on a cloud of pure physical sensation. She could hear the steady beat of rain outside the tent but it had no reality for her. Nothing in the world existed or mattered except the world of excitement that Temple had created for her within his arms.

A fine sheen of sweat glistened on Connie's skin when Temple positioned himself between her thighs. She opened her eyes, which were soft and languid with passion. A shaft of tenderness pierced his heart.

"Connie—I would not hurt you for the world." His voice was harsh.

"I know that, Temple." She licked her lips and her eyes fluttered shut once again.

"Look at me, Connie, open your eyes. I want you to look at me while I love you." Waves of moist heat emanated from the juncture of her silken thighs where his own flesh throbbed and waited with need.

She opened her eyes as he asked. He raised himself and took his weight onto his forearms while he pressed his hot hardened flesh against her.

"Keep looking at me, Connie." His voice was husky and low.

"I will." She gripped his shoulders. Nervous tension combined with barely harnessed desire telegraphed through her fingers. He was all power and passion and it took her breath away.

Temple closed his own eyes for a moment, while he tried to master the lust swirling and surging within him. Connie hissed in pain and his eyes flew open. She was staring at him with a wide, questioning expression and he knew that he had caused her pain.

"I'm sorry." If he could have prevented this one minute of discomfort he would have. "It will last only a moment—then it will be gone. I promise. Do you trust me?"

"Yes." She managed a quivering smile.

His tenuous control was slipping, but finally she began to relax beneath him.

"That's it, Connie, slow and easy." Temple swallowed hard and steeled himself. He would not allow himself to weaken until he brought her as far as she could journey this first time. He saw her lids flutter. "No—don't close your eyes, darling."

She opened her eyes and he pushed his shaft past the warm barrier of flesh. Her sharp intake of breath and a welling of tears ripped at the heart he thought was impenetrable to such things. Passion and some feeling that Temple did not want to examine flooded through him. She managed a trembling smile and raised her head to kiss him.

Pride and happiness that he was her first lover poured through him. But then a voice inside his head asked if he were man enough to be her last.

"Temple, that was..." She gasped and arched higher.

He felt the gentle nudge of her against his hips and nearly let himself go. Only his great desire to see her satisfied held him in check long enough. Then when her tense body began to grow less rigid he drove into her as hard as he dared. And while the storm raged outside, Temple allowed himself the bliss of loving sweet Connie.

Lightning illuminated the inside of the tent with a blue-white flash. Temple looked at Connie, sated and languid within the crook of his arms. He leaned over and kissed her forehead.

"Thank you," he said softly.

Her eyes came slowly open and the most beautiful smile Temple had ever seen blossomed across her face. "For what?"

"For asking me to stay."

"There is still a lot of night left." She nuzzled closer and twined her fingertips in the hair on his chest.

"Why, Constance Honoria, I do believe you are trying to tempt me," he said in mock horror.

"Is it working?" she asked.

He took her hand and wrapped it around his rigid shaft. "What do you think?"

Connie yawned and stretched her forearm but came in contact with a rough jawbone. She blinked and came wide awake. Temple was indeed beside her and the events of last night were not a delicious and forbidden dream.

"Morning." His voice was gruff as it vibrated through her nude body.

"I—I'm sorry to wake you," she stammered, not really embarrassed about what had happened between them, but unsure of how she should act after so brazen a display.

"You didn't. I've been awake for a while." He opened one eye and his lips turned up at the corners in a grin. "Sounds like the rain has finally stopped."

"Uh, yes, it has." Connie levered herself up, clutching the blanket to her chest. She saw Temple's brows come up and knew he was amused by her awkwardness.

"I'll close my eyes if it will make you feel better," he teased.

Heat scorched her cheeks. "If you don't mind?"

"Not at all, Connie." He met her glance. With his pet name for her feeling like a soft caress, she nearly tumbled back into his arms. She shook herself and sat up. When Temple closed his eyes, she scurried across the tent floor and found her gown. She slipped the fabric over her head. "All right, you can open them now."

"I already did." He was sitting on the edge of the bed staring. He had been watching her the whole time.

"Temple, you are unscrupulous and cannot be trusted!"

"Temple is a pirate, awrk." The squawk came from inside the shawl-draped cage.

Constance was grateful for the bird's interruption. It gave her an excuse to be doing something besides staring at Temple. "Livingstone is ready to get out for a while."

She went to the cage and took off the shawl. Livingstone ruffled his feathers and stretched his wings. When she opened the door he hopped out upon her shoulder.

"Connie, you are a lovely, awrk, creature," he squawked.

"What did he say?" Temple stood, and Constance felt her eyes riveted to his nude form.

"I—I guess he was listening."

"Taste every inch…awrk." The bird paced up and down her arm.

"Damn mimic," Temple commented.

"He gets bored, I think."

Livingstone flapped from Connie's shoulder to the crate where the lantern still burned. She bent near the chimney and blew it out, not knowing what to say to Temple since her pet had obviously decide to mimic their words of passion.

"We must have forgotten to do that last night."

"We were busy with other—" Temple speared her with a glance that was openly carnal "—more plea-surable pursuits."

"Sweet, sweet, Connie, awrk. Look at me—open your eyes." Livingstone said loudly.

Constance longed for something to say, but she seemed tongue-tied. She knew it was ridiculous to be acting like a prim maid in light of what had happened, but now with Livingstone repeating what they said she felt her cheeks burning with heat. Temple flashed a narrowed gaze at Livingstone just as the bird hopped to the tent floor and meandered through his discarded clothing. When the bird flapped back to the crate he held a folded white paper clasped in his sharp beak.

"Oh, Temple, he has your letter." Constance snatched the paper from Livingstone's hold before he destroyed it. She held it out to Temple. "I guess you forgot to read it."

He grinned at her second reference to how forgetful they had been, but Connie's expression of distress made him remain silent. She was fidgeting and her cheeks blazed with heat each time he caught her eye.

He didn't know if he should laugh or wring the damned bird's neck, but watching Connie blush prettily only made him want to get her back into his arms—he certainly wasn't interested in reading some damned letter. But he took it from her hand and ripped it open.

Temple scanned the page and Constance saw his mien change in the blink of an eye. "Is it—bad news?" She took a step toward him.

Without a word he stood up, leaving the letter open on the cot. His nakedness seemed to be inconsequential to him as he strode across the floor and picked up his trousers where Livingstone had been rummaging through them. Constance, however, was not so unmoved by the sight of his lean muscular body. A flaring hunger entered her middle. When he pulled his trousers over his narrow buttocks she felt a pang of disappointment. He still had his back to her when he slipped on his shirt. Constance glanced away before he turned and caught her leering at him.

Her gaze fell upon the open letter. The handwriting was large and unfamiliar. Without conscious thought she found herself reading the letter.

Mr. Parish, after our meeting I did a little digging of my own. I have unearthed some facts concerning the crime that occurred ten years ago. Contact me as soon as possible—it could be important for your career. Thaddeus Ball.

She picked up the page. "Temple, who is Thaddeus Ball and what crime is he referring to?"

Temple's shoulders stiffened. He felt the burning lump in his throat grow. Last night he had actually believed that he and Connie might find a future together, but the blackmail note had squelched that idea.

He continued to dress, pulling his suspenders into place without turning to face her. He could not face her—could not tell her the sordid story of his past, or how it kept tainting his life. How could he tell her? If she knew what he had been like in his youth—the things he had done—she would be ashamed of him, and the one thing he could not withstand would be Connie's rejection.

"Temple?" she asked more insistently. "What is this all about?" When he finally turned, she saw something haunted in his eyes, something that made her take a step backward.

"Mr. Ball is referring to the reason I left ten years ago."

"A crime?" She glanced at the letter held in her trembling hand. "You left because—you committed—a crime?" The words came out in a stuttering jumble. Connie was about to add, *I don't believe it,* but the icy rage that flared in his eyes froze the words in her throat.

Cold seeped into his bones while Temple stared at Connie. He had hoped she would give him the benefit of the doubt, allow him to explain everything before she judged him, but she was truly C.H.'s daughter. Her reaction was quick and decisive. Just like C.H.'s—and just as wrong.

"Is it so easy to imagine me doing something criminal, Connie? Even for you?"

"Temple, I never meant… The letter said…"

"Never mind, I understand. It's probably for the best anyway. This never would have worked." His lips twisted upward on one side, giving his expression a painful ironic appearance. Temple looked at her for half a minute before a harsh epithet left his lips. His gaze fell on his hat, and he scooped it up and strode toward the tent flap without a backward glance or another word.

"Where are you going?"

"Back to my side of the cut—I momentarily forgot my place—and my goal. I won't make that mistake again." He stopped at the mouth of the tent. His shoulders grew more rigid. "Goodbye…Connie," he whispered as he ducked out the flap.

For one crazy moment she nearly ran after him, but then she remembered all the newspaper accounts about him. He had been called a bounder, a man who would use any weapon, take any liberty to get what he wanted.

She stared at the rumpled blankets on the cot and a deep hollow opened in her soul. Temple had used his skill as a seducer to get her where he wanted her— now he was headed back to the dig and the bones that had been his goal all along.

Temple made his way down the slope while anger and sadness built inside his chest. He had been a fool to think that Connie would see him differently than the rest of the world.

He should have known better.

"Just as I should have seen Thaddeus Ball for what he was," he grumbled. He remembered Thaddeus Ball clearly. The eager young reporter had not looked like the kind of man who would resort to blackmail, but the letter was clear enough. Temple shook his head in amazement. He had been wrong about Ball, but what tore at his heart was that he had been wrong about Connie.

She believed him capable of every sin—every crime. His judgment of other people's character was off by a mile. Just as faulty as their assessment of him. The pain of it tore at his heart, but he pushed the feelings aside. He had worn a thick coat of armor for years and only sweet Connie had been able to get past it.

"I will never make that mistake again. Never, by damn."

He was halfway across the cut, lost in his misery and anger, before he realized that he was not wading in hip-deep water. He stopped and glanced around in confusion. The ground was wet and muddy, sprigs of silt-coated grass poked up here and there, but there was no standing water.

Temple squinted down at the rough water-marked edge of the cut, where the two sides of the gorge had met only yesterday. Now instead of the pointed end of this meandering canyon, he saw an open cut. The sides had been eaten away by the force of the rainstorm and rising water, and a new wash had been created at the end of the old one where the water had emptied into the lower flatlands beyond the canyon.

Temple looked at his digging site. The canvas was gone of course, swept away with the flood, as well as the mound of dirt that had been piled beside the hole. He felt his breath lodge in his throat as he hurried forward. He had to be the first one back to New York. Montague's endowment had taken on more importance in the past few minutes. Temple paused and swallowed hard. He took a deep breath and looked down.

There in beige stone, washed clean by the torrent, was the beautiful four-foot-long skull with the rows of sharp recurved teeth. But now it was not alone—there was more much more to his miraculous find.

At the base of the skull, well-formed and completely intact vertebrae curled backward. As usual the dinosaur had contorted in the last throes of death. Below the skull the animal's ribs and shoulders connected to what had once been a set of exquisitely formed and highly functional flippers. Now the delicate bones that once propelled it through the ancient oceans were connected to the remains of three-inch-long petrified claws.

The dinosaur was glorious—and unknown. Temple's gaze slid over the bones again. They extended only slightly farther back than the ribs. It was not an intact skeleton; the hips and tail section were missing. But then the odds of finding a whole dinosaur in as good a condition as this were slim.

He took off his hat and stared reverently at the front half. It was splendid, ready to packed into a crate and taken back to New York.

"I have won." His flat voice seemed to echo through the sides of the ravaged canyon.

No matter what dirt Thaddeus Ball had dug up, or what Dandridge University had told the papers, Temple was going to win Montague's prize.

At last he was the winner. All he had to do was return to New York and spend the rest of his life trying to forget that he had fallen in love with Connie.

He had never felt so alone.

Chapter Eighteen

Constance stared at the tent flap, unable to move. She tried to swallow the hard hot lump that had mysteriously taken shape, but it lodged stubbornly in her throat.

"Stop being silly." Her voice cracked and broke with a flood of disappointment. She sniffed and pulled herself up straighter.

She had asked *him* to stay with her. It wasn't as if he had begged her on bended knee. The daylight had come and banished all her romantic illusions as it had driven away the rain. Now it was business as usual, and the most important thing to Temple, as it had always been, was proving himself the better digger and garnering Montague's money.

Constance stiffened while she absorbed that fact. She forced herself to walk to her trunks and pull out some clothing. She had been unwise to give her body and affection to a rogue like Temple. Her father had called him a pirate for years—she should have listened. One hot salty tear snaked its way over her cheek, but she brushed it away with the back of her hand.

"I will not cry," she told herself between clenched teeth. By drawing in a shuddering breath she managed to hold back the tears, but none of the sorrow. A great raw gulf opened inside her bosom while she hastily pulled on her father's purloined shirt and a pair of his trousers. Mechanically she combed her hair and arranged it into a functional knot on her head.

Constance stepped outside. The sound of horses' hooves and the jingle of harness startled her. Peter Hughes urged his stocky team toward her tent. The wagon wheels were caked in mud and the sides of the wagon were splattered.

"Howdy, Miss Cadwallender." He held his hand aloft in greeting. Constance forced herself to smile at him even though her face ached from the effort. "I thought you might be getting low on supplies."

"That was very kind of you, Mr. Hughes." Constance stepped forward. Her boots sank into the top layer of muck and made her progress slow. "But you didn't have to go to all that trouble. I could have waited until the mud dried a bit."

"No trouble, miss, no trouble at all." He wrapped the reins around the hand brake and jumped down. His trouser legs were tucked into his boots and he marched through the mud without care, obviously accustomed to this kind of environment.

She kept her eyes firmly on Peter Hughes, not wishing to allow her gaze to stray anywhere near Temple. She knew if she turned and looked at him, even briefly across the wash, she would burst into a torrent of humiliating tears.

Temple was on his hands and knees, chipping away the last bit of limestone around his find when he heard Peter Hughes's voice. He had seen the wagon coming earlier and had intensified his efforts to free the skull from the sandstone. He had undercut the soil and rock surrounding the specimen on every edge and was confident he could lift it out in two flat sections. It would be easy to transport back to Morgan Forks and then by train to New York.

He stood and found himself staring at Connie. He was not prepared for the impact the sight of her would have on him. His belly lurched and plummeted while a cold clammy sweat enveloped him. Temple didn't want to look at her—but he couldn't take his eyes from her. She was beautiful, almost fragile looking with her father's trousers and shirt hugging her slim body. Her shiny rain-washed hair was tightly bound on her head.

He felt that strange sizzling compulsion to set the dark tresses free. But he could not.

She thought he was a thief. She had no respect for him. Even though he ached with love for her—even though he would have gladly spent his days trying to understand her eccentric habits, being blamed for every predicament she got herself into, he could not allow himself one kind word or gentle gesture.

Connie, with her soft brown eyes and seductress's body was the only thing standing between him and his prize—between him and a long overdue measure of respectability. His pride would not allow him any other course but to continue forward toward his goal.

The sound of another horse and wagon drew Temple's attention to the horizon.

"Son of a—just what I need—Holt Morgan." Temple swore a little under his breath. But he was being foolish. The cowboys in the back of the Flying B wagon would have the bones packed in no time.

Temple took off his hat and dragged his hand

through his hair. He stared down at the bones, the wonderful unique bones, and realized that he was miserable.

Constance gratefully allowed Holt and his men to take charge of putting her site in order. The water had brought in a thin layer of silt to cover all she had found. She looked across the cut and felt a cold dull ache settle beneath her heart.

Temple was so busy he had not once even looked her way. It was as if the night they had shared meant nothing to him. While she watched the morning sun capture the silver and gold of his hair, a new insight came to her.

She was another of Temple's many conquests. She shivered involuntarily at the thought.

"He charmed me into my own bed," she whispered to herself. And while she watched him and Peter loading two crates into the back of the wagon, fury and pain mingled in her soul.

His shirt stretched taut across his back.

She willed herself to banish the memory of how those muscles felt beneath her palms. Anger and a sense of betrayal gained force as she observed him. He was a pirate—and he had stolen her heart. The knowledge that he had done it so easily and most probably as just another way of ensuring his success was what brought fury cresting in her mind.

His trousers hugged powerful thighs.

She was furious at both her own weakness and Temple's lack of feeling for her. And she found herself galvanized into action. She strode to the site and hopped down beside a cowboy who was digging.

"Give me the spade," she snapped. "I don't have

much time to get these bones crated and get back to New York.''

Constance angled the surface of the spade until it was almost flat and then she scooped up a layer of silt. Whether because of her fervent prayers, or some small degree of skill on her part, she was rewarded by the presence of bones.

''Quick, use the brushes and clear away this dirt.'' She heard the excitement in her own voice and without conscious thought found herself looking up, eager to share her find with Temple. When she saw him, tying ropes on a wooden box in the back of Mr. Hughes's wagon, her breath lodged in her throat.

''If I thought it would open his eyes, I'd go knock him down for you.'' Holt's deep sympathetic voice startled her. She looked up and found him staring at her.

''I don't know what you mean.'' Constance blinked rapidly to stay the hot tears stinging the backs of her eyes.

''Do you love him that much?'' Holt yanked the checked kerchief from around his neck and handed it to her.

''Is it that easy to see?'' There was no use in denying her feelings—at least not to herself.

''Ma told me. At first I didn't think it was true—didn't want to believe it was true, I guess.'' Holt gave her a sad smile. ''But the way you look at him...only a blind man wouldn't know it.''

She managed a trembling smile. ''You are nearly right. Temple is not blind, but the only thing he can see is these.'' She pointed at the bones that were rapidly being unearthed by the cowhands.

''What can I do to help, Miss Constance?'' Holt's green eyes were sincere.

Constance glanced at Temple once more. Then she knew what she wanted. "The rain has destroyed my chance of proving my theory." She frowned and stared at the muddy earth. "But it would be my greatest pleasure to see Temple Parish humbled. If I can get these bones crated and back to New York before he does, then I will win Montague's endowment for the Dandridge. It would mean a lot to me to be able to keep my pledge to my father—in spite of—everything that has happened."

Holt smiled. "I understand, miss. Leave it to me and the boys. These bones and you will be on the next train out of Morgan Forks." He touched her shoulder lightly with his fingertips before he started barking orders.

Constance stood back, content for once to let someone else be competent and responsible.

Temple felt the urgency in Connie's camp. He could not hear or see anything specific, but he had been on enough digs to know that she had found what she was searching for. He scuffed his boot into the damp soil and tried to forget the way she had looked at him— the way she sounded when she read Ball's letter.

But he couldn't.

She thought he was a street rat, just like everyone else. Temple tightened his hands into fists while the pain of her words ebbed. He narrowed his eyes and looked at Connie's slender form across the ravine.

As long as he had the name, he might as well play the game, he thought bitterly.

Temple turned away and started planning—designing a way that he could not possibly lose the prize.

Chapter Nineteen

The strained silence was wearing on Peter's nerves. Temple had not said a word since they'd packed up his tent and headed back toward Morgan Forks. In fact, the only time he even seemed aware of where he was, was when Peter had to double back and find a way around an arroyo that was still running with muddy water.

"You look like a man heading for his own funeral," Peter quipped.

Temple's head came up and he stared at Peter in silence. The look in his eyes brought back a wave of memories. The haunted expression of pain and loss gave Temple's eyes an edge as sharp and cold as ice. It sent a shiver through Peter just to look at him.

"Sun's getting low." Temple's voice was flat and emotionless.

"Guess it's time to stop for the night." Peter found a little rise and eased the wagon up. Then he set the brake, wrapped the reins around the iron railing of the seat and hopped down. Temple didn't even complain about the delay, he just followed Peter almost as if he were sleepwalking.

All the while Peter was tending the team he watched Temple. It was almost scary to see him like this. He was like a hollow shell. While Peter observed the younger man, he came to a decision. He would have to tell Temple about the night in Central Park.

Temple sipped the bitter coffee and stared out over the Montana prairie. The golden glow of another campfire no more than two miles away held his attention. He stared at the fire until his eyes burned from the strain but still he could not look away.

It was Connie and Holt Morgan's fire.

The assurance that Holt would keep her safe filled him with an uneasy calm. Even now, knowing that she was not far behind and might possibly claim Montague's endowment, could not completely erase his need to protect her. It made him angry to admit it— but he had feelings for Connie. Just how deep those feelings ran he couldn't say—didn't want to know— because it was pointless.

In her eyes he would always be someone without roots or scruples. He would never have her respect, and without that he didn't want her love.

He drained the cup but continued to sit and stare at the winking fire.

"It's almost as dark and quiet as it was that night, ain't it?" Peter stood at the edge of the light.

"What night?" Temple grated out.

"The night the statues were smashed in the park."

Temple's head came around and his eyes narrowed. Peter could see him focusing, reaching into the fog of the past.

"How would you know?" Suspicion rumbled in his question.

"I was there," Peter said softly. "Look at me close, boy. Don't I look a little familiar?"

For the first time, Temple really looked at Peter. His skin was weathered—like that of most of the men in Montana. The clothes on his lean body were not any different than those worn by any other man Temple had seen here. Peter looked like a prospector, or a teamster. But as Temple looked, tiny little things caught his notice. Peter wore lace-up shoes instead of boots. He wore a cloth cap, not a wide-brimmed hat. And he did have a way of pronouncing words that hinted at a long-ago abandoned accent.

"I've watched you all day, boy. You've got that same look in your eye."

Temple was on his guard, curious yet wary. "What look would that be?"

"The look you had in your eye that night. I saw that you were ready and willing to die for what you believed. I don't think you could help yourself—I don't think you can help yourself now. You are like a dog that's been trained for the pits, Temple. Once you set yourself on a course you don't know how to stop, to turn back. Even if it is tearing your heart out to keep going forward."

"How do you know so damned much about me?" Temple stood and tossed the empty cup aside. "Just who in the hell are you, anyway, Peter Hughes?"

Peter took a deep breath and sat down on a nearby boulder. Temple stood above him, glowering.

"I was like you, Temple. I lived on the streets— did what I could to get by." Peter looked at him and smiled. "There was a time I thought that money would buy me the respectability I had not been born to. I was wrong. And you are wrong."

"What the hell do you mean?"

"You can't take the money and the credit, not if it means hurting Miss Cadwallender—"

"The only thing I'm interested in is the money. And you are right about one thing, Hughes, money does buy respect. I've tried to earn it by hard work and it hasn't meant a tinker's damn. Now I'm going to do what I've been accused of for years. I will cheat, steal and even break Connie's heart to get Montague's prize, I promise you that." His voice was hollow and cold.

"I don't believe it—I won't believe it, 'cause if it's true then I saved your hide and left New York for nothing that really mattered."

The fire reflected off the craggy weathered face, and Temple truly did recognize him. Peter Hughes was the man who stopped the bullyboy from bashing in his skull that night in Central Park.

A strange feeling crept up his spine and out into his limbs. It was a sensation he was not accustomed to. It was the knowledge that he owed this man a long over-due debt of gratitude.

"What do you mean, Hughes?" Temple's curiosity was stronger than his sense of dread and for that reason he kept asking questions.

"Until that night—in the park—I had never known anyone, seen anyone, who was willing to die for an idea. But you stood your ground, shouting how it was wrong to destroy something beautiful, how it was a crime against the people to shatter those statues. You were ready to have your head smashed in, willing to die if need be, to protect those stupid models because you thought they were beautiful."

"I was a stupid kid," Temple grumbled, while

memories buffeted him like an icy wind. "I know better now."

"No, you were the smart one—back then." Peter grimaced. "Up until that moment I had only been surviving. I had never been alive until a skinny boy stood against a dozen of the Tammany thugs in the dark. I wasn't the same after that. You changed me." Peter stared at Temple with the fire of accusation in his eyes.

"I changed you? How?" Temple didn't want to hear it, but he couldn't stop himself from asking. Now that Peter had opened the floodgates that had held his memories in check, they were pouring out of control. Temple remembered his hunger, his loneliness, his desperate desire to belong. A shudder coursed through him when he realized that though he had grown older and taller, those cravings were still with him, perhaps even stronger now that he had confronted Connie's true opinion of him.

For all the years he had wandered the earth, looking for some way to win C.H.'s respect, he had believed that little Connie cared for him—accepted him. But time had changed her, too. She had grown into a woman and now she thought of him as a guttersnipe, just like her father.

"I was ashamed of what I had done, smashing those wonderful things. That was why I saved your life—that and the look in your eye. I left New York right after that night. I traveled as far as Boss Tweed's stolen money would take me, looking for a different life, a better me." Peter stepped a little closer. "That's why I know what you're going through now, son."

"You don't know anything about me," Temple challenged. "You don't know how hard I've worked to gain respect."

"I know the newspapers are full of stories about you. In fact they are calling you the most noted scientist and explorer of the year."

"That doesn't matter." Temple cut his hand through the air in a gesture of dismissal. "That isn't what I want."

"Why?"

"Because there was only one person's respect I've been trying to earn. I don't care what the world thinks of me—all I care about is..." He shuddered and the words stuck in his throat.

"What, Temple?"

"All I care about is C.H.'s respect. I want him to know that I didn't do what they accuse me of. I want him to know I've worked hard. That's what matters. And the only way I can prove it to him is to beat Connie." The words wrenched from him as he made the admission both to Peter and to himself.

"I have been in your shoes, I know what you are feeling, but I'm asking you—begging you. Make the right decision, Temple, or it will haunt you for the rest of your life. If you take the wrong path now, thinking all that money and fame will give you what you've been chasing—you'll regret it." Peter dragged his hand down his face and sighed as if he were weary. "Respect is hard earned, and maybe in your case it is long overdue and lacking, but don't let yourself sink back into the sewer, boy. Remember how you felt that night—find that kind of courage inside yourself again."

Temple stared at Peter for one long painful moment. Then he uttered a string of oaths and stomped off into the night. The silence hung around him like a shroud.

Only the blink of Connie's campfire penetrated the darkness.

Morgan Forks looked just the same except for the main street, which was now a river of mud. Temple grimaced when he realized that Connie was only an hour or two behind him. Once again they would be forced to occupy the rooms over the hotel.

"When is the train due in?" Temple asked Peter.

The old man's frown deepened and he refused to look at Temple, but finally he answered. "Early tomorrow morning. Why?"

Temple tried to ignore the disappointment that emanated from Hughes. The old fool didn't know what he was talking about and he didn't know Temple. "I'm in a hurry, that's why."

Peter snorted, and in spite of himself, Temple felt his gut knotting with something that felt uncomfortably like guilt—or maybe it was shame for what he knew he was planning to do.

As soon as the wagon rolled up in front of the small building that doubled as train depot and telegraph office, Temple hopped out. He strode inside, surprising the elderly man standing behind the desk. Temple would have known in a crowd that he was a telegraph operator. He wore black garters on his sleeves, had long quick fingers and beady sharp eyes—just like every other operator in every office Temple had ever been in.

"Can I help you?" He adjusted garters that didn't need adjusting.

"I want to send a telegram." Temple dug into his trousers until his fingers closed upon some coins.

"And then I want to unload a couple of boxes. Where can I put them where they will be safe?"

"There's a woodshed in the alley beside the office. Has a floor and a roof—will that do?"

"That'll do." Temple hitched one leg and propped his elbows on the tall counter. "What day is this?"

The operator pointed to a calendar hanging on a nail behind him. "Monday. Who do you want to send the telegram to?" The little man stuck the end of a pencil in his mouth and prepared to jot down the message.

"Mr. Thomas Jones, care of Ashmont University, New York City. Say that Temple Parish has won. Tell him that I will be in New York Thursday afternoon by two o'clock. Tell him to meet me at Ashmont's offices—and to alert Mr. Montague so he can bring the press and the funds."

"Is that all?"

"Yes, that's all." Temple placed three silver dollars on the counter. "Is this enough?"

"Yea, that'll do." The little man was already busy tapping out the message. Each time the machine beneath his finger clicked, Temple winced.

He turned and walked out into the mire of Morgan Forks's main street. A strange empty ache had settled in his belly. Peter was still sitting in the wagon seat.

"I can unload the crates over here." Temple walked to the side of the telegraph office and looked inside the shed. As the operator had promised, there was a floor. The area was clean and dry.

He walked to the end of the wagon and slid out the first crate. It was heavy, but manageable. He glanced up and saw Peter watching him. "No, there's no need for you to help, Hughes, I can get them both," Temple snapped irritably.

Hughes chuckled. "I thought you could. You seem to be real good at taking care of things all by yourself. I wouldn't want to butt in where I wasn't wanted."

Temple stopped long enough to glare at Hughes, but when he saw the man's mischievous smile widen, he knew it was pointless to say any more. He picked up the second crate and positioned it beside the first.

A noise drew his gaze to the end of the street, and he stepped back into the sunlight. He half expected to see Connie and Holt pulling into town, but it was just a buckboard with a man and a boy. They stopped in front of the mercantile while Temple heard himself expel the tense breath he had been holding.

"Are you thirsty?" Peter Hughes had climbed down from the wagon and now leaned against the wall of the telegraph office.

"I could use a drink," Temple said. He found himself wanting company, or perhaps he just didn't want to be alone with his own thoughts. "How about you, Hughes, would you like to share a bottle?"

Peter's brows shot up. "A bottle, eh?"

"That's what I said. Look, if you don't want a drink, just say so. It wouldn't be the first time I've had to drink alone."

"Don't get yourself worked up." Peter stood away from the building. "I'm feelin' a little dry."

Temple stepped off the small stoop and sank into the thick mud. He realized that his worn leather bag was still stowed under the wagon seat. The mud made a sucking sound when he turned back to get it. When he looked up, he saw the glint of sunshine off metal in the distance.

Connie was coming.

He wasn't sure he could face her.

Chapter Twenty

Temple took another pull on the whiskey bottle. The sound of a coyote howling outside of town halted the peeps and croaks of the critters sharing space with him inside the woodshed.

He sat up, hitched his boot heel up on the edge of the crate and looked out at the blue-black night. The sound of laughter drew his attention to the saloon across the street.

Against his will, he found his eyes climbing the wooden structure to the windows on the second floor. A light burned in one window.

"Connie's room." His words were slurred, his tongue thick from the whiskey. He had been too much of a coward to face her, so he had paid for the bottle and slunk into the woodshed like the street rat she thought he was. Now he was trying his damnedest to get roaring drunk, so he would not think about Connie. He wanted to be so numb that he would not remember what it felt like to hold her, or how his heart beat a little harder inside his chest each time he thought about her.

He had not succeeded.

* * *

Constance walked to the narrow window and looked down into the dark street. Holt had finally left her, after he had made sure she had dinner and was settled safely in the small room with a tub full of hot water for a bath. He and the bartender had carried her crate up the stairs, while the men lined up at the bar stared with gaping mouths. She wondered why they reacted so strangely. Heat climbed to her face when she glanced down and realized she was wearing mud-spattered men's trousers.

She had made a spectacle of herself in front of Temple and now she had provided amusement for the residents of Morgan Forks. A sad litany of her achievements. But no matter how much she had suffered, nothing she had been through had lessened her anger at, disappointment in or love for Temple Parish.

She stepped away from the window and started peeling off her clothes. Heavy clumps of mud clung to her trousers as tenaciously as the memory of Temple's touch clung to her flesh. Her sturdy traveling dress was also filthy, wadded up and stuck into a corner of the crate to cushion her find. The only clothes that had not been ruined on this expedition were the fashionable frocks.

Once she was naked, she stepped into the hot water. From sheer necessity she would have to wear one of those dresses tomorrow. The thought brought back the look on Temple's face and the sound of his voice when he told her she was pretty.

Hearing him say it had made her feel pretty. She could not remember a time in her life before that moment that she had ever even considered that she *might be* pretty.

Constance removed her spectacles and laid them on

the bare wooden floor beside the tub. She scooted deeper into the narrow space, hoping the hot water might remove the lingering tingle from Temple's love-making. She leaned her head back against the rough staves and willed herself to forget the taste of his kisses. She scrubbed with the hard milled soap until her flesh turned bright pink, and still her skin tingled with the memory of his caress.

How had she allowed herself to become entangled in Temple's charms? she wondered. But then she chided herself for the thought. Her muscles ached, her head ached, and her pride had been deeply wounded.

Temple had done nothing but be himself—he was long on appeal and short on judgment. At least all the newspapers had made it seem so throughout the years when one debutante after another had been linked to him. No, she could not blame Temple entirely. It had been her own foolishness that brought her to this point. She had been determined to show him she was no longer a child. She had primped and plotted and in her own clumsy, inexperienced way had done everything she could to seduce him.

"And now I am paying the price for my folly." She splashed water on her face and soaped her hair.

What was done was done. Tomorrow morning she was getting on that train and heading to New York to claim Montague's endowment.

She had not seen him in town today. Holt had suggested that he might have found another way to travel, in an effort to beat her home, but she refused to think about it now. She had found the bones; now all she had to do was get them back to New York first. Then at least she would have that small victory to comfort her while her heart was breaking.

* * *

Before sunrise the high-pitched screech of brakes on metal rails echoed through Temple's head. He opened one eye and saw a white cloud of steam congeal in the darkness beyond the woodshed. A dull pounding ache settled at the base of his skull when he sat up.

"Couldn't get drunk, but I sure got the hangover," he whispered to himself. He winced at the sound of his own voice but he managed to make it to his feet and sling his leather valise over his shoulder. When he staggered out into the darkness, it was quiet, save for the blowing sound of the steam engine.

Temple looked down the tracks and saw nobody. The train obscured his view of the saloon and the room above where Connie now slept. He grated his teeth together, against the pain in his head and his continued passion for a woman who held only contempt for him.

He staggered down the row of cars, peering inside each one as he passed. The baggage car was loaded with trunks and boxes. He paused for a moment while he considered what to do. He didn't want to leave his crates alone for a minute, but he didn't want to be around when Connie's crate was loaded either.

Temple went farther down the train until he found another car, empty with the big doors standing wide open. A pile of straw was in one corner and it looked as if someone might have used it for a bed.

Temple tossed his valise inside while stars danced in his pounding head. Then he made his way back to the shed, and gritting his teeth against the whiskey-induced agony, he picked up one of his crates. Cursing the whole time for being such a fool to let himself fall in love with Connie, he lifted it through the wide door and slid it across the rough planks. He repeated the trip, all the while mumbling under his breath. When both crates were inside, he jumped into the car and collapsed in the narrow space between the crates and the wall.

He had the straw for a bed, his leather bag for a pillow and his guilt for company. He squeezed his eyes tight and prayed he could sleep off the feeling that a blacksmith had taken up residence inside his skull. All the while trying to forget that he was planning to break Connie's heart.

Peter downed the cup of bitter coffee before he glanced at the empty staircase. He figured Miss Cadwallender was up and around, and had expected to see her down here before now. For one minute he entertained the idea that she had decided to stay—to avoid Temple—to let him win by default. But the thought was no sooner in his head than he was discounting it. She had too much spunk for that.

Still there was nobody on the stairs. Perhaps she needed help getting loaded. He had heard the curious speculation surrounding her and the crate most people were sure had to be a coffin. It never ceased to amaze Peter that folks would take the most ordinary incident and blow it into something dramatic.

While he was grinning at the notion, he saw a flutter of petticoat on the top stair, then a dress the hue of pink posies, with stripes the color of rich cream running through the shimmering material. As she descended the narrow staircase, a little more of her was revealed, until finally he was looking at her from toe to the top of her glossy head. Her dark hair was coiled and caught by a simple comb, the only jewelry she wore was a pair of cameo earbobs.

Miss Cadwallender gripped the railing with a slender gloved hand and carried the birdcage with the other. She took another step slowly—as if she were not used to the feel of the dress and full petticoats.

Peter couldn't help grin. Just when he had grown used to seeing her covered in mud, wearing men's trousers, she emerged looking more beautiful than a lady had a right to.

"Miss Cadwallender, you make an old fellow's heart skip a beat." Peter lounged against the newel post at the bottom of the stairs and watched a Montana sunset appear in her smooth cheeks.

"Thank you, Mr. Hughes." She took the last few steps quickly, as if his compliment had made her uneasy.

"The train is loading. I thought you might need some help with your crate." He took the wire cage from her as he spoke.

"Yes, I do." She glanced back up the stairs.

"No need to worry yourself. Let me get you on the train and I'll see it is loaded into the baggage car for you."

"That is very kind of you, Mr. Hughes, but I can find my way to the train alone," Constance assured him.

"Oh, I know that, miss, but the mud is ankle-deep. You'll need help crossin' the street to keep your skirt dry and you'd never be able to manage this thing." He nodded at the cage.

Constance's brows knit together. She glanced out the streaked window as if to verify what Peter said. "Oh, I had forgotten about the mud,"

"It's not a problem, miss. Just give me a minute

and I'll bring the wagon up to the door and then deliver you right to the train car."

"You are very kind, Mr. Hughes. I won't forget all you have done." She touched him on the back of the hand with her glove-encased fingers and for the first time in years, Peter couldn't think of a thing to say.

Constance stood at the door of the saloon and waited while Mr. Hughes instructed two men about her crate. Then he disappeared down the street to what she supposed was the stable. In minutes he was turning his wagon around in front of the saloon.

"There you are, miss." He grinned and reached out to give her a hand. Livingstone's cage was already in the middle of the seat. She settled herself stiffly beside the bird, painfully aware of the fact that she would probably never see Mr. Hughes again.

"Mr. Hughes, I'd like to give you—" Constance dug into her reticule.

"Don't go insultin' me by offerin' me more money. I've been paid more'n enough for what I've done for you. You just get yourself back to New York and show Temple Parish what a lady can do—when she's given the chance."

She looked up and met his eyes. Her bottom lip trembled slightly. "Oh, Mr. Hughes—I—I,"

"There now, don't go makin' me feel bad by cryin'. I never could abide a weepin' woman." He cleared his throat but the hot lump remained. "Here we are—just like I promised."

Constance looked up to find she was looking directly at the train steps. A cloud of steam billowed out from the engine.

"You just step straight across." Peter offered his hand to steady her and she did as he instructed. "Do you want the bird with you or shall I see him to the baggage car?''

"I would be more comfortable if Livingstone were in the baggage car. I have packed some bread and seeds and have a small container of water in a pouch for him.''

"I'll take care of it. I'll make sure the man in the baggage car knows all about him. They are bringin' your crate over now, I see. I hate goodbyes, so I think I'll just leave you now and see to the loadin'.'' He met her gaze. "You take care of yourself, understand?''

"Yes, Mr. Hughes, I understand—and you too.'' She smiled at him for half a minute, then she turned and disappeared inside the train car. He saw her ease into a seat before he urged the team on. The men were just carrying her crate across the street when Peter arrived at the baggage car. He was about to have the men load the crate when he heard something. Curiosity made Peter walk toward the open car and peek inside. He saw a familiar pair of mud-caked boots.

"Bring that crate over here, boys.'' Peter snatched up the birdcage and the packet of food and water. He stood back while the men pushed the crate into the car. "I'll see you boys at the saloon in just a bit—then we'll settle up—if that's all right with you.''

The men nodded in agreement and trudged back into the muddy street. Peter stepped farther inside the dim car. As his eyes adjusted to the lighting he looked around for a place to set Livingstone's cage. He finally put it and the packet of food on top of one of the other two crates adjacent to Miss Cadwallender's.

"Well, Livingstone, it looks like you are goin' to

have company on the trip home.'' Peter jerked off the oilskin covering.

Gingerly Peter lifted Temple's hat from his face. The smell of whiskey wafted up.

"Pickled, that's what he is, Livingstone, pickled." Peter shook his head and replaced the hat. "I would love to see the look on his face when he finds you and Miss Cadwallender's crate ridin' with him." Peter chuckled to himself. He didn't believe that Temple had changed from that defiant boy who had faced down the Tammany thugs—and he was willing to bet Miss Cadwallender's happiness to prove it to him. "And if you have any influence on the boy, talk to him, Livingstone—talk to him and change his mind." Peter chuckled as he slid the door shut. He stood back and watched as the conductor walked by, shouting that the train was getting ready to leave.

Peter glanced at the car while a smile tickled the corners of his mouth. "I've done all I can do, now I'll just have to wait and see how it all turns out." Peter watched the train swaying down the track until it was no more than a dark speck on the horizon.

Temple slowly became aware of the rocking motion. His mind was foggy—thick from the effects of the whiskey. He turned over, seeking a more comfortable position.

"Awrk, Temple is a pirate."

The familiar grating sound brought his eyes open with a start. He put one elbow on a crate and levered himself up. That made the anvil and hammer inside his skull quicken their unrelenting tempo.

"Sweet, sweet, Connie. Open your eyes while I love you, awrk."

"Oh, God—I am in hell." Temple moaned. "I died and God has sent me to Hades." He dragged his hand through his tousled hair and blinked at the apparition of the bird.

"Temple is a pirate," the bird rasped again. "Awrk, pirate—pirate. Lovely creature...taste every inch of, awrk, your body, awrk."

"Oh, Lord, I never dreamed there would be Livingstones in hell." Temple heard the misery in his own thick words. "Why me?" He glared at the bird as if he expected a lucid answer.

"Awrk. Connie's a beautiful lady. Kiss me, awrk."

Temple struggled up, and clung to the edge of the crate, willing his stomach to stop churning. He couldn't remember when he'd felt worse. The swaying of the train made his vision blur and his mouth felt as though a herd of camels had bedded down inside it.

After a couple of attempts he staggered unsteadily to his feet and managed to reach the door. He couldn't decide if he wanted to retch or jump.

"But if I'm already dead, it makes no sense to kill myself." Thinking made his head throb more. He opened the door a few inches and gulped in air. It was spiced with the smell of wood smoke.

He glanced up toward the engine, but grit and half-dead embers forced him back inside. He clung to the facing of the doorway, trying to piece together recent events.

"I can't be dead. It hurts too much to be dead." He closed his eyes and tried to will his reason to return. Finally he dredged up the memory of climbing inside the empty train car.

But now the car was far from empty.

He stared dully at the birdcage and then his gaze

slid to the oilskin cover lying beside it. A small card attached bore the name C. H. Cadwallender. Temple frowned and counted the crates again.

"Three, and one of them Connie's." He was puzzling over that when the train whistle blew again causing the blacksmith's hammer to beat against the anvil with agonizing speed. He flopped down on top of one of the crates, cradled his head in his palms and closed his eyes.

"Temple is a pirate," Livingstone chirped happily. "Look at me while I love you...lovely creature, awrk."

Suicide no longer seemed like a viable option, but as Temple glared at the ebony fowl through half-closed eyes, murder became a strong temptation.

Chapter Twenty-One

Connie stared out the window but she was only marginally aware of the images sliding by. Mud gave way to grassy prairie, cultivated fields became quaint towns and factories, but still her mind and body were in conflict with each other. While she tried to school her thoughts and plan her meeting with her father and Mr. Montague, her senses rebelliously conjured up images of Temple.

She saw his body shimmering in the lake. Hard muscles rippling beneath the surface of the water mixed and swirled with her recollection of him striding across her tent, proud and unembarrassed at his nakedness. With a moan she buried her face in her gloved hands.

"I can't keep thinking of him. He is out of my life. I have the bones—"

The conductor walking down the aisle paused with his hand on the edge of her seat. "Miss, is there anything wrong? Is there anything I can do?"

Constance glanced up, mortified that she had been talking to herself. "No. I mean, yes—yes, there is. At the next stop would it be possible for me to send a telegram?''

''No, miss. We only stop at Thompsonville to take on water.'' The middle-aged man smiled when she sighed with disappointment. ''I could send one for you.''

''Oh, I would appreciate that—if you're sure it's not too much trouble.''

''No trouble at all.'' He pulled a stubby pencil and a scrap of paper from his coat pocket. He handed them to Constance. ''You write it out and I'll see it gets sent.''

''What time will we reach New York on Thursday?''

The conductor flipped open his watch and peered at it as if that information was contained on the round face. ''We should be pulling into the station by eight-thirty, miss. If we don't have delays unloading, you should be on your way by nine o'clock.''

Constance nodded while she wrote the message to her father. When she reached New York he and Mr. Montague could meet her at the offices of the *Sentinel*. She would have the press waiting to greet her—and to write up the account of her success. Even though proving her theory would have to wait for another expedition, there would be no possibility of Temple winning the prize—none at all.

She watched the conductor fold the paper and put it into the outside breast pocket of his coat. His gait was uneven as he swayed down the aisle of the train car. Just as he reached the connecting door, she rose from her seat, undecided about sending the telegram.

Constance watched the conductor disappear into the next car. She sagged down in her seat, still torn. She wanted to win in order to keep her promise to her father and help Dandridge. But she questioned if some of her motivation was not revenge against Temple for spurning her. The thought made her squirm uncomfortably in the seat.

Constance tried to occupy herself by watching the other passengers in the crowded car, but her mind was elsewhere. Now that she had allowed herself to think of Temple, she could not concentrate on anything else.

She twisted her gloved fingers together and wondered if he would hate her for what she was doing—but then what did it matter? He did not love her or he would not have left her tent after they had made love. Constance stared out the window and wondered how she could be the winner and have such a hole in her heart.

Hours later Constance was still gazing mindlessly at the passing landscape. The sun had set and most of the car was nodding in slumber. A child whimpered from somewhere in the train car and was followed by the comforting murmurs of a woman's voice. She sighed heavily. She would remain unmarried, would never know the joy and tribulation of raising a child.

Would never know the touch of a man again.

She was in love with Temple Parish. Constance Honoria Cadwallender had given herself to the pirate. The man who only cared about fame and fortune.

One hot tear threaded its way down her cheek. She leaned her forehead against the cool glass and closed her eyes while the train clattered on through the night.

The lurch of the train car jarred Temple awake. He opened his eyes and found himself staring at the wire cage. Livingstone stretched his wings and fluffed his feathers.

"Good morning, bird." Temple stood and realized that the train was going much more slowly, perhaps even coming to a stop. The night's sleep had cured his headache, and the bread and water had sufficed as dinner for both of them.

"I will never drink again," he promised Livingstone while the train continued to snap and lurch, not stopping completely but making progress only by intermittent jerks. The whine of the metal wheels on rails was interspersed with hissing steam and the grind of couplings absorbing the strain between each car.

"We must have reached New York." Temple raked his hand through his hair and put on his hat. Then he opened the sliding doors and peered outside.

The rays of the morning sun momentarily blinded him. He hung on to the side of the car and blinked until his vision returned to normal. The Sixty-Fifth Street station loomed in front of him. Ribbons of rails crisscrossed below and beside the train that threaded its way through the maze of engines, cars and cabooses. Metal clanked in protest as cars were dropped off and others were coupled on. Men in greasy clothing swarmed in and out of the tangle of steel. The train rolled a few feet farther and Temple saw a wagon up ahead. A red-haired man in bib overalls, with bulging biceps, held the reins of an impatient draft team.

"Good morning," Temple shouted while he leaned a little farther out the open door. The man's head came up and he scanned the train, searching for the source of the voice.

"Yeah, it's mornin' but I don't know how good it is." Splotches of freckles ran across his wide nose.

When he opened his mouth Temple saw an uneven gap between his front teeth.

"Problems?"

"Aw, I came for a load of freight, but now it's delayed. Damned New York train yards—a man can hardly make a livin'." The man turned away, disgusted with his plight and uninterested in any further conversation.

"Is your wagon for hire now?" Temple continued to hang on to the door while the train inched spasmodically along the maze of tracks toward the back of the wagon.

The teamster's head came around once again, the mention of money having regained his attention. "Could be. What'cha got?"

The train was barely moving now, lurching as steam coiled back from the engine. One of the huge sorrels stamped an iron-shod foot. The flaxen mane caught the sunlight as the animal tossed its head, obviously as tired of waiting as the man holding the reins.

"Some wooden crates—"

The man pulled gently on the reins, trying to calm the fractious team, and Temple saw heavy muscle cord in his forearm. "How many and where are you headed?"

Temple turned and looked at the crates. His gaze slid from his pair to Connie's larger one. He felt his gut ball up and he tightened his jaw against his own thoughts. He turned back to the teamster while Peter Hughes's voice echoed through his head.

He was at the crossroads of his life. Now he had to decide what kind of man he really was.

"Three. I have three crates. I need to transport them to Ashmont University on West Seventy-Ninth."

"I know the place—near that highfalutin museum of unnatural history, ain't it?"

"Something like that." Temple grinned at the man's misnomer.

"Must be mighty valuable if you rode with them."

"Let's just say I didn't want to lose sight of them." Temple decided to press on before the teamster called the train bulls to check his story. Tramps and men who rode the rails were treated to the blunt end of a bat first and questioned after the fact. "I'll pay double for your wagon."

The teamster wrapped the reins around the hand brake and jumped down. "Sure, I can haul them for you." He hopped across the tracks until he reached the door where Temple stood. "Slide them out and I'll carry them across."

The train was moving so slowly it was almost imperceptible as Temple shoved his two crates to the door. The behemoth easily lifted one up to his shoulder. Within seconds he was back for the second. And then finally he returned for the third—Connie's crate.

"I'll help you with this one, it's bigger." Temple jumped to the ground.

"Much obliged." The teamster grabbed one end and Temple the other. Little weight was on Temple's end and he realized the man could have handled it alone with no difficulty. As soon as it was shoved inside the dray Temple returned to the car and snagged his valise. The teamster watched Temple for a moment, then he stuck his head in the dim confines of the car.

"Mister?" the teamster called. "What about this?"

Temple stopped, frowning. He watched the man vault into the car. One beefy fist held the oilskin-covered cage aloft. "This must be yours too." The man was looking at him with suspicious narrowed eyes.

Temple had forgotten about Livingstone after he had slid the cover over his cage. He nodded while guilt folded over him in an icy wave. "It is—I mean he is. I nearly forgot him, can't do that. Bring him along, and thanks." Temple wasn't really happy about bringing the chattering bird, but he couldn't leave the poor creature alone in an empty car.

The teamster hopped down from the slowly rolling car. He ambled to the wagon and handed Temple the cage. He was whistling a happy tune by the time he levered his massive body back into the seat of the wagon. Within moments Temple was watching the tangle of tracks and engine's belching steam disappear into the distance.

Temple leaned back against one of the crates. He would have to send the bird to C.H.'s house after he collected Montague's check. Or maybe he would deliver Livingstone himself, and give C.H. the opportunity to congratulate him in person.

Constance stared out the window at the collection of trains. She had thought they would be pulling up to the platform soon but so far the engine continued to tug and jerk at irregular intervals. She saw the conductor's blue hat and waved at him.

He nodded and made his way to her, stopping along the way to answer a question or pull his watch from his coat pocket. "Yes, miss?"

"Have we arrived yet?"

"Yes and no. I'm afraid there is some congestion up ahead. We have to wait for another train to clear the roundhouse and then we should be able to let passengers off. I'm sorry for any inconvenience this is causing you." He looked sincere in his apology.

"What time is it?" Constance thought of the telegram she had sent to her father, requesting that he have Filbert Montague meet her at ten-thirty.

"It is half past nine, miss. Is that a problem—I could send word to someone if you need me to."

"No. If we are going to be able to get off momentarily it should be all right. Thank you." Constance settled stiffly back into her seat. She sighed, glad that she had put extra seeds and plenty of water in Livingstone's cage. As long as she could hire a wagon—and there seemed to be plenty of them sitting idle outside her window—then she and the crate would make it to the *Sentinel* offices on time.

Twenty minutes later the young man she had hired to haul her crate of bones was using his horse and wagon to cut a path toward the baggage car.

"I'd like for you to drive me all the way to the *Sentinel*'s office on Stryker's Lane."

"No problem, miss." The young man tugged down the brim of his cap and concentrated on negotiating the train tracks. Finally the horse gingerly picked its way across one more crisscrossed set to the baggage car of Constance's train.

"It is a large wooden crate and a covered birdcage. There should be a tag with the name C. H. Cadwallender attached to both." Constance stood up in the seat and craned her neck to see inside. The young man leaped up inside the car and spoke with the train employee who was sorting mailbags and steamer trunks. Constance saw him push his cap back on his head and frown. Then he shook his head. The young man returned to the door of the baggage car.

"He says there ain't no such crate in here, miss. He says there ain't been nothing like that loaded or unloaded the whole trip."

"But it has to be. It must be there." Constance gathered her skirt and jumped down to the ground. She walked to the baggage car and peered up at the boy. "Please, look again. It must be here."

The boy looked doubtful but he returned to the baggage handler. Constance felt her stomach balling up while they spoke. She could tell by their expressions that her crate was not here. And she knew exactly why.

"Temple Parish—" She turned on her heel while she thought about how she was going to tell her father that she had lost the endowment to the blackest-hearted pirate since Captain Kidd.

Thaddeus Ball watched the aging professor's eyes return again and again to the clock on the wall. He clasped his fingers behind his head and leaned back in the lumpy chair. Miss Constance Cadwallender was late—very late.

"I cannot imagine what has happened to her. She has been raised to be punctual above all else." Professor Cadwallender focused a sharp don't-dare-contradict-me gaze on Thaddeus.

"Oh, I'm sure she has, sir." He leaned forward until the legs of his chair hit the bare floor with a thud. "But as it seems she is almost an hour and a half overdue, perhaps we should begin to send inquiries."

Professor Cadwallender's brows rose in astonishment. "Exactly what do you mean, young man?"

"I mean that something may have happened—to detain her."

Filbert Montague, who had remained silent in a well-padded chair throughout the vigil, stood. "I think you may be right. And even though you disavowed the telegram from Mr. Parish as a hoax, I now have to wonder who was pulling whose leg." The millionaire stared at C.H. as he spoke. "If the young woman shows up with bones in her possession, as you promised, then let me know. Otherwise, you can join me at Ashmont University, where Mr. Temple Parish has promised to deliver my dinosaur. Good day to you, gentlemen." The man nodded before he picked up his gloves and hat. The glass in the door rattled when he shut it behind him.

"I don't think he was too happy."

"Neither am I." The professor growled. "Something dire must have happened. Honoria has never disappointed me in her life and I doubt she would begin now."

Thaddeus watched emotion play across the man's face. "Where are you going?"

"I am going to Dandridge to see if they have heard from my daughter—and if I have not seen her by two o'clock then I will go to Ashmont University to find out what that scoundrel Temple Parish has done with her. I will have the truth out of that pirate if I have to bludgeon him to get it." C. H. Cadwallender leaned heavily on his cane as he bustled out the door.

"And here I thought I had already written the story of the century about Temple Parish," Thaddeus commented to the reporters who had gathered near his desk. "I must say, that man makes news wherever he goes." Thaddeus smiled and stood up. He grabbed his hat off the wooden rack, shoved a fresh pencil in his pocket and headed out the door.

"Where are you going, Tad?" the editor asked.

"I think I better find Temple Parish before I lose the scoop of my career."

Chapter Twenty-Two

"Miss, is this where you wanted to go?" The cabbie turned to face Constance in the open carriage.

She glanced up, stunned to see that she had ridden from the station, where she had paid the wagon driver for his time, all the way to the *Sentinel* offices on Stryker without being aware of it. "What?"

"I asked if this is where you wanted to be?"

Constance looked at the newspaper office in misery. She could imagine the smug faces of the reporters when she explained to Mr. Montague that the bones had been lost—stolen.

"I can't face them, not now," she mumbled. Images of Temple's face, wreathed in a victorious smile, assaulted her.

"What's that? I didn't hear you, miss."

"I've changed my mind. This is not where I want to be." She glanced up at the confused driver. "Take me home. Take me to Twenty-Seven Gramercy Place."

"Yes, miss." The cabbie turned and flicked the reins. The horse trotted off and Constance sank back against the seat in misery. She had lost her heart, the endowment and now very likely her father's trust—and all to Temple Parish.

The carriage clattered over the uneven stones of the tree-lined street. Spring had turned to summer while Constance was in Montana. The bright hues of four-o'clocks and daisies drew her eye, but brought her no joy.

She glanced up the lane at the dour brown blocks of granite that made the solid walls of her home. The ivy had once again twined its way through cracks and crevices on the craggy stone. It had entirely engulfed the trellis that stood on either side of the wide twelve-step stoop that led to her front door.

In her youth Constance had hidden within the protective shelter of those vines, springing out to startle her father just before he put his foot on the last step. She stared at the spiky green leaves of the Virginia creeper and longed for the simplicity of her childhood.

"Here we are, miss." The cabbie's voice drew her attention. She exited the open carriage before he could help her out and avoided his curious gaze by occupying herself with finding money with which to pay him. Finally she pulled out some crumpled bills, not knowing how much was there, and handed them up to him with trembling fingers.

"Thank you, miss." He touched his cap before he left.

Constance turned and started walking. She stared at the myriad cracks in the old walkway as she started climbing the steps. When she was halfway up, she finally raised her head and looked up at the house.

Her breath caught in her throat. Livingstone's cage was nestled in the shade of the ivy, sitting on three wooden crates stacked one atop the other. One crate had a card attached to it with her name on it. She rushed forward, confused by what she saw.

"Livingstone! Are you all right?" She opened the door of the cage and plunged her hand inside.

"Connie is a beauty." The bird squawked while it hopped from perch to perch nearer her hand. "Kiss me...kiss me."

"What did you say?" Constance drew her hand back and shut the cage. She stared at Livingstone in astonishment.

"He said you are a beauty." Temple's deep voice brought her spinning around. She stared into bloodshot brown eyes.

He gave her a lopsided smile. "It was a long trip—I spent quite a while listening to this damned stupid bird, but at least this time I agree with him."

"What are you doing here?" Constance didn't know whether she wanted to slap him or run into his arms. His smile twisted and the image of swaggering swashbuckler invaded her thoughts. She took a step backward, not trusting him or herself. "I would have thought you'd be accepting Mr. Montague's money—or have you already done so since you made sure I could not?" The pain of betrayal made her words sharp with accusation.

He shook his head and flopped down on the third step below her. "I deserve that, Connie, that and much more."

"Yes, you do." She sat near him and stared down at his motionless form. He dragged off his hat, exposing his thick wild hair. "How could you, Temple?"

He looked up at her and shrugged. "I have worked

like a dog for the past ten years for one reason, Connie.''

"Money."

"That's what I thought, but Peter made me see the truth. I've been around the world and back again for one thing.'' He smiled. She was so pretty with indignant fury coursing through her. He wanted to claim her lips and feel her rage turn to passion, but he couldn't do it, not yet.

Constance felt her knees turning to liquid so she forced herself to look away. Temple's gaze was as hot and persuasive as it had been the night in her tent.

"I wanted to earn C.H.'s respect—"

"I hate to interrupt, but..." A young man stood blushing on the sidewalk below the bottom step.

Temple was up before Constance could react. "Damn it, Ball. I am sick of people like you." He took a menacing step toward the startled man. "I didn't do it—do you understand? I am innocent of the damned thefts. Rake me over the coals in the papers again, bring me up on charges. I just don't care anymore.'' Temple's hands were balled into fists and Constance wondered if he were going to pummel the man. "I did not commit those thefts from Dandridge ten years ago."

"Oh, I know that," Thaddeus said evenly. "I've known for some time." He blinked at Temple curiously. "Didn't you get my letter?"

Temple froze on the spot. Constance saw confusion in his eyes and she recalled the letter that had ultimately led to his leaving her. "Yes, I got it. Weren't you planning on blackmailing me?"

Thaddeus Ball laughed and shook his head. "Hardly. I followed the leads and they took me right to the guilty man. It wasn't even very difficult. If you had kicked up a fuss ten years ago everyone would have known the truth.'' Ball frowned up at Temple. ''Why didn't you?''

Temple glanced at Connie and then he touched the scar on his cheek. ''I didn't want to see Connie or C.H. embarrassed.''

''What is this all about, Temple?'' Constance rose to her feet. ''For years Papa has been avoiding my questions. I think I have earned the right to know what went on between you two—and why.''

He gave her a sad look. ''All right, Connie.'' Temple was ready to bare his soul to her. He was prepared to let her see all of him, the street rat he used to be and the man he was now. He prayed she could forgive him.

Thaddeus Ball pulled a pad from his coat pocket. He drew a pencil from his shirt pocket. ''Do you mind?''

''I guess not.'' Temple drew his knee up and rested one muscled forearm on it. Connie closed her eyes and told herself not to notice.

''Why did you walk away ten years ago?'' Thaddeus poised his pencil above the paper.

''C. H. Cadwallender took me off the streets, gave me a home and only asked one thing of me.'' Temple paused. ''He asked me to stay on the right side of the law.''

''But you said you were innocent.'' Thaddeus frowned.

''I am innocent of the thefts from Dandridge.'' Temple glanced over at Connie. He swallowed hard and searched for the courage Peter had spoken of.

''I don't understand,'' Thaddeus said.

"Christmas was coming. I wanted to buy something for C.H. and Connie with money I earned myself. I had gone back to work for certain businessmen." Temple's brows furrowed together. "I ran bets from the gambling halls for the bare-knuckle fights."

"Oh, I see." Thaddeus scribbled quickly.

"I hid the gifts at Dandridge University. I was caught there late at night shortly after the thefts had been discovered." His fingers unconsciously went to the scar again. "All I had in my pockets, after they—uh—subdued me, were the gifts, but given my background, it was assumed I was the thief."

"But I still don't understand why you didn't demand an investigation."

"C.H. had taken a lot of criticism from his colleagues when he took me in. He would have been ridiculed, embarrassed by an investigation. I didn't want to put him or Connie through that kind of humiliation." Temple glanced at Connie from under his lashes. "Besides, I didn't want C.H. to know that I had broken my promise to him."

"So you left the university under a cloud of suspicion and you have been living with that lie ever since." Thaddeus's voice rang with bemused wonder. "It's a lot to go through, Mr. Parish, just to preserve Professor Cadwallender's reputation."

"I agree, it is a lot to go through." C.H.'s deep voice drew the attention of all three people. He stood beside the thick curtain of ivy. It was obvious he had heard the entire story. Temple rose to his feet and faced his old mentor.

"Papa—I—" Constance started to explain why she had never arrived at the *Sentinel* but he raised his hand to silence her.

She felt tension ripple across the space that separated him from Temple.

"Sir." Temple met C.H.'s stony gaze.

"I should have known you were innocent."

"Yes, you should have—but that was a long time ago. I've spent too many years trying to live down that lie and live up to your expectations."

"I don't know what to say, Temple, except that I'm sorry. I failed you."

Constance saw her father's strong chin quiver and she felt his pain and his guilt. Temple stared at C.H. without moving and she found herself pitying them both. Then suddenly Temple mouthed an oath and reached out to C.H. The two men embraced each other. A part of her leaped for joy while another part of her burned with envy. Thaddeus Ball cleared his throat and Constance could see he was as touched by the gesture as she was herself.

"I've missed you," C.H. mumbled as he released Temple.

"I've missed you too, sir." Temple grinned and slapped C.H. on the shoulder. "I could have used your advice more than once."

C.H. waved his hand but Constance saw the pleased grin spread across his face. "I doubt that. You have carved yourself a niche, and you've done it all on your own. Since Honoria did not show up at the newspaper office, I assume you have won Montague's endowment as well."

"If winning that endowment will earn your respect, Papa, then I guess Temple will be a happy man." She wrung her hands together. Both her professional pride and her woman's heart were breaking, while another part of her was glad that at last Temple had found his prize.

"I didn't get a chance to finish what I was telling you, Connie." Temple leaned back against the cushion of leaves. "I finally realized there was something I want a whole lot more than Montague's money or C.H.'s respect."

"What could that possibly be?" She was nearing tears, torn by her sense of betrayal and her body's traitorous reaction to having him so near.

He looked up at her and every trace of humor left his face. He looked suddenly boyish and vulnerable. She fought against her own weakness and met his gaze. Only her pride kept her from falling into his arms.

"I want your love, Constance Honoria,"

"How can you say such a thing when you stole my bones—made sure I could not win? It's easy for you to ask for my love now that you have cheated me out of the chance of beating you fairly."

"No, I haven't."

"You haven't what? Stolen my find and my chance or broken my heart?" Her nose felt as if it were going to run and she swiped at it with the back of her glove.

"I couldn't go through with it, Connie. I took your crate and fully intended to steal your discovery, claim it right along with mine, but I couldn't do it." His shoulders seemed to sag and he looked as if he had just confessed a great sin to her.

"I don't understand." Constance moved closer and sat down beside him on the cold concrete steps as she had when they were children.

"They are all here, Connie. I never met with Montague. I never went to Ashmont. I couldn't break your heart, at least I never meant to. You are the most important thing in the world to me. More important than fame or fortune, or even C.H.'s damned respect.'' He reached out and took hold of her hand. ''I'm giving my bones to you, Connie. Take them, use them, throw them in the Hudson River.''

C.H. made a choking sound and Thaddeus Ball shuffled his feet in embarrassment, but Temple didn't care. His pride had kept him from being happy for too long.

Constance stared at Temple in silence. Never in her life had she felt such an outpouring of love, or been more incapable of expressing it.

''Please, say something, Connie.'' Temple scanned her face with hungry eyes. ''For the love of God, tell me that you don't hate me. At least give me that much.''

''Oh, Temple.'' She felt a tear cascade over her lower eyelid. ''I don't hate you. I love you, you've been too blind to see that.''

''I love you...I love you,'' squawked Livingstone.

Temple grinned. ''For once that damned bird took the words right out of my mouth. I do love you, Connie. More than anything.''

He pulled her into his arms and kissed her hard. She felt the delicious tingle of excitement when his unshaved cheeks gently scraped against her own. Her pulse accelerated when he speared his tongue into her mouth. She felt herself floating out of control, somewhere in the clouds. Slowly he ended the kiss and pulled away.

''I really hate to interrupt but my story no longer has an ending.'' Thaddeus looked from Temple to

Connie. "What are you going to do about the endowment, Mr. Parish?"

"I told you to call me Temple." He grinned and
pulled Connie into the crook of his arm. "You'll have
to ask Miss Cadwallender about that. I have given my
find to her to do with as she wishes."

"Oh, Temple, I can't take credit for your work. If
we can't share the endowment then I don't want any
part of it."

Constance saw her father's wide-eyed expression of
horror, but to his credit he remained silent. He leaned
on his cane and pinched his mouth into a straight line.

"Just knowing that you were willing to give it up
for me is enough." She caressed Temple's weathered
jaw with her gloved hand.

"Relax, C.H., the money isn't gone yet. If Connie
is willing, I have a plan that I think will benefit us
both."

She nodded at him and he couldn't resist kissing
her once again.

"Good." Temple lifted Livingstone's cage off the
top crate. "I have been dying to see what you found,
Connie. Do I have your permission to take a peek?"

She grinned at his childish enthusiasm while her
father elbowed his way nearer the crate. They were
much alike, these two stubborn men she loved beyond
reason.

"Go ahead, take a look." Constance watched while
her father, Temple and Thaddeus Ball pulled her crate
out and pried open the lid.

"Remarkable, Honoria. I am very proud of you,
darling," C.H. said as he deposited a kiss to her forehead.

"I've never seen anything like them," Thaddeus

Ball assured her, then he made more quick notes on his pad.

But Constance wasn't listening to them. She was watching the look on Temple's face. A feeling of dread crept up her spine while his brow furrowed deeper.

"Temple? What is wrong?"

He stood and raked his hand through his hair. "I don't believe it."

She climbed the steps until she was standing on the landing beside him. "What? What is wrong?" Constance leaned over and looked at her find. The long vertebrae that shaped the tail seemed intact. And the delicate bones in each of the wide splayed flippers had not been damaged during the trip home.

"Drag that crate of mine over so we can open them all up."

Thaddeus stuck the pencil behind his ear and yanked one of the boxes over closer to C.H. while Temple moved the other. Thaddeus yanked off the lid and they all bent over to take a look at the bones.

"It is unbelievable," Thaddeus said.

"Never saw anything like it in my life. Why, the odds against this happening must be astronomical," C.H. said while he leaned on his cane.

"Now look at these." Temple opened the last crate. All of them leaned over the box and stared inside.

Connie's brows rose in surprise. "Amazing."

"That's one word for it." Temple grinned. They both glanced back inside the crates. And then suddenly they broke into gales of laughter.

"We found the same dinosaur." Connie chuckled. "All the time I was trying to keep my find a secret and you had the front half of the same extinct creature.''

''You know what this means, don't you?'' Temple asked.

''No.'' Connie shoved her spectacles up on her nose and he caught himself smiling wider.

''It means we must collaborate—work together.''

Her expression fell, but she quickly recovered and schooled her features. ''Of course, you are right. For the good of the universities we must join forces and claim Mr. Montague's endowment.''

''Seems only sensible,'' C.H. agreed.

''It will make a nice ending to my story.'' Thaddeus pulled the pencil and pad out and once again began scribbling.

Temple grinned at Connie and pulled her closer. ''That's not exactly what I meant.'' He gently lifted off her spectacles.

''I can't see when you do that,'' she objected half-heartedly, but he continued and ignored her.

''The kind of partnership I am interested in is a bit more permanent.'' He pulled out the comb holding her hair and the great shiny mass tumbled to her shoulders.

''Temple, what on earth—?''

''I am asking you to collaborate with me forever, Connie. I want you to be my wife.'' He folded her into his arms until they were standing almost nose to chin on the steps.

''Wife?'' She blinked like a little owl. ''You want to marry me?''

''That is the customary way in which one takes a wife, yes.'' Temple stared into her eyes and found himself counting the flecks of gold among the mahogany.

"Oh—I see," she whispered.

"I knew all along that you didn't need those spectacles," he joked before he bent and kissed his fiancée.

Epilogue

"Read it again, Peter." Bessie leaned her chin into her hands and sighed. She was sitting backward in a chair with her hands splayed across the wooden back. Peter smiled at the girlish look of contentment that clouded her eyes. The small crowd that had gathered at the mercantile to hear the account had all dwindled away except for Holt, who stood by the pickle barrel.

"One more time and that is enough." Peter tried to sound stern but it wasn't easy with Bessie looking like that. "My throat is gettin' dry."

Holt snorted and shifted positions, clearly bored with both the newspaper article and the company. Peter cleared his throat and started to read.

"Temple Parish, noted scientist and explorer, stunned the scientific community today by unveiling a new species of ichthyosaur. The animal, which will be known as Filbertous montagueous-aquatus, was revealed at a press conference at Ashmont University. While accepting the endowment and personal award from philanthropist Filbert Montague, Parish continued to shock the group by announcing the find was shared equally by his competitor, Miss Constance Honoria Cadwallender. While the assembly was speculating on the exact nature of their collaboration, Mr. Parish announced that he and Miss Cadwallender will be married immediately.''

Bessie sighed and Holt grumbled an epithet. Peter stifled a chuckle and read the rest of the article.

''When asked what he planned to do with the money he had earned, Mr. Parish replied that he was taking his wife on a trip around the world. His response to the question of what he would be seeking on that trip was the cryptic reply 'my wife's laughter.' ''

Peter turned the paper over. A small item caught his eye and he scanned it quickly. The article was a terse account of the arrest of Andrew Pollock, formerly professor of languages at Dandridge University. The article went on to say that Professor Pollock had been stealing from the university over a period of ten years.

''Miss Constance is too good for him. He doesn't deserve her,'' Holt mumbled sourly.

''Holt, if a woman waited to give her love to a deservin' man, then we'd all be as extinct as those dinosaurs.'' Bessie chuckled and stood up from the chair.

''Actually, the men who are the least deservin' usually need love the most,'' Peter commented while he folded away the newspaper.

Bessie turned and stared at him. A strange expression rippled through her green eyes. "You know, Peter, there may be hope for you yet."

Peter looked at her and grinned. A burst of excitement shot across the space between them. "I'm countin' on that, Bessie."

Holt moaned and looked toward the ceiling of the mercantile as if he were in pain. "Oh, no. Not again."

*   *   *   *   *

Coming in December
from Harlequin Historical

A Warrior's Bride

Award-winning author Margaret Moore
creates another exciting story
set in medieval times!

A WARRIOR'S BRIDE (ISBN 28995-2)
available wherever Harlequin Historicals are sold.

WELCOME TO *Love Inspired* ™

A brand-new series of contemporary inspirational love stories.

Join men and women as they learn valuable lessons about facing the challenges of today's world and about life, love and faith.

Look for:

Christmas Rose
by Lacey Springer

A Matter of Trust
by Cheryl Wolverton

The Wedding Quilt
by Lenora Worth

Available in retail outlets
in November 1997.

LIFT YOUR SPIRITS AND GLADDEN YOUR HEART with *Love Inspired* ™!

Steeple
Hill™

LI1297

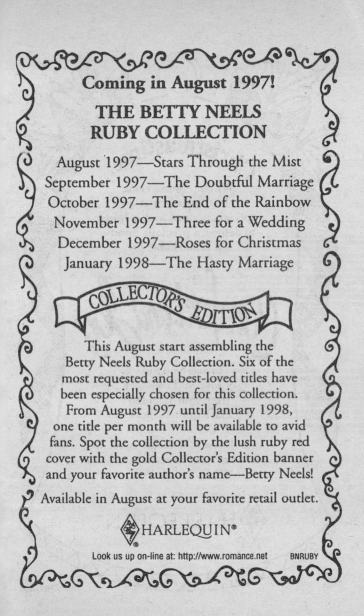

Coming in August 1997!

THE BETTY NEELS
RUBY COLLECTION

August 1997—Stars Through the Mist
September 1997—The Doubtful Marriage
October 1997—The End of the Rainbow
November 1997—Three for a Wedding
December 1997—Roses for Christmas
January 1998—The Hasty Marriage

COLLECTOR'S EDITION

This August start assembling the
Betty Neels Ruby Collection. Six of the
most requested and best-loved titles have
been especially chosen for this collection.
From August 1997 until January 1998,
one title per month will be available to avid
fans. Spot the collection by the lush ruby red
cover with the gold Collector's Edition banner
and your favorite author's name—Betty Neels!

Available in August at your favorite retail outlet.

HARLEQUIN®

Christmastime...

When rediscovering
lost loves brings a
special comfort, and helping
to deliver a precious bundle
is a remarkable joy.

Comfort and Joy

brings you gifts
of love and romance
from four talented
Harlequin authors.

A brand-new Christmas collection,
available at your favorite retail store
in November 1997.

HARLEQUIN®